Praise for *Next to Las...*
and Craig Johnson's Lon...

~~~

"A smart, thoughtful mystery from an author who's incapable of being boring, and who's writing at the top of his game."

—*Newsday*

"Johnson's affecting story is a winning combination of suspense, situational comedy and cosmic awe. We greatly admire the author's hero, who never wavers, even when faced with the seemingly implausible."

—*The Wall Street Journal*

"It's the scenery—and the big guy standing in front of the scenery—that keeps us coming back to Craig Johnson's lean and leathery mysteries."

—*The New York Times Book Review*

"Vietnam War vet Walt shows few signs of age in this consistently entertaining series."

—*Publishers Weekly*

"Like the greatest crime novelists, Johnson is a student of human nature. Walt Longmire is strong but fallible, a man whose devil-may-care stoicism masks a heightened sensitivity to the horrors he's witnessed."

—*Los Angeles Times*

"Johnson's trademarks [are] great characters, witty banter, serious sleuthing, and a love of Wyoming bigger than a stack of derelict cars."

—*The Boston Globe*

"Stepping into Walt's world is like slipping on a favorite pair of slippers, and it's where those slippers lead that provides a thrill.

Johnson pens a series that should become a 'must' read, so curl up, get comfortable, and enjoy the ride." —*The Denver Post*

"Johnson knows it's Walt his readers crave, and he delivers."
—*Booklist*

"A Walt Longmire novel is like going on a ride-along with an old friend, watching him ferret out the bad guys with wit and humanity (and more than a few bullets), while we swap stories and catch up on old times." —*Mystery Scene*

PENGUIN BOOKS

NEXT TO LAST STAND

Craig Johnson is the *New York Times* bestselling author of the Longmire mysteries, the basis for the hit Netflix original series *Longmire*. He is the recipient of the Western Writers of America Spur Award for fiction, and his novella, *Spirit of Steamboat*, was the first One Book Wyoming selection. He lives in Ucross, Wyoming, population twenty-five.

By Craig Johnson

The Longmire Series

The Cold Dish

Death Without Company

Kindness Goes Unpunished

Another Man's Moccasins

The Dark Horse

Junkyard Dogs

Hell Is Empty

As the Crow Flies

A Serpent's Tooth

Any Other Name

Dry Bones

An Obvious Fact

The Western Star

Depth of Winter

Land of Wolves

Next to Last Stand

Daughter of the Morning Star

Hell and Back

The Longmire Defense

Also by Craig Johnson

Spirit of Steamboat (*a novella*)

Wait for Signs (*short stories*)

The Highwayman (*a novella*)

Stand-alone E-stories
(Also available in Wait for Signs)

Christmas in Absaroka County (*four stories*)

Divorce Horse

Messenger

CRAIG JOHNSON

NEXT TO LAST STAND

PENGUIN BOOKS

PENGUIN BOOKS
An imprint of Penguin Random House LLC
penguinrandomhouse.com

First published in the United States of America by Viking,
an imprint of Penguin Random House LLC, 2020
Published in Penguin Books 2021

Copyright © 2020 by Craig Johnson
Penguin Random House supports copyright. Copyright fuels creativity, encourages diverse
voices, promotes free speech, and creates a vibrant culture. Thank you for
buying an authorized edition of this book and for complying with copyright
laws by not reproducing, scanning, or distributing any part of it in any
form without permission. You are supporting writers and allowing
Penguin Random House to continue to publish books for every reader.

ISBN 9780525522553 (paperback)

THE LIBRARY OF CONGRESS HAS CATALOGED THE
HARDCOVER EDITION AS FOLLOWS:
Names: Johnson, Craig, 1961– author.
Title: Next to last stand / Craig Johnson.
Description: [New York] : Viking, [2020] | Series: The Longmire series
Identifiers: LCCN 2020013739 (print) | LCCN 2020013740 (ebook) |
ISBN 9780525522539 (hardcover) | ISBN 9780525522546 (ebook)
Subjects: GSAFD: Mystery fiction.
Classification: LCC PS3610.O325 N49 2020 (print) | LCC PS3610.O325
(ebook) | DDC 813/.6—dc23
LC record available at https://lccn.loc.gov/2020013739
LC ebook record available at https://lccn.loc.gov/2020013740

Printed in the United States of America
5th Printing

Netflix is a registered trademark of Netflix, Inc. All rights reserved.
The series Longmire™ is copyrighted by Warner Bros. Entertainment Inc.

This is a work of fiction. Names, characters, places, and incidents
either are the product of the author's imagination or are used fictitiously,
and any resemblance to actual persons, living or dead, businesses,
companies, events, or locales is entirely coincidental.

For Kathryn Court,
editor, publisher, and dear friend.

There are not enough Indians in the world
to beat the Seventh Cavalry.

—GEORGE ARMSTRONG CUSTER

ACKNOWLEDGMENTS

The story of Cassilly Adams's painting *Custer's Last Fight*, approaches the drama of the historic moment it depicts and is something I've wanted to write about for some time. Although I've been interested in the Battle of the Little Bighorn, I never developed the mania that seems to overtake those who fall under the spell of the monumental incident that took place just up the road from my ranch. There has been so much written and rewritten on the subject that it seemed like a mountain too tall to climb, until I stumbled onto something that triggered my interest . . .

Other than seeing Budweiser reproductions hanging in every bar and saloon in the West, I happened on the painting in a literary sense in the *Norman Maclean Reader*, a collection of essays, letters, and other writings by, in my estimation, one of the most eminent men of letters in the West. A portion of the book is dedicated to an unfinished Custer manuscript that the great writer either gave up on, or simply discovered he didn't have time to write. The Cassilly Adams painting is referred to numerous times, and its social implications intrigued me to the point that I started off on the first of many steps in climbing Mount Custer.

One source was Christopher Kortlander, ambassador and diplomatic agent for the Crow Nation and his extravagant Custer Battlefield Museum in Garryowen, Montana. Mr. Kortlander is licensed to reproduce the Otto Becker revision of Adams's *Custer's Last Fight* through Anheuser-Busch in a beautiful, museum-quality print, which is available through the museum at www.custermuseum.org.

There have been numerous books written on Custer, *The Little Bighorn Battle*, *Sitting Bull*, and *Crazy Horse* just to name a few, and I can say that I have now read the majority of them—and not all of them are good. The ones I'll mention here are the cream of the crop, so that any readers who wish to follow in my footsteps will have a ready-made trail marked for them.

For an overall, clear view of the historic events that led to the battle, the battle itself, and the ramifications that followed, Nathaniel Philbrick's *The Last Stand* would be hard to beat, with James and Jim Donovan's *A Terrible Glory* coming in at a phenomenally researched second. Stephen E. Ambrose's *Crazy Horse and Custer* was another wonderful read that brings the epic event down to a human scale, along with the venerable *Son of the Morning Star*, by Evan S. Connell. There are others that encompass a larger scope, such as *The Custer Myth* by Colonel W. A. Graham and *The Custer Reader* by Paul Andrew Hutton, but I have to admit that I most enjoyed the native narratives for their polar perspectives. We're fortunate enough to have amazing works such as James Welch's *Killing Custer* and my good friend Joseph M. Marshall III's *The Day the World Ended*; along with the anthologies of Lakota and Cheyenne voices such as *Custer's Fall*, collected by David Humphreys Miller; *Cheyenne Memories of the Custer Fight*, compiled by Richard G. Hardorff; and *Lakota Noon*, compiled by Gregory Michno. Osprey Publishing's offering, *Little Big Horn 1876: Custer's Last Stand*, is a concise guide to the battle for those not wishing to climb the mountain but loiter among the foothills.

This book wouldn't have been quite so enjoyable without my many visits to the Brinton Museum in Big Horn and the Buffalo

Bill Center of the West over in Cody, two museums that if you happen to be passing through the wilds of Wyoming, you should make a point of experiencing.

Thanks to Mary Sue Williams and the staff at the Wyoming Home for Soldiers and Sailors—yes, she really does exist—and the staff and rangers up at the Little Bighorn Battlefield National Monument for answering my continual questions in my numerous visits.

Finally, thanks to all my friends and comrades on the Northern Cheyenne and Crow Reservations for being the filter through which all this information had to pass.

This book marks a beginning and an end within the Longmire canon with the retirement of my dear friend and editor at Penguin Random House, Kathryn Court, who took a chance years ago on a cowboy novelist from a town of twenty-five and became the godmother of then unknown Walt Longmire. Through her careful mentoring, the good sheriff has achieved dizzying heights, and a great deal of my success can be traced to her. I'm sorry to see her go but understand that life is made up of transitions and this is another. I will miss her dearly.

Thanks to my agent and confidant, Major-General Gail Hochman and her second in command, Brigadier General Marianne Merola. Thanks to Colonel Margaux Weisman, Lieutenant-Colonel Victoria Savanh, Major Ben Petrone, Lieutenant Mary Stone, Master Sergeant Eric Wechter, and Corporal Francesca Drago.

A special thanks and welcome to Chief Mule-Skinner Brian Tart, president of Viking and Penguin Publishing, who takes over the reins of editing me. We'll keep our eyes to the horizon where new adventures await along with many novels to come.

Finally, to my wife, Judy, the Scout, who finds the sign of my heart no matter how rocky the trail may be.

1

Years ago, on one particularly beautiful, high plains afternoon when I was a deputy with the Absaroka County Sheriff's Department, I propped my young daughter, Cady, on my hip and introduced her to Charley Lee Stillwater. Charley Lee was one of the Wavers, as they were called, the old veterans who sat in front of what was originally Fort McKinney, which then was called the Wyoming Soldiers' and Sailors' Home until the name was changed to the Veterans' Home of Wyoming, to wave at passing traffic.

Charley Lee put Cady in his lap and sang old cowboy tunes to her all afternoon—she'd been enraptured.

On the drive home, the five year-old asked, "Has Charley Lee been out in the sun too long?"

I'd smiled. "No, honey—he's a different color than us."

She thought about that one, her hair swirling in the wind. "He's brown."

"Well, yep, he is. Like your uncle Henry.

She spoke with the certainty of one well acquainted with her colors. "Uncle Henry is tan."

"Um, yes, he is."

"What are we?"

"We're white."

The future lawyer studied her hand and then me as if I was trying to get something over on her. "We're pink."

"Yep, but they call it white."

She'd been silent for a moment and then proclaimed with solemnity. "That doesn't make any sense."

"Few things about skin color do, Punk."

Fort McKinney was built in response to the intense reaction caused by the defeat of Lieutenant Colonel George Armstrong Custer and his Seventh Cavalry at the Battle of the Little Bighorn in 1876. It was one of many forts constructed to combat the fanciful Indian menace that was sweeping across the high plains, even though the Indian Wars were over with by the time Custer may or may not have saved the last bullet for himself.

By 1894 it was pretty well figured out that wild Indians weren't really much of a threat and the fort was closed; in 1903 the grounds and structures were handed over to the state of Wyoming.

It's about a half mile along the cottonwood-lined entrance from the fort's front door to State Route 16 that winds its way through Durant and up into the Bighorn Mountains range, but Charles Lee Stillwater would make the trip every morning and every afternoon in his electric wheelchair to sit by the red-brick sign that read VETERANS' HOME OF WYOMING and wave at the sporadic traffic.

That's how I had met Charley Lee, an exuberant man who liked to refer to himself as "the last of the Buffalo Soldiers" down to the Union kepi he wore on his head. Of all the men in their modified wheelchairs at the entrance to the home, he was the one who waved as if his very life depended on it.

I always waved back, and one day, when I served as a young deputy under former sheriff Lucian Connally's command, my curiosity got the better of me, and I'd stopped for a visit. Maybe it was because I was freshly back from Vietnam or maybe I was still in need of a little enlisted conversation, but I'd driven the Bronco Lucian had assigned me into the pull-off, handed out Reed's Root Beer candies to the small group, and leaned on the fender to talk with them. It became a routine that became a habit during the slow afternoons special to rural law enforcement, and one I continued with through today.

"He was born in Saint Louis, Missouri, July Fourth, 1923, to George and Lula Stillwater, and was the older of two sons," Kenny Cade offered from his wheelchair. A chief petty officer, he was a small man and a bundle of energy who had lost his legs when a jet had run over them. It was a little cool this morning, so Kenny was wearing his khaki N-1 Deck Jacket, the faux fur pulled up near his tanned face. "He worked at the family general store his parents owned, but when a traveling negro baseball team, the Indianapolis Clowns, stormed through the town, Charlie threw out twelve base runners and hit three lingering curveballs so far into the weeds that no one could find them. He played pro ball after that."

I leaned against my truck and nodded. "How did he end up in the military?"

"Pearl Harbor."

"Oh."

Someone driving by honked their horn, and I watched as the men all waved.

Kenny continued, "Yeah, he joined up and they sent him to Fort Bliss, Texas, in '42, where he shoveled shit in the stables and slung shit on shingles at the commissary."

"He hated Texas." All four of the men in wheelchairs nodded as I turned to Army Command Sergeant Major Clifton Coffman, who nudged his boonie hat back on his head.

"Why?"

"Said it was too hot, but hell, you shovel shit or shingles anywhere for four years and I defy you to like it." Kenny continued. "When he got back, he became the starting catcher for the Kansas City Monarchs, also working part time in the textile mills. He married Clara, a widow with two children. And they had one of their own, whom they named Ella."

I nodded. "I knew her. She was a nurse?"

"Yep. Charley Lee was well on his way to becoming an all-star when the 999th Armored Field Artillery requested his assistance in a little get-together along the thirty-eighth parallel."

"Hell, I think they just promised him he wouldn't have to go back to Fort Bliss." Ray Purdue smiled, the air force master sergeant always seeming to be sharing a joke with only himself. "Korea had to be better than Texas."

They all nodded some more.

Marine Sergeant Major Delmar Pettigrew rubbed a knob below his knee where his right leg used to be before a malfunctioning hand grenade had removed it and its twin to the left. "Order 9981."

They all nodded some more.

"What was Order 9981?"

Another horn blew, and the Wavers waved again.

Ray lowered his arm and then squinted a pale blue eye in concentration. "In 1948, President Truman issued Order 9981 that all branches of the US military be desegregated, but some all-black units remained until the mid-fifties." He continued.

"By April 22, 1951, UN forces were trying to recover from a counteroffensive launched by the Chinese People's Liberation Army. It was Charley's 999th's job to support South Korean infantry in what would be the Chinese army's spring offensive."

Clifton stared at the pavement between his missing legs, lost in a Jeep wreck during the Tet Offensive. "They got their ass shellacked for one full day before they were ordered to fall back because the Chinese were advancing south across the Imjin River. They redeployed at Kumgong-ni and began firing on the pursuing Chinese only four thousand yards away."

"Four thousand yards?"

His eyes shifted to me. "Did I stutter, Lieutenant? Anyway, the observation outposts began being overrun and communication wires went silent on 'em."

Delmar sighed. "They abandoned their asses."

Kenny pulled at an earlobe as if trying to pull the story back. "When a reported battalion of South Korean infantry a thousand yards to the west turned out to be a singular soldier, Charley Lee and the rest of the 999th loaded up a convoy and headed south, hoping for the best."

Delmar sighed. "They didn't get it."

They all nodded.

"What happened?"

Kenny, who seemed the most knowledgeable of Charley Lee's past, continued. "Falling back to Pobwon-ni, they found that that village had been captured and they were gonna be surrounded. They had about a hundred Chinese infantry hiding in the rice patties on either side of the road, and the 999th was getting hell with heavy submachine gunfire. Hell, all our guys had was howitzers, so the convoy was sorely lacking in short-range defensive weapons."

Clifton smiled. "Charley Lee started catching and throwing the Chinese incendiary grenades back at 'em, but they started taking mortar fire and the damned vehicles were blowing up left and right."

Delmar shook his head as he watched a blonde in a convertible drive by. "So, Charley Lee jumps in the M39. I mean, shit was on fire everywhere, and this Korean truck blows up in front of him. Well hell, he'd driven through enough cornfields back in Missouri and figured he could drive through rice patties, so he did."

Kenny made a face. "Ran over at least a dozen Chinamen and then made it back onto the main road but not before taking machine-gun rounds in his left thigh, right hip, and foot."

Ray pulled out a pack of cigarettes and lit one with a decorated Zippo he struck to life on his own stump. "That was the end of his ballplayer days."

Kenny went on. "He rolled back to the textile mills and coached Little League and high school baseball before retiring back in Missouri. After his wife died, his daughter, Ella, brought him here."

Somebody on the road honked, and they all dutifully waved. "How did he die?"

Delmar laughed. "High-stakes bingo game Saturday night that Charley Lee won out and began laughing. He laughed so hard that he set to coughing and went off to bed and never woke up. All I could think was that was how I wanted to go."

Another car horn blew, and the four men waved at the passing driver, all of them grinning.

Looking up and down the road that led into the mountains,

I couldn't help but feel a wave of sadness overwhelm me. Deaths up at the Fort are a common albeit sad occurrence that almost never necessitated the involvement of the Absaroka County Sheriff's Department, unless unfired ammunition or weapons were found. Because the staff knew Charley Lee was a friend and like a surrogate grandfather to my daughter, they contacted me as a professional courtesy.

Having gotten the inside story from the Wavers, I climbed back into my truck.

Delmar, my fellow marine, shouted, "When are you gonna bring us beer, like you used to?"

I hit the ignition, laying an elbow on the sill. "Sorry boys, but I'm not allowed. Carol says it might interfere with your medication."

"Interferes with our having a good time."

Turning in a circle and driving by the front opening of Fort McKinney, I glanced at the boys out enjoying the summer sun in front of the redbrick sign, but was distinctly aware of a gap in the middle, where a fifth electric wheelchair used to always sit, for all the world reminding me of the missing-man aerial formation used by squadrons to salute a fallen comrade.

I continued on toward one of the two remaining original buildings, the old fort hospital, now serving as the visitors' house, the other being an honest-to-goodness chicken shed that was on the National Register of Historic Places.

I opened the other windows a bit and climbed out of the three-quarter ton truck, reached back, and stroked my sidekick and perennial ham-finder on the head. "I'll take you for a walk when I get back, okay?"

His big Saint Bernard/German shepherd/dire wolf eyes stared back at me.

"I will, honest—this shouldn't take that long."

Closing the door, I walked toward the front entrance of the Dutch hip, gable-style building, and paused to take off my hat as I knocked on the door. At the flagpole to my left a staff member was lowering the flag to half-mast.

Inside, I walked by wicker furniture and an abandoned mid-game checkerboard on a small table. I watched as the maintenance man tied off the flag near the AGM-28 Hound Dog air-launched cruise missile that was the centerpiece of the Fort's static museum.

I stood there for a moment, saluting, when I heard footsteps approaching from behind and turned to find Carol Williams, who functioned as both a caretaker and an administrator.

The small woman with the silver hair leaned against one of the posts. "You been out there talking to the Wavers?"

"They gave me the lowdown on Charley Lee."

"Do they still ask you to bring them beer?"

"Every time."

She shook her head. "I'm sorry, Walt, but if the Feds ever found out . . ."

"That's all right, I'm not so sure I want them drinking and driving those aftermarket contraptions of theirs."

"Amazing, isn't it? It's a competition among all of them hopping up the motors and using different tires; Delmar stole the motor off of one of our washing machines to try to put in his wheelchair." She sighed. "Boys." After a moment she stood up on tiptoe, studying my face. "I heard about it, but I hadn't seen it—that's some scar."

"Thanks."

She crossed her arms. "I think Charley Lee was one of the

last Korean War veterans we had—moving on into Vietnam now."

"You trying to tell me something?"

She smiled. "I just think about all the history being lost."

"When an old man dies, a library burns to the ground."

"Voltaire?"

I shook my head. "An old African proverb."

I held the door as she motioned for me to follow, and we ducked into the main building. "We'll head over to Charley Lee's room in a moment, but I'd like to show you something first."

We walked down a short hallway hung with black and white photographs from a time when this was an actual fort. "Charley leave a bazooka or flamethrower in his footlocker?"

"Something like that." She stopped at her office where Gene Weller, the security guard, stood at the door. "Hi, Gene."

"Hey, Walt."

Carol paused to pull out some keys and unlock her door.

"Having a security problem here at the Fort?"

She gave me a knowing look, but I had no idea what it was I was supposed to know. "C'mon in."

Her office was a small room with more photographs and a certificate of commendation for Chief Petty Officer Williams on the walls. There was a bookshelf of mostly military history crowned with a large, handmade model of the USS *Missouri* and a very clean and orderly desk where, sitting on a leather blotter looking somewhat out of place, there was a large, battered Florsheim boot box with a rubber band holding the lid closed.

I stood in front of the desk, looking down, my hands on my

gun belt, the web of my thumb resting on the hammer of my Colt. "So, it's not bigger than a bread box."

She sat in her chair, rested her elbows on the blotter, and laced her fingers to provide a cradle for her pointed chin.

"I take it you've already opened it?"

"I have. It was on the top when we pulled out his footlocker. I secured his room, brought the box back here, and called you."

I nodded, reaching down, gave her one last look, and then slid off the rubber band and flipped the top.

Inside was a white plastic grocery bag carefully wrapped around a symmetrical bundle that took up the whole box. I glanced at Carol again and then peeled the plastic away to reveal scores of bills taped together in small bands.

I withdrew one of the packets after noting not only the number but also the denomination. "Hundreds?"

"All of them."

"In bands of one hundred?"

"Yes."

I glanced at the box again to see if it was really completely full. "How many packets?"

"I haven't emptied it, but estimating from the size, I'd say one hundred."

Peeling a bill from the packet in my hand, I held it up to the overhead light. "I'm no expert, but it doesn't look counterfeit to me."

"Me either." She shook her head. "You can see why I didn't go any further without you being present."

"Boy howdy." I nudged the box with a forefinger. "Any note in here? Receipt for deposit or withdrawal—anything?"

She shook her head slowly. "Nothing that I saw, but then I didn't go all the way through it after I saw what it was."

I studied the stack, about a half-inch thick. "Usually the bands have a bank name, but these are blank." I nudged the box as if poking it might get it to give out with some answers. "No writing on the box?"

"Florsheim Midtown, plain-toe zip-boot, brown, size twelve." She stood. "Do you want to head over to his room?"

I stared at all the money. "A cool million."

"Now you know why I called you."

"So . . ." I returned the bill to the packet, reinserting it among its brethren, then replacing the lid and rubber band. "Fifty-fifty?"

It was a small room, smaller than I would've thought, but there were so many books and stacks of paper and file folders in the place that it was probably twice the size it seemed once you emptied it out. "So, Charley Lee was a hoarder?"

"Of sorts."

His motorized wheelchair stood by the door at attention like Tiny Tim's abandoned crutch. There was a window overlooking the back of the building where the creek ran, and I could see what was possibly the only chicken coop on the National Register of Historic Places near one of the small ponds where the lodgers sometimes fished in summer.

There was a built-in closet with some drawers, and I was surprised to see a Texas flag tacked up on the wall among all the other stuff. "Funny, all the Wavers say he hated Texas."

Carol shrugged. "He figured out that there were some of our residents who took umbrage with Texans as much as they did people of color, so I think he took pride in both just to annoy them."

There was a lot of art on the walls, including an arresting portrait of a southwestern Buffalo Soldier standing in front of a Navajo blanket, Henry rifle on his shoulder. I stepped closer to examine the painting and thought the individual looked remarkably like Charley Lee himself. "This is an extraordinary painting."

Carol nodded. "Yes, he had remarkable taste."

Moving on to look at some of the others, I was surprised to discover that they were also actual paintings and not prints. "This is quite a little gallery he had here."

She pointed to a half-buried barrister bookcase. "There are also some artifacts in there. Charley Lee was one of our best amateur archaeologists, finding all kinds of things in the parade grounds and even stuff in the old stable, and I know people have been going through that place for a hundred years."

I stooped and peered at the rest of his mementos—spurs, cartridges, a belt buckle, square head nails, an old pair of wire-rimmed glasses, and a strange rattle with a hide-made head, miniature horns, and a tuft of buffalo hair. Opening the case, I picked up and studied the beaded, leather-covered stick and shook it, listening to the rattle. "Cheyenne."

Carol gestured under the twin bed. "The locker is under there."

I pulled the green-painted wooden box from under the bed, slid it between my legs, and turned it to face me. "Not very heavy." I studied the clasp. "No lock?"

"No."

"Wow." Flipping the metal strap up, I lifted the lid, laying it back far enough for the small chain at the left to hold it open. There was a tray in the top, just as I'd remembered from my time in the Corps, with a few dividers. I picked up some photographs, which I studied. There was one of a beautiful young woman seated in a 70's Pontiac with a hand stretched forward attempting to block the camera's eye.

I held it out to Carol. "Ella, his daughter?"

She nodded. "I think so."

There were a few other photos, including a more formal one of another woman in a long dress whom I assumed had been Charley Lee's late wife. "What emergency contact information do you have for him?"

"Nothing."

"Nothing?"

She shook her head. "He had a wife whom I would think is dead and Ella, his daughter."

"No contact information?"

"We know Ella moved to California but after that, nothing."

I glanced around the room. "Oh, I don't envy you."

"I'm betting there's going to be not much hope of finding his scattered family, even if they're still alive, but I think Ella got married out there. Not sure if she had children, though, but that might be the place to start."

"Check the hospital, I'm sure they've got records." Replacing the photos in their cubby, I scanned the rest of the tray that held a few medals and decorations, three old bottles, and a couple of baseballs, signed by guys whom Charley must've played with back in the day. "Somebody should research this stuff. Heck, one of these could be signed by the black Babe Ruth for all we know."

Carefully lifting the tray, I sat it on the bed beside me. "So, the box was just setting here?"

"Yes."

"Hmm." I glanced back in the footlocker at the neatly folded clothes and what looked to be an old army blanket, blue with red trim. "Cavalry blanket from the Civil War or the Indian Wars." Pulling some of the clothes out, I sat them on the bed beside me. There was an army dress uniform that would've gone with the Florsheims and a couple of dress shirts and ties so thin you could've used them as shoestrings.

No letters, no notes, no journals, or anything else that might've given us a clue as to how Charley could've come by the pile of cash.

The only thing left was the blanket, so I lifted it from the corner and watched as a few mothballs fell out and bounced on the tile floor, headed for the woodwork, but stymied by the stacks. Their smell filled the room, and I was about to put it back when a stiff piece of material slipped from the folds.

Carol and I looked at each other.

It was canvas, a little over a foot square, not in the best shape, but there was an image on one of the sides. It was pretty rough, but the paint was vibrant and the image very clear— some kind of Indian warrior in full headdress looking down at a mustachioed cavalryman; both men are locked in a death struggle. There was a cloud of what might've been smoke covering the Indian's groin, and he had his hand around the soldier's throat. The blue-clad horseman was grabbing the chief's arm with a look of grim determination even as the Indian was bringing a war club down on his head. The decimated headdress on the Indian was strange looking, almost like one that a Seminole might have worn, but as far as I knew they never wore headdresses.

"It's a painting, or part of one."

Carol came over. "It looks old."

"Yep."

"Any signature or date on it?"

"Not that I can see." I glanced around the room at the assembled art. "Now, with all this, why didn't he have this one on his wall too?"

"Maybe it had sentimental value."

I studied the oddity. "It's old . . . and strange." Turning it, I looked at the edges. "The canvas is unpainted on the ends, so it wasn't cut from a larger piece."

"Do you think it has something to do with the money?"

I shrugged. "Possibly, possibly not, but I can take it someplace and have it analyzed—maybe run it over to the Brinton in Big Horn. Maybe the museum can tell us what it is, or what it's worth." Glancing around at the paintings, I had a thought. "Did he have any kind of safe-deposit box?"

"We don't know."

"Did he have a will, or anything?"

"I've been going through his files, and he has it marked that he does." She glanced around the room at the stacks. "But we haven't found it yet."

I joined her in the looking, wondering where you'd start, and glad it wasn't my job.

"There's no way to trace it."

I gestured toward the box of money, now on the banker's desk. "It's money, I thought that's what you guys did."

"I'm afraid I'm not going to be much help." The young banker, Wes Haskins, shook his head and adjusted his glasses. "The bills are not serialized, they're just random, and the binding tabs have no identification on them at all."

I leaned against the closed door. "Can you give me something to go on?"

"Florsheim makes a nice shoe . . ."

"Wes."

He picked up the loose stack and studied the binder. "The tabs are self-adhesive, so I'd say no older than the nineties, but we can run it through the counter and get a date on the bills themselves to give you a general idea of the age."

"Okay."

"One thing."

"All right."

"We're going to have to alert the state and the IRS." He looked down at the box. "Over ten thousand dollars, and it has to be reported, and this is a lot more than ten thousand."

"Great. And where are they?"

"Over in Sheridan."

"Alert away, but I've got a question—does Charley Lee have a safe-deposit box here at the bank?"

He leaned back in his chair. "You'll have to go through probate or get a warrant for that kind of information, Walt."

I sighed. "The old president would've just told me."

"I could go to jail."

I glanced across the street at my offices. "Not mine."

There was a pause, and then he spoke. "Yes."

"Yes, what?"

"Just, *yes.*"

"Charley Lee Stillwater does have a safe-deposit box here at the bank?"

"I didn't say that."

"So, he doesn't?"

"I didn't say that either."

"You said *yes.*"

"Yes, I did."

"Concerning?"

"Just *yes.*"

"Right, got it." I reached out and dumped the entire lot on his desk, carefully unpeeling the grocery bag and placing it back into the box before putting the top back on and rubber banding it. "I think . . ."

"One more thing?"

I tucked the box under my arm and opened the door. "Yep?"

He pointed at my package. "That is the current bag used by the IGA, here in town."

"You're sure of that?"

He pulled an identical bag from under his desk and placed it on top of the mound of cash. "Jen packed my lunch in one today."

"This is one of the worst movies I've ever seen."

Henry Standing Bear, owner, proprietor, and best friend, glanced over his shoulder at the whooping and hollering emitting from the vintage Sony Trinitron above his head. "Yes, in the canon of truly horrible Custer films this is perhaps one of the worst."

"How do you suppose they got Robert Shaw to be in it?"

Producing another can of Rainier on my Red Pony Bar & Grill coaster, he crushed and pitched the empty into the recycling bin. "I would imagine, and this is only a guess, that there was drinking involved."

My undersheriff, Victoria Moretti, studied the side of my face. "We could've all had bonuses."

Ignoring her, I continued looking up at the screen where Custer and his men fired a ridiculous canon at some really embarrassingly dressed Indian extras. "I think they filmed this one in Spain."

"We could've all had new vehicles."

Continuing to watch the movie, I pontificated. "I guess they couldn't afford horses."

She lifted her wine and saluted the TV. "We could've all taken a cruise to Italy."

Taking a sip of my beer, I gestured toward the actors. "From the outfits, what tribe would you say those Natives are, Henry?"

The big Cheyenne swept his hair back and paused polishing a glass long enough to glance up at the screen. "Gener-a-kee, I would say."

Finally giving up, Vic turned and watched the screen for a moment. "So, that happened around here, right?"

"What?"

She smiled and turned to look at me. "The Little Bighorn thing."

Henry sat the glass on the towel on the bar in perfect symmetry with the others. "The Battle of the Greasy Grass."

She glanced at me again.

"That's what the Natives call it."

"Same battle?

"Yep." I shrugged. "They won it, so they can call it whatever they want."

She sipped her drink. "I've heard a bunch of stories, but what really happened?"

I glanced at the Cheyenne Nation, who suppressed a smile. "Well, there are a lot of versions."

"So, tell me yours—the *Reader's Digest* edition."

I sighed, glancing at the Bear again. "Are you going to interrupt? Because if you are, then you get to tell it." He placed two fingers to his pursed lips, indicating that he would remain quiet, so I began in rote largely repeating what had been taught to me from textbooks in the sixties. "Not long after the aborted treaties of the Black Hills, an area of great spiritual importance to the Lakota, gold was found there, and hostilities recommenced."

The Bear shrugged. "The white men lied."

After a moment, I continued. "A large contingent of Lakota . . ."

"And Cheyenne."

"And Cheyenne, defeated General Crook at the Battle of Rosebud Creek."

"The Battle Where the Girl Saved Her Brother."

I threw up my hands. "I quit."

He folded his arms and cocked his head. "You are doing very well."

"You said you wouldn't interrupt."

"I am simply giving a general sense of perspective—a cultural play-by-play, if you will."

I took a sip of my beer and began again. "General Terry had been dispatched to deal with the Indians even though their exact location and number were unknown. He sent Custer out to find them with strict instructions that he should not attack but wait for Terry's much larger force." I glanced at Henry, but he said nothing. "Custer was a dashing and flamboyant commander . . ."

"A devious and irrational bundle of manic depression who finished last in his class at West Point—in short, a horse's ass."

"Who hoped to deal with the Indian Problem himself in hopes of getting out of trouble with President Grant."

The Cheyenne Nation spoke out of the corner of his mouth. "Under oath, called the brother of Grant a liar and thief."

"And hoped to advance his own political career with a personal victory."

"Like all true horse's asses, he hoped to go into politics."

"Custer found the Indians . . ."

"Or the Indians found him."

I took a sip of my beer. "And split his forces into three parts, ordering Major Reno . . ."

"A drunk."

"To deliver the main attack while Custer and roughly two hundred riders attacked the flank. It was only when they came into view that Custer realized the size of the Indian camp, which was enormous. Nonetheless, they continued the attack, were beaten back, and quickly surrounded and killed."

"Except for Custer, who killed himself."

"Or not."

"He shot himself."

"Henry, the bullet wound was in his left temple and he was right-handed."

"Then his brother shot him."

I turned back to Vic. "Custer's brother-in-law and nephew were also killed in the battle, and it's believed in some circles that Tom may have shot the mortally wounded general to keep the Indians from capturing and torturing him more."

"Which they most certainly would have, the torture of choice being cutting the victim's genitals off and placing them in their own mouth, but in the case of Custer the women pushed awls in his ears puncturing his eardrums so that in the Camp of the Dead he would be deaf as he had been in this world." He took a sip of his drink.

"Mo-na-see-tah, Custer's Cheyenne wife, warned the Lakota women that the Long Hair was family and that they should not mutilate him."

"Custer's what?"

The Cheyenne Nation nodded succinctly. "But I believe they cut off a little-finger joint and shoved an arrow up his penis."

"Not to change the subject . . ." I shook my head. "But what leads you to believe that his brother shot him?"

The Bear continued to sip his soda water. "I have a brother."

2

"Russians."

"Russians?"

"Russians."

I stared at the old man in the US Navy "Dixie-cup" hat as he smoothed out his spaghetti-stained cardigan. I waited for him to add more, but he didn't, so I felt compelled to ask, "And Kenny, where did Charley Lee meet these Russians?"

He gestured all around us. "Why, right here."

Leaning against my truck, with Dog's massive head sticking out of the passenger side window beside me, I glanced up and down Route 16, my eyes lingering on the snowcapped peaks of the Bighorns' Cloud Peak Wilderness area. "He met Russians here on the highway?"

All four men nodded. They were once again parked in their wheelchairs next to the Veterans' Home redbrick sign.

"What, they were driving by in a staff car with big red hammers and sickles on the doors and he flagged them down?"

The rail-thin one in the thick glasses and air force ball cap, Ray, snickered. The one in the cardigan, Kenny, gave him a look to silence him but that did little good. "He talked to the Russians a lot."

"More than one Russian?"

"They was sometimes two."

"Two Russians."

Delmar, dressed in the rayon marines jacket, joined in. "Say, shouldn't you be taking notes on all this?"

The other three nodded. "S'matter of national security."

"That's right."

I calmly pulled out a notepad and pen and pretended to write things down. "So, two Russians?"

They all four nodded.

"Did you catch their names?"

They all four first looked at one another, then back at me, and then shook their collective heads.

"What did they look like?"

They all looked at one another again, and then the individual in the green fatigue jacket and boonie hat, Clifton, volunteered, "Russians. They looked like Russians."

I closed my notebook. "What, long gray coats and furry hats?"

Ray, the one in the air force ball cap that had the scrambled eggs embroidery on the front, nodded. "Furry hats, yeah."

"What did they look like? I mean besides the furry hats?"

Delmar, the marine jacket, spoke up. "One was a blonde woman, little bitty thing, and the other was an old fella with a mustache . . ."

Ray interrupted. "He wasn't a Russian."

Clifton took exception. "The hell he wasn't, he talked Russian, damn it."

"He talked English too, does that make him British, you moron?"

Delmar clarified. "She was Russian, but he was an American."

After a moment they all nodded in unison.

Ray thought it important to add, "She was cute too."

"Age?"

"Younger than us."

I paused, but figured they were beyond getting their feelings hurt. "That doesn't narrow the field much, guys." I stepped back and petted Dog. "Not to change the subject, but did you fellows ever see Charley Lee with a shoebox?"

They all stared at me.

"Right." Pocketing the notebook and pen, I pushed off the fender of my truck. "You guys have anything else you'd like to add?"

Clifton smoothed his brim and looked up at me. "You gonna catch who killed poor ol' Charley Lee?"

"Well, as far as we know, Mr. Stillwater died of natural causes."

They looked at one another and then back at me. "That's what they want you to think."

"Right." I fished my keys out of the pocket of my jeans along with my watch. "Coming up on noon . . . don't you fellows need to get back in for lunch?"

"Yer damn right . . . it's walleye fillets today with tartar sauce and Tater Tots."

Delmar agreed. "The only thing better is pizza night."

Kenny in the cardigan led the way, pivoting in his motorized wheelchair and sailing back for the complex of buildings in the distance.

I watched as the remaining three peeled off in formation and motored their battery-powered way next to the rolling dales of the picturesque drive that ran alongside the main entryway, the hopped-up wheelchairs looking like a convoy with each one flying a different tiny flag.

Watching the little procession go, I couldn't help but wonder how I'd decorate my own wheelchair someday.

"Are we done yet?" I turned to find my undersheriff, having woken up from her nap, scrubbing her eyes with the heels of her hands. "I'm hungry."

"Evidently, it's walleye fillet day."

She pushed Dog aside and hung out the window in what most people would consider a gorgeous, high-plains, mid-June day. "So long as there's tartar sauce and Tater Tots. I'm all about the Tots." She glanced around, her eyes traveling down the foothills to the Powder River Country that stretched farther than any human eye could see. "Holy shit. I'm glad it's summer."

Following the lead of the wheelchair brigade, I said nothing.

She turned her head and looked at me. "Aren't you glad it's summer?"

"Yep."

"I mean, you've been talking about it for months."

"I have?"

"Yes, you've been complaining about the ice and cold ever since you got back from Mexico a few months ago."

I turned to look at her and then glanced around at the almost phosphorescent leaves of the trees and the lush grass of the irrigated state property. "I guess I haven't noticed, or maybe it's not what I thought it was going to be."

"What the hell did you think it was going to be?"

I took a deep breath and let it out slowly. "Different." Walking around the front of my truck, I climbed in and closed the door behind me, fastening my seatbelt and firing up the big V-10. I turned to look at her again. "What?"

"You are so weird lately."

"Lately?"

She shrugged an admission. "Weirder. I mean you're not freezing up like you were so much, but you seem distracted all the time."

Pulling the selector lever into gear, I spun the steering wheel and started down the long drive toward Fort McKinney proper, aware that she was still looking at the side of my face. "What?"

"I have a question."

"More?"

"It's a personal question."

"All right."

"When you were down there in Mexico . . . And you can level with me on this."

"Okay."

She lodged herself against the passenger seat and continued studying me. "Did they shoot your dick off?"

I almost ran off the road. "What?"

"They shot it off, right?"

"No . . ."

"Because I haven't seen the thing in months, and I'm just thinking that it must be gone because . . ."

"It's fine, it's there, and it's fine, thank you . . ."

She placed an elbow on the sill and propped her head up, the fingers threaded into the thick blue-black hair as she adjusted her sunglasses and gazed out the windshield. "Let me finish."

"I'd rather you didn't."

"Look, I'm no Gina Lollobrigida . . ."

"Actually, you are."

She sat up, folding a tactical boot under herself and lowering her Clubmaster Ray Bans to study me with the tarnished gold eyes. "Then why haven't I even seen the damn thing for months?"

"Look . . ."

"What, do I need to reintroduce myself, take a number, or what?"

"I've told you it's not you . . ."

"I really thought something was going to happen last night after we left the bar, but you just put me in my unit like I was last week's groceries and then patted me on the head and sent me on my way."

"I'm sorry."

"I don't want you to be sorry—I want something else."

"I'm getting that." Turning right, I drove past the flagpoles and the visitors' center, parking closer to the offices and living quarters. "Look, can we discuss this some other time?"

"I want to do something more than just talk about it."

"Okay."

"So, I've got another question."

I switched off the ignition and unbuckled my seatbelt. "Another one?"

"Yeah, what were you thinking about out there on the road after the Four Horsemen of the Metropolis rolled off?"

Relieved at the change of subject, I sighed. "I was wondering what I'd be decorating my wheelchair with when the time comes."

She studied me for a long while and then smiled a voluptuous grin. "Me. I'll wear slinky outfits and drape across your lap like Mata Hari." She dropped her sunglasses back onto her nose with a forefinger, and I was once again reminded of just how dangerous looking she could be. "You know what the greatest exercise against looming mortality is, right?"

Watching Carol approach from the administration building, I nodded and climbed out, happy to have somebody else to talk to and something else to talk about.

Across the way, the Doors played "Riders on the Storm," which segued into Creedence Clearwater Revival's "Fortunate Son" from a pair of speakers lodged in the window of one of the second-story apartments.

"How'd it go?"

I turned to her. "Well, the investigation seems to have taken an unexpected and international turn in that Charley Lee was evidently meeting with the KGB out by the front entrance."

She covered her face with a hand as Vic came around to join us. "Oh God, I'm so sorry."

I shrugged. "They're a funny group."

"They were so adamant about talking to you, I should've known." She smiled. "The Wavers, we originally called them Waves, but they didn't like that."

"How about Wacs, as in wack jobs?" Vic leaned on my truck and glanced up at the speaker, wailing away into the all but empty parking lot. "So, who's Wolfman Jack?"

Carol looked that way, and I noticed there were all kinds of vintage rock and roll stickers applied to the entire window so that you couldn't see inside at all. "Oh, that's Magic Mike Bursaw, he's kind of our unofficial radio station. He's got walls lined with records from the sixties and seventies—goes nonstop all day."

"Kind of nice."

"Yeah, we had a new guy come in over at administration who asked if we could get Mike to turn it down. We told him he could go ask Mike if he wanted to, but that the last guy who tried to touch Magic's stereo came away with three broken fingers and a bloody nose."

I gazed at the covered window. "Violent, is he?"

"Only if you touch his vinyl."

I nodded. "Any progress on Charley Lee's room?"

"Quite a bit, actually. I stuck around last night and sorted through all the personal correspondence and then stacked all the books in the hall outside."

"Aren't you afraid that somebody will take them?"

Carol glanced at Vic. "They're art and history books; if they were *Playboys*, I'd be worried."

My undersheriff looked perplexed. "These guys don't read history books?"

"Not military history. I guess they've seen too much of it themselves."

"I hear its walleye for lunch?"

She smiled. "You're welcome to join us." Her smile faded just a touch as she studied Vic. "I can have a few trays brought to Charley Lee's room, that way you can avoid the common area."

"Why would we want to do that?"

She nodded toward my undersheriff. "She's going to cause quite a stir, and you're going to have about fifty guys wanting to sit at your table."

"Ah, maybe we'll take your advice."

"You remember where Charley Lee's room is?"

"One twenty-four."

"Right. I'll get the lunches for you guys and meet you over there in about ten."

"Deal." We walked through a dayroom, went past another reception desk next to a communal fireplace, and down the hallway.

Vic studied the stickers and memorabilia fastened to the doors along with the residents' names on plastic plaques. "Reminds me of dorm rooms."

Noting the army, navy, air force, and marines stickers, I added. "With a little more of a military twist."

Charley Lee's room was easy to spot with the books stacked along the wall beside the door; hundreds of them. Stepping past, I leafed through a few at the top. "*Gardner's Art Through the Ages, Western Art of the Twenty-First Century, Jansen's History of Art, The Image of the Black in Western Art, Volume V, Landscape and Western Art* . . . Charley Lee was something of an aficionado."

"Certainly liked art too." Vic picked up a few others before noting the look on my face. "What?"

Turning the open page toward her, I pointed at the copious notes in the margins, written in a careful hand. "He should've been teaching somewhere." Turning the pages, I continued reading. "These notes are really insightful, and his use of artistic terms is nothing short of impressive."

"Did he go to school for this stuff?"

"Not that I know of." I stared at the stacks. "Must've been self-taught."

"You think he bought and sold paintings—that's where the money came from?"

"I don't know, but you'd think something like that wouldn't have gone unnoticed around here." Placing the book back into the stacks, I opened the door and flipped on the light, finding the place a lot more orderly than the last time I'd seen it. "I'd say Carol's been working overtime."

There were plastic milk-case style file folders and manila envelopes that filled a few old beer cases stacked neatly on a hand truck by the door. Slipping a few folders from the plastic containers, I looked at the writing on the envelope that read *Correspondence Between CLS and the Buffalo Bill Center of the West.* There were more with other illustrious names like the Booth Western Museum, the National Museum of the American Indian, the Brinton Museum over in Sheridan County, the Gilcrease Museum in Tulsa, the Eiteljorg in Indianapolis, and the Denver Art Museum.

"Pretty amazing, huh?" We turned to find Carol, who was holding two trays, in the doorway.

"I'll say, and a pretty amazing job on your part in filing all this stuff."

She shrugged, handing each of us a tray with the aforementioned walleye, tartar sauce, and Tater Tots. "My father was an accountant."

Sitting on the bed, I watched as Vic sat in the guest chair and Carol leaned against the wall by the hand truck. "So, what was all this correspondence about?"

"A lot of trading information about artists and their art. Sorry to be so vague, but to be honest, I didn't read any of it. As soon as I ascertained who it was, I just piled it into the appropriate files or boxes and moved on to the next." She glanced around. "If I'd started reading, I don't think I would've gotten very far in getting it cleaned up—there were even letters he'd written back and forth with the Budweiser Corporation in Saint Louis."

"No personal correspondence among family members?"

"There were some letters from his daughter, but not much. They're in the second carton there."

"You didn't run into any more treasures or artwork?"

She shook her head. "Only what's on the walls." She glanced around. "Some of it's relatively valuable, but nothing worth a million dollars."

Starting on my lunch, I threw a chin toward the painting of the Buffalo Soldier standing in front of the Navajo rug. "What about that one?"

"I can't say for sure because I'm certainly no expert, but I'd say that one is relatively new from the look of the paint; the style and everything . . . Doesn't it almost look like a poster for a movie or something?"

"In fact, it does. It also looks remarkably like Charley Lee." Leaning forward, I studied the canvas. "And there's no signature."

Vic broke off eating with a piece of walleye on the end of her fork, which she extended toward the art. "Has anybody looked on the back of the thing?"

Carol once again shook her head. "I was concentrating on getting a pathway cleared so we could walk in and wasn't so much worried about what's on the walls." She turned back to me. "Anything on that one we found in the blanket?"

"I haven't pursued it just yet, but there are at least two museums here in the state with which he was in correspondence, so I guess I'll start there." I continued eating and unscrewed a bottle of water she'd provided and took a swig. "Any sign of a will?"

She smiled. "There was an envelope in his personal file that had a piece of notebook paper in it from 1994, not notarized, leaving all his worldly possessions to one Bass Townsend."

"And who, pray tell, is Bass Townsend?"

"That, is a very good question."

Vic made a face. "So, if we don't find somebody to give this money to, who gets it?"

"The federal government." I turned back to Carol. "Any word from the tax folks over in Sheridan?"

"They want to know which institution has the money."

"I bet they do . . . What, they're worried that a Wyoming sheriff is driving around with a million dollars in a shoebox?"

"Something like that."

"The Bank of Durant, right down the street here."

"Security box for Charley Lee?"

"Yes, well, I think yes. I'll go have a talk with Verne Selby and see if I can't get a warrant." I looked back up at the painting. "What do you do with the personal items if there isn't anyone to forward them to?"

"Generally we keep any artifacts for the museum display in the dayroom and just donate the things that aren't of much value, but with these paintings and books . . . Especially the military history and art—I don't know what we're going to do. There's a ton of books on Custer and the Little Bighorn."

Vic chimed in. "I hope they're better than the movies."

Carol looked at me. "We caught a really bad double feature at the Red Pony last night." I glanced out the door. "Did you see all the notes in the margins of the books?"

Carol sighed. "I did. I pulled all the pieces of paper from them, but I don't know what to make of all those notes."

"We need somebody who knows something about art to go through them."

"Any ideas?"

"The closest would be the Brinton over in Big Horn." I

glanced out the door again at the tall stacks of books and at the bathroom where even more books sat on top of the toilet. "Good thing you've got a hand truck."

I listened as the judge imitated the banker. "It'll have to go through probate."

"That'll take months, if not years."

"Possibly." I glanced around the chambers of His Honor Verne Selby. "If you don't mind my asking, Walter, what are you looking for?"

"A copy of *Bleak House* to throw at you."

He nodded. "That might hurt—as I recall it is a long book."

"There isn't anybody, Verne, no contacts, nothing—just a handwritten will leaving all his worldly belongings to a Bass Townsend."

"Well, that's inconvenient."

"And it's a million dollars."

"Expensively inconvenient."

"I don't think we've ever had anything like this happen in the county before."

He leaned back in his weathered leather chair and glanced down Main Street from his second story window. "We've had large estates that were liquidated, private assets, but usually there's someone who comes forward. I'm assuming that a public announcement will be made in the *Courant*?"

"Today, along with the obituary."

"Well, perhaps someone will come forward with some information."

"And if they don't?"

He straightened his mustache in a very cinematic, Clifton Webb way and then spread his hand. "The coffers of the state and nation will be replenished."

"Along with a bunch of lawyers."

"Jarndyce and Jarndyce." He turned back to study me, and I let him for a good long while. "How are you doing, Walter?"

"Annoyed."

"More than usual?"

"Meaning?"

He studied me with the pale, patient blue eyes. "There's been talk that you've been more distracted and agitated than usual."

"From whom?"

He waved in a vague sort of way. "Just general talk."

Repositioning myself in his chair, I thought about it. "Well, I'm still getting over some of the physical damage from Mexico, I only talk to my daughter once a week if she can tolerate it, and I'm not so sure I like being a sheriff anymore—I think that about covers it."

He nodded. "Still have your dog?"

"I do."

"Good—always good to have a dog."

"Maybe it's time, Verne."

"Possibly." He leaned forward and rested his arms on his desk. "I understand the Basque contingency has been in contact with your deputy, the young man, Saizarbitoria."

"Yep, he talked with me about it."

"That's good, that's good."

"He's a capable young man."

"Yes, but is he sheriff material?"

"I think so."

"What does he have to say about standing for sheriff?"

I laughed. "Mostly he wants to know if I'm stepping down."

"And are you?"

"I haven't made up my mind yet."

There was a long pause. "What would you do with yourself, Walter?"

I stood, sliding my chair back into position beside the other one and looking around at the old barrister bookcases. "I don't know. Maybe head up to Fort McKinney and wave at cars."

"It affects you, going up there, doesn't it?"

"It does."

"I don't hardly ever remember Lucian Connally going up there at all."

"He doesn't."

"Ever?"

"Ever."

"I suppose we all deal with mortality in our own way." He glanced up at me. "Do you still play chess with him at the home for assisted living?"

"The old folk's home, he calls it . . . Tonight, yep."

"How is he doing?"

I walked over to the bookcases and stared at the perfectly uniform tomes, tan with maroon stripes, like soldiers on parade. "Not as sharp, and he doesn't get out that much, which I suppose is my fault."

"I should go up there." There was a pause as he thought about it, and the room seemed to grow smaller. "But you and I both know I won't."

Staring at my reflection in the glass, I watched my lips tighten. "No, Verne, probably not."

———

"You keep leadin' with that queen and you're gonna get yer ass kicked."

"It's my queen and my ass."

Lucian Connally retrieved his tumbler from the small table to our left, sipped his Pappy Van Winkle's Family Reserve, and licked his lips so as to not lose a drop. "Yes, it is."

"Are we celebrating something?"

He lifted his glass. "June sixth, 1944."

"That was last week." He continued to hold his glass out to me.

I nodded and touched the rim of mine to the old Doolittle Raider's. "D-Day."

He studied me. "Any dates you recollect from that war of yours?"

"January thirtieth, 1968." He looked at me, puzzled. "Tet Offensive."

He angled a knight toward the border. "Any good dates?"

I mustered out "August third, 1972," and thought about it. "I've got a question for you."

"Shoot."

"Do you remember the day your plane got shot down?"

"I remember the minute."

"The day you were captured by the Japanese?"

"Yep, why?"

"George Orwell used to say that the English people do not retain among their historical memories the name of a single military victory."

"Commie."

I laughed. "In his own way he fought a battle against totalitarianism that is as long-lasting as Churchill's, against the language of fascism at least."

His dark eyes came up to mine. "What in the hell are you talking about?"

Angling left, I took his bishop. "Human nature. I mean, when you think about it, hardly any of the epic poems or books are about victorious battles—*The Iliad, The Charge of the Light Brigade, The Lost Battle, A Farewell to Arms, Drummer Hodge . . .* "

He grunted. "In answer to your question, successful and prosperous cultures have the luxury of looking back at death and defeat with a sense of nostalgia, having won the overall war."

I moved my monarch after his rook.

"You don't think it's just a form of atonement for having participated in war in the first place?"

"Not if it was a good war."

"Define the term *good war.*"

"The ones we won."

"So Korea was not a good war?"

"That was a tie."

Pursuing with the queen, I noticed his knight lying in ambush. "The Indian Wars?"

He studied me and then lifted his glass, taking a long, slow sip. "You mind if I ask where all this horseshit is coming from?"

"One of the residents up at the Veterans' Home passed away a couple of nights ago, Charley Lee Stillwater."

"The colored fellow?"

"Uh, yep. Anyway, he had a lot of Custer books, and then there was one of the movies on at Henry's bar last night with Robert Shaw, I believe."

As expected, he brought out the knight.

"My God, that one was horrible." He made a face. "But not as bad as Ronald Reagan in *Santa Fe Trail*, where they had him as Jeb Stuart's goofy buddy in 1859, when everybody knows Custer didn't graduate from West Point until 1861."

I angled my queen away. "My point being that the preoccupation with Custer . . ."

He touched his knight again and then settled on his king, sensing a danger. "Was personal propaganda is what it was, a brilliant campaign by a widowed wife; Libby Custer was relentless."

Drawing on his distracted attention, I moved my own king back.

"She assembled her husband into a shining example to American youth, turned him into a hero. Heroes are big business, just look at all those ball-playing assholes on television selling shoes, soap, soup, and nuts."

Bringing my queen back, I tightened the noose. "I don't follow."

"In the later part of the nineteenth century, we were moving away from a community and regionally based economy to a national one. Nationwide business is big business and for that you needed an image, and men like Custer fit the bill. Hell, he was on cigars, soap, and posters. I even had a pedal-car with his name on it when I was a kid."

"What if the image was false?"

Ignoring the queen, he moved his king again. "Who's to say if the image was false?"

"He was actively engaging in genocide, Lucian."

"Says who?"

"History." Nudging my queen forward, I announced. "Check."

He looked disgusted.

"Either way, there's right and there's wrong."

"Easy to say, sitting here playing chess in comfortable chairs and drinking my antiquarian bourbon."

I moved my queen again. "Check."

The old sheriff sighed. "I don't think he was as blundering an ass as he's portrayed, but in the heat of battle he made a dreadful miscalculation." He reached out and toppled his king. "And for that, he paid the highest price that can be paid."

I lifted my glass. "Remember the Alamo."

He lifted his. "Amen, brother."

3

"It could either be a bad copy or a proof of some sort."

"Proof of what?"

"No, just a proof, like an artist study."

I watched as Barbara Schuster handled the canvas with white gloves in the conservation area of the Brinton Museum, carefully extracting it from waxed paper sleeves, and I felt bad about hauling the thing around rolled up in my jacket pocket. She reached up and adjusted a desk lamp with a circular fluorescent light and magnifying lens that was attached to the large table that dominated the room. "Well, from the action of the subjects I would say that this is a study of a painting of a western battle sometime in the mid- to later part of the nineteenth century. The cavalryman is outfitted properly . . ."

"The Indian looks a little odd."

"Yes." She lowered her glasses on her nose. "Artists of that period, having never actually met an Indian, sometimes had some rather fanciful ideas as to their appearance. Many times the study would be done in an attempt to deal with problems involving light, color, form, perspective, composition . . ."

"Costume?"

"Yes, that too."

"He's kind of a combination of tribes, isn't he?"

"Yes, but like I said, a lot of times artists simply used their imagination, resulting in subjects that are somewhat far-fetched, but if this is a study for a larger work, then the final version might look completely different." She flipped a toggle on the lamp, and I watched as it switched to a black light.

"So, there's no way to tell who the artist might be or what piece of art this might've been a study from?"

"I'm afraid not." She turned the canvas under the glow lamp again. "It's for a work in progress and sometimes a great deal of the vitality of a piece of art can be gleaned from these types of studies, lending a fresh discovery or excitement to the work. It's almost like notes on how the artist became aware during the creation of the art, allowing us the opportunity to be a part of that creative process, but there would be no reason to sign it if that's the case."

"There's no way this is a work of art unto itself?"

"Doubtful. I mean if you look at the quality you can see that the artist did this in something of a hurry and left out a great deal of detail, giving the impression that it is a work leading to an actual painting if it was anyone of real repute." Folding her arms, she sat back on her stool. "This was probably never meant to see the light of day."

"What's it worth?"

She stared at me. "Excuse me?"

"What's it worth, a ballpark figure?"

Her eyes went back to the square of canvas and crusty pigments. "I'm no authority and those types of financial assessments are usually made by experts in the field or people who can break up the molecular aspects of the paint or the canvas itself . . ."

NEXT TO LAST STAND ~~~ 43

"Just a basic idea."

"Without any trace of the artist or history—I really can't say."

"Is it worth a million?"

"A million what?"

"Dollars."

"Goodness gracious, no." She looked at me and laughed. "If you were planning on retiring on this, I'm afraid you're going to have to stick with being a sheriff."

I leaned in and looked down at it. "So, even if it was a prominent artist and a noteworthy painting it wouldn't be worth that kind of money?"

"Well, if you were to, say, find one of Michelangelo's studies of the male model of the *Libyan Sibyl* from the ceiling of the Sistine Chapel it might be worth that much, but even then, you'd have a hard time certifying it."

"Why?"

"The final rendering was female—art changes and artists change their minds." She glanced at the painting again. "And in all honesty, even though the artist is certainly capable, he or she was no Michelangelo."

"I see. So, a couple hundred bucks?"

"At best."

"Okay."

"Do you mind if I ask what gave you the idea that it might be worth a million dollars?"

"Just hazarding a guess." I reached down and scooped the thing up along with the coverings. "You mind if I keep this stuff to protect it?"

She stood. "Not at all, and if you want a second opinion, we have a number of specialists in the field, appraisers who can perhaps determine the exact worth. Count von Lehman, for one."

"*Count* von Lehman?"

She smiled. "More of our shirttail Sheridan County royalty."

"He's really a count?"

"Papal indulgence—he used to teach up in Bozeman and over at Sheridan College after he formally retired." She smiled. "I once asked our conservationist, Larry Lowe, what kind of count von Lehman was and he said No Count, but you might have him take a look at it. Last I heard he was living over near Story in some strange house he built."

I patted the packet surrounding the orphan art. "Not for a couple hundred dollars, I don't think."

"Well, if you decide you want to hang it on the wall of your office, Larry can stretch it onto a frame for you—old canvas can be awfully brittle."

"I'll keep it in mind." Pulling some of the books from a satchel on the stool beside me, I sat them on the counter. "These are a few of the books he had. Any idea if they might be worth something?"

She examined the books, opening one and flipping through the pages. "Harmsen Collection Volume Two: *American Western Art, Visual Art of the Lakota, Early Illustrators of Western Art* . . . There's some call for these, but not so much since they've been written in." She looked up at me. "The owner?"

"Was."

"Oh."

"From the notes in the books, would you say he was educated in art?"

She opened the book again and started reading. "Possibly. If you want to leave some of them with me, I'll go through them and see what I can find."

"You're sure that's not too much trouble?"

"Not at all."

We took the elevator down to the ground floor, walking past the life-size display of Bradford Brinton. "The new digs are pretty amazing."

"It's a long way from William Moncreiffe's original ranch house, huh?"

"When did he sell the place to Brinton?"

"1923."

"Before my time."

"Mine too." She extended a hand when we stopped at the glass doors at the front of the relatively new museum. "I'm sorry if this turned out to be a disappointment, Walter, but it's a bit of unusual excitement I suppose?"

"The actual owner passed away over in Durant at the Veterans' Home, and I thought we should get a general idea of what it's worth."

"Still, not your usual line of work."

I placed the art under my arm and extended a hand. "Nope."

She took my hand, and we shook. "Well, if I can be of any further assistance at all, don't hesitate."

"I won't and thank you again." Heading out the door, I looked toward the edge of the parking lot where Vic sat on a bench watching Dog, who was standing in Little Goose Creek.

Walking down the stairs, I angled toward the two and stopped beside her, placing my hands on my hips. "Did you let Dog go swimming?"

"It was his idea." She didn't move, her head lying back with the sunglasses covering her eyes reflecting the intermittent sunshine that sparked through the thick-leaved cottonwood trees. "I guess he needed cooling off, or he decided to go fishing."

"The inside of my truck is now going to smell like wet dog." I glanced around at the beautifully sculpted grounds near the little town of Big Horn in neighboring Sheridan County. "You missed a beautiful museum."

"Yeah, I just don't like museums that much. I spent my whole childhood back in Philadelphia going to museums and, of course, visiting the Liberty Bell."

"See the bell a lot?"

"Every school year since sixth grade—we're on a first-name basis." She stretched her legs out and crossed her boots as Dog dipped his head and gulped a gallon or two. "I don't know what the big deal is, I mean, it's got a crack in it."

"So I've heard."

"What did they say about your painting?"

"A couple of hundred bucks at best."

Her eyes went back to Dog. "Sell it to 'em, and we'll go have lunch."

"I don't think they want it."

"Too bad." She stood and stretched, her uniform shirt coming loose and revealing her lean torso. "So, who is this Bradford Brinton guy?"

"Born in Illinois, Brinton got a degree from Yale and went into business with his old man as vice president of the Great Detour Plow Company, which merged with J. I. Case Threshing Machines."

"Case, as in *the* Case?"

"Yep. He enlisted and took part in the Meuse-Argonne and

Somme offensives in WWI and bought this ranch in 1923. He was married and had two daughters and died in Miami, Florida, in 1936 of acute pancreatitis when he was fifty-six." I glanced around. "He left the ranch to his sister, and she used it as a summer home until 1960, when she turned it and the artistic contents over to the Northern Trust of Chicago, who administered it as the Bradford Brinton Museum."

She peered down the creek as Dog ambled across the bank and looked up at us. "And that's the ranch house, down there, that we drove by?"

"Yep."

"What's the other one, farther down?"

"From what I'm to understand, his whoopee house."

"Whoopee house?"

"He sometimes had women and liquor brought in."

"You cowboys . . ." Shaking her head she turned and looked back at the state-of-the-art, sixteen-million-dollar museum as Dog drew closer. "And who built that?"

"Forrest E. Mars Jr."

"And who is Forrest E. Mars Jr.?"

Dog began shaking, filling the air with droplets that coated us. "Have you ever eaten a Mars Bar, Milky Way, or a bag of M&M's?"

She wiped off her glasses with a shirttail. "Sure."

"Then in some small way you helped foot the bill for that museum."

"Mars, as in Mars." We started back for my truck with Dog in tow. "So, Sheridan County is the Main Line of Wyoming?"

"In what way?"

"Old money."

I thought about it. "I guess so."

I looked out over Lake Desmet, the three-thousand-acre body of water that runs along the Bozeman Trail at the base of the Bighorn Mountains, but I couldn't see it even though I felt as if I were floating on it. Someone was talking to me, but I couldn't seem to respond. It was as if I opened my mouth I might drown.

"Maybe he won the lottery."

I jerked my mind back in hopes that she might not have noticed its absence. "What?"

She glanced at her wristwatch. "That was a short one, only three minutes—maybe you are getting better."

I sipped my iced tea but said nothing.

She gazed out at the small waves being decapitated by the wind. "Who the hell knows, maybe ol' Charley Lee just invested wisely."

I rested the iced tea back on the table. "And the books and partial painting don't really mean anything?"

"I'm just saying there may not be any mystery to all this." She looked out the Lake Stop windows at the restless water. "It seems like you want there to be?"

I shrugged. "I just want that million dollars to go to the right person, and I'd like to know where it came from."

"Not your job."

"What's that supposed to mean?"

"That's what we have lawyers and bankers for, not to mention the IRS."

"I'm trying to help them along."

"You're trying to do their job, which is why you're pissing them off."

"I'm not pissing anybody off." There was a disturbance on the deck as a mother and father bickered, their voices rising.

"Then where's your warrant?"

I shrugged. "I'm working on it."

She sipped her Diet Coke but then turned and gazed at me. "What did Verne Selby say?"

I gestured out the window. "He basically told me to go jump in said lake."

She turned, self-satisfied, as we both studied the landscape past the combative parents.

Our food arrived, and we sat there eating, relatively silent, staring through the glass at a few of the other tourists seated on the deck outside, their children making bright noises and racing about like barn swallows.

"Is having kids overrated?"

I was surprised by the question but quickly recovered before stuffing more pork carnitas into my mouth. "It has its moments—kind of like a tornado that goes on in your life for twenty years."

She took a fry from her plate and popped it into her mouth. "Sounds like fun."

I chewed and thought about it as we watched the argument outside become even more heated. I was about to turn away when the woman, having waited until the man had gone to the railing to say something to the children below, looked directly at me and mouthed two words.

HELP ME.

"Heard from your daughter lately?"

A long moment passed as the man returned and leaned in toward whom I assumed was his wife. "No, I guess she's busy."

"Yeah."

He was quick, and we could hear the report of the blow as he smacked her, her face turning as she lifted a hand of her own to cover up, then turning to look at him in shock.

I was already off my stool when the woman stood and backed away to the left, turning and running into the building and disappearing into the bathroom.

Vic was standing to my left as I started off. "I'll check on her."

I said nothing but continued toward the end of the bar and took a left, pushing through the glass doors and moving toward the umbrella-covered table where the angry man sat watching the two kids playing in the sandbox below the deck.

"Excuse me?"

He turned, and his eyes blinked only once.

"Could I see some identification, please?"

He continued to stare at me.

Pulling my light jacket back, I revealed my star and kept very strong eye contact with him. "I need to see some ID. Right now."

Nodding a response, he hunched up and removed his wallet from his back pocket and flipped it open, pulling out a license and handing it to me with as much indifference as he could muster. But in the action his jacket gaped, and I could make out a snub-nosed revolver tucked into his belt.

Continuing to watch him, I glanced at the card and read, "Mr. Dean Gibson, San Jose, California?"

"Yeah?"

I glanced back and could see Vic returning with the woman, a hand on her arm. "Do you mind coming with me for a moment?"

He shook his head. "I'm not leaving my kids out here."

As the two women arrived, I gestured toward the red-eyed one who had mouthed the words to me through the picture window. "Is this your wife, Mr. Gibson?"

He glared at her, but she wouldn't look at him. "Yeah."

"Then I'm sure she and my deputy won't mind looking after the children while you and I talk?"

He glowered at the woman for a few seconds and then redirected his scowl at me as he stood. "All right, let's get this over with."

Gesturing for him to precede me, we walked toward the parking lot, and I quietly slipped my hand down to unsnap the safety strap on my Colt. When we got to the farthest table, I stopped with my hand on my sidearm.

He turned to look at me, stuffing his hands into his jeans and rocking back and forth in his running shoes, exhibiting a little anxiety before smiling and breathing a quick laugh. "Listen, this isn't what it looks like."

I glanced at the license in my hand and waited a few seconds before responding. "And what's that, Mr. Gibson?"

"She gets a little mouthy sometimes, and I can't have that in front of my kids, you know?"

"No, Mr. Gibson, I'm afraid I don't. The state has pretty clear rules about that kind of physical abuse."

"Look, it's not like I make a habit of hitting her, all right?"

"The unauthorized application of force to another resulting in harmful or offensive contact and seeing as how you did it under the eyewitness of law enforcement . . ."

"Oh shit, come on."

Ignoring his remark, I continued. "It's entirely at my discretion as to whether to charge you with aggravated assault and or battery."

He said nothing more but just stood there, studying me.

"Are you armed, Mr. Gibson?"

He looked away and then brought his eyes back to mine. "No."

I let that one set for a while, hoping he'd change his mind but pretty sure he wouldn't. "You sure about that?"

He ran a hand through his hair and then dropped the hand to his belt buckle within easy reach of the revolver. "Yeah, I'm sure."

I gave it another long pause as I closed my fingers around the stag grips on my Colt.

Figuring he had no other options, he made his move, snatching for the revolver in his waistband. But my hand was just as quick, closing around his as I brought the large-frame, semiautomatic up with the other hand and slammed it under his chin, sending him over the railing backward as the .38 fell onto the deck and skittered off the edge.

I was around the railing and grabbing the front of his jacket as he tried to get up, swinging a roundhouse at me that glanced off my head and removed my hat. In the instant that my vision was blocked, he brought a foot up, catching me in the knee as I brought the Colt back around to hit the side of his head this time.

Falling into a parked car, he kicked at me again, this time catching me in the crotch, which I guess had been his target all along.

The air went out of me, along with the will to stand upright and not puke, but I was able to get a hand on his ankle as he slithered from the hood of the car. We both tumbled onto the surface of the gravel parking lot, and he kicked me again as I gripped my way up his legs, pounding him with the butt of the Colt. He finally quit kicking, and I was able to grab the collar of his jacket and lift his face up to mine.

I was screaming something at him, but I wasn't sure what it was—something about women and children and guns.

"Walt!"

His head lolled to one side, and I was pretty sure he wasn't listening.

"Walt!"

Somebody was yelling my name from a long way off.

"Walt!"

Releasing my grip, I dropped the man and fell to the side, resting my back against the wheel of the car next to us. Taking a deep breath, I brought a hand up to my face and could feel the scuffed flesh at my jaw where he'd caught me at least once.

"Walt!"

I turned and looked up into the sun where a dark figure was outlined, holding a Glock 9mm on the two of us. "Yep?"

"You okay?"

I took another deep breath and felt the nausea fading, just a bit. "Peachy, how 'bout you?"

I stared at the partial painting of the bonneted native that was laid out on the bar.

Henry Standing Bear lowered his face to look under the brim of my hat at my jaw. "A good fight, huh?"

I looked up from the artist proof. "Depends on what you'd call good."

"You won."

Vic leaned forward, studying the other side of my face as Dog raised up between us, eager to go home. "The amazing thing is you never loose teeth—that's handy and less expensive."

The Bear leaned back, picking up the remote and lowering the volume on the TV in the otherwise empty Red Pony Bar & Grill. "So, he was kidnapping his own family?"

"What used to be his family back in California." I gestured toward Vic, who had the story down a little better than me. "Divorced, right?"

She nodded, and I noticed she was getting a little tipsy. "About a year ago, but I guess he never took it to heart. They went their separate ways, and she moved back to Ohio and took the kids with her. About a week ago he got a wild hair and drove to Dayton, grabbed her and the kids at gunpoint, and started back for San Jose with them."

The Cheyenne Nation frowned. "How did you spot him?"

I shrugged. "She mouthed the words *help me* as I was looking at them through the window."

Vic nodded and reached down to pet Dog, who had settled between our barstools again, giving up on going home. "Top-flight police work."

I shrugged. "I like to think I'm pretty keen as to what's going on around me. I guess I could've waited till she used signal flags or a carrier pigeon."

Vic leaned in a little farther. "How's your chin?"

Picking up my Rainier, I took a swig and then held the cool can against the scraped skin. "I think I need a face transplant."

"See if you can do something about that little piece of ear that's missing too."

"Thanks."

"Or that scar that dissects your eye."

"Okay, that's enough." I glanced up at the TV. "What the hell, we're watching this again?"

The Bear glanced over his shoulder. "This is a different one."

"Which Custer is this?"

"Either Errol Flynn or Ronald Reagan . . . I think Reagan is Custer and Flynn is Jeb Stuart." He studied the screen. "Or the other way around."

"Errol Flynn played Custer in one of these."

He snapped his fingers. "This is the one. I believe it is *They Died with Their Boots On*, or as we like to call it on the Rez, *They Died with Their Facts Wrong*."

"I think *Santa Fe Trail* is the one that Lucian dislikes."

The Cheyenne Nation studied the screen. "I can see why, the tone of the movie was pro-slavery, which I found off-putting back in the sixties and do not find any less so now, come to think of it."

"What's with all these Custer movies?"

"It is the week of the battle, and TMC is showing a Custer film every night." He restored Vic's dirty martini. "Personally, I am awaiting *Little Big Man* on Saturday."

We all studied the screen with no sound. "From the landscape, it looks like they fought the battle down in Wheatland."

"Yes, and too many chiefs and not enough Indians. Look at the number of warbonnets; you would have thought the Seventh Cavalry was being attacked by an entire nation of chiefs." Fetching his soda water from the bar back, I watched as he added a strong dollop of gin. "These movies make me drink." He took a swig as the swarms of Indians galloped in and out of the screen in a sort of mindless way. "The battlefield does not look anything at all like the Little Bighorn Country and no credit is given to Gall's infantry and Crazy Horse's cavalry, which neatly hemmed Custer's command in and then finished them off."

We watched as the cinematic Flynn, the last man standing, took a bullet to the chest as yet another warbonneted chief grabbed the stanchion of the Seventh and rode off into the black and white sunset of, well . . . Wheatland. "You think Custer was the last one killed?"

"Do you mean was he the last one to shoot himself?" He shook his head. "I do not." He glanced back at the map of North and South Vietnam on the wall behind him. "You remember what it was like when we were choppered into Khe Sanh and the VC overran the barricades?"

Grunting into my beer, I nodded my head. "I remember it most vividly."

"I would imagine it was like that, only a great deal worse."

Sitting there safe on my barstool, I thought about that day and more important the night—the confusion, the terror, the futility, and finally the exultation as we'd made it, the last being a luxury the Seventh Cavalry hadn't received.

"I hope you two Westerners don't mind, but this Custer stuff bores the shit out of me." Vic, uninterested in the conversation, reached out and turned over a *Durant Courant*, flipping a few pages as she sipped her drink. "You want to know what Custer was thinking there at the end?"

The Bear volunteered. "Where did all these Indians come from?"

"Exactly." She pulled the paper in closer. "Hey, your buddy Charles Lee Stillwater is in here."

"The obituary?"

"Yeah." She read and then surmised. "Doesn't sound like

the *Courant* filched out any more information than we already know."

"No name and address of survivors?"

"No." Vic stood, a little unsteady. "I think I have to go to the bathroom."

"Are you okay?"

"Yeah, I just need to go to the bathroom, all right?"

The Bear studied her. "There is a Custer shrine in the men's facilities and seeing as you two are my only remaining customers, you are welcome to visit it."

She placed a hand on the bar to steady herself as Dog rose again, hope springing eternal. "A shrine, in the toilet?"

"Yes."

She trundled off, walking the wooden floors of the Red Pony Bar & Grill like they were the deck of a pitching ship heading 'round the Horn. "Boy, you Cheyenne know how to hold a grudge."

"Well, you have to remember that my people were only given citizenship in 1924." Watching her go, he turned to me. "She drank a lot tonight."

I reached down and petted Dog as he sat, not completely giving up on calling it a night. "I think today was hard on her."

"Because?"

"Kids were involved; she had to sit with them and the wife while I dealt with this Gibson guy." Studying the partial painting, I pushed it toward him. "You want something new for your shrine?"

He turned the canvas and looked at the two combatants. "So, I take it this is not an antiquity of great value?"

"According to the Brinton Museum, a couple hundred bucks at best."

His eyes came up, and he continued to study me. "How are you?"

I sighed. "Waiting on a vision."

"As we all are." He glanced after Vic and then waited a moment more before introducing another mildly hurtful subject. "How is Cady?"

"All's quiet on the southern front."

"But you have spoken to her?"

"Not for a couple of weeks, no." I stared at the surface of the bar, at all the little stains, nicks, and dents. "Charley Lee was one of her favorites."

He turned to the bar back and punched NO SALE on the mammoth, brass cash register, popping open the tray and then shutting it in the beginning ritual of closing the bar I'd witnessed a million times. "If things are slow, why not go down there?"

I gestured toward the closed money tray and started to get out my wallet. "What do I owe you?"

He gestured toward the canvas. "I will take the painting for my bathroom."

I nodded, raising my beer as he lifted his own drink and we toasted. "Deal." He nodded, and I thought about Cady. "I'm not so sure she wants me down there."

"She loves you."

"That, as you well know from your own dealings with family, does not mean she wants my company."

"We could go steal your granddaughter—we Cheyenne have a longstanding tradition of such things."

"And then I can go share a cell with Dean Gibson when my daughter and assistant attorney general get through with me?"

"I will come visit you in Rawlins."

He glanced over my shoulder, and I turned to watch Vic weaving between the chairs and tables, finally making it to her stool as I took her elbow and helped her get a good seat. "I think I'm drunk."

"Yep, I think you are."

She glanced at Henry. "Too much firewater."

He nodded. "Could be."

"I've never been in the men's room before; that's some shrine you got in there."

Slipping off my stool, I stood as Dog raised his head to look at me. "I'll be right back, then we'll go home, okay?"

Disgruntled, the *Canis dirus* lowered his massive head back to the floor.

Crossing past the pool table, I entered the alcove and took my customary right to the bathroom door with the sign that read BRAVE, across from the one on the other side of the hallway that read BRAVER, which sometimes confused the tourists. A famous quote from the Lakota chief Red Cloud states that men do that which is difficult while women do that which is impossible.

I'd been in the restroom of the Red Pony so many times that I didn't even see all the stuff, but it was testament to the Bear that no one ever molested or stole the things hanging there. There were a few pieces of graffiti that had been scrawled on the walls, proclamations such as *Crow got the land and Lakota got the glory, while the Cheyenne did the fighting!* Or pithy remarks like *Custer wore Arrow Shirts!* Or, *Custer got Siouxed!*

Finishing the business at hand, I continued to look around at the hair-pipe breastplate, a faded-blue kepi, and a dented bugle and wondered how much of the stuff was real.

There was artwork too. A Kevin Red Star, a Joel Ostlind,

and some more predictable alcohol-oriented prints, including the ubiquitous *Custer's Last Fight*, a Budweiser poster complete with cardboard frame that I'm pretty sure has hung at one time or another on the walls of every bar and saloon in the entire American West.

Zipping up, I stepped over to the sink and washed my hands, still looking at the mass-market poster over my left shoulder. I pulled out two paper towels and dried my hands as I turned to look at the dramatic display I'm sure I'd seen there the entirety of my adult life.

Tossing the paper towels away, I leaned in and examined the piece.

At the bottom, printed into the cardboard frame, was a plate that presented *Custer's Last Fight* as a gift from the King of Beers. My eyes couldn't help but go to the center where a long-haired Custer, replete with windblown red scarf, gripped an obviously empty revolver by the barrel and swung a sabre.

Two things as just a start—Custer had cut his hair before the battle, and the Seventh Calvary expeditionary force had not been issued sabres for the action. As to the scarf, I'm pretty sure that wasn't correct either.

Such is the nature of nitpicking when it comes to military history, the first and foremost inaccuracy being that there were no survivors of what has long been referred to as a massacre when in all actuality there were thousands. They just happened to be natives.

Staring at the image of the man, historically correct or not, I couldn't help but wonder at the decision-making process that had led to his death—the personal, professional, and political demons that had rushed him headlong to his destruction on that sunny hillside on June 25, 1876. And as I stepped back a bit in order to take in a broader scope of the print, I also thought about how few times historical figures actually died alone, but at the same time, how many other lives they took with them.

Just as with the movie on the television in the bar, there seemed to be an awful lot of warbonnets scattered across the battle in the poster, and even stranger were the Zulu-style shields the natives carried. The cavalrymen were definitely getting the worst of it, with some being clubbed, some stabbed, some shot, and more than a few already being scalped.

It was about then that my gaze drifted to the left.

There, in the corner of the print, was a strangely familiar, bonneted native raising a war club in preparation of bringing it down on a soldier who hung on to his other arm.

4

"It took a year to complete back in 1885 and was over sixteen feet wide and nine feet tall." Holding the large art book open, I read from page two, an alphabetical advantage when researching an artist by the name of Adams. "He was born in Zanesville, Ohio, the son of William Apthorp Adams, a lawyer who traced his ancestry back to John Adams of Boston, one of the Founding Fathers."

Sensing a disinterest, I raised my head to peek over the mountainous landscape of books between me and my undersheriff, who was sprawled across the surface of the Absaroka County Library table as if she were collapsed from boredom. "Can we go shoot something? Because if we don't, I think I'll just shoot myself."

Ignoring her, I continued reading as the nice young lady from the front desk appeared with a few more books, depositing them onto the table with a smile and then leaving without a word. "He studied at the Boston Academy of Arts, under Thomas S. Noble, and later at a Cincinnati art school and served in the army during the Civil War, where he was wounded while aboard the USS *Osage* at the Battle of Vicksburg. Late in the 1870s, he moved to Saint Louis, where he found work as an artist and engraver, and I guess it was there that he painted *Custer's Last Fight*."

She raised her head, propping it up with a hand, elbow on the oak surface. "I'm bored."

I gestured toward the miniature mountain range of books between us. "Doesn't any of this interest you?"

"No."

I went back to Dorothy Harmsen's *American Western Art*. "As models, he used actual Sioux Indians in battle dress and cavalrymen in uniforms of the period." Pulling another book from the pile, I flipped a few pages, revealing the painting, Custer escaping the fold between two pages by a scant inch. Studying the thing, I sighed. "I'd say he was relatively accurate with the cavalrymen, but half the Indians look like Zulus."

The first having failed, she tried another tack. "I'm hungry."

"He created it for two members of the Saint Louis Art Club, which took the painting on the road and charged people two bits to see it."

"Can we go eat?"

My eyes were drawn back to the two-page spread and then to the cardboard version I'd procured from the bathroom of the Red Pony Bar & Grill. "It didn't make as much as they hoped and was sold to a saloonkeeper there in Saint Louis who hung it in his barroom."

She snapped a finger and leveled it at me. "There's an idea, let's go have a drink."

"But the saloon went bankrupt, and the painting was acquired by the largest creditor: a small, local brewery owned by one Adolphus Busch."

Her interest perked, if only a little. "As in *the* Anheuser-Busch?"

"Yep. In 1895 the brewery gave the painting to the Seventh Cavalry, but evidently it was destroyed in a fire in 1946." Closing the tome, I placed it on a stack and reached for another. "This is incredible history."

Slapping a hand on top, she thwarted my progress. "This is incredible bullshit—who cares, Walt?"

Sliding the book toward me from under her hand, I flipped it open, working my way through the directory. "I do."

"It doesn't change anything. You've got the guy, who I assume died of natural causes?"

"Isaac hasn't finished the autopsy just yet."

"I don't see what our official involvement is at this point."

"A million dollars in an oversized Florsheim shoebox."

She sat back and looked at me. "That's going to end up going to the IRS—case closed."

I lifted the folder that held the partial painting. "And what, pray tell, do you make of this?"

"I, pray tell, make nothing of it." She leaned forward, lowering her voice. "It's a stupid copy somebody did of a famous painting. Get it framed and put it on your wall or give it to Henry to put in his bathroom shrine to Custer."

Opening the folder, I studied the canvas. "I want to get it professionally looked at."

"Where?"

"Cody."

"Why Cody?"

"The Buffalo Bill Center of the West."

"You're going to drive that crusty piece of canvas over to a museum in Cody?"

Nodding, I gathered up the books and stood, carefully placing the partial painting and the valueless cardboard version under my arm. "I've made up my mind."

"Can we have lunch first?"

"I was thinking tomorrow, after I've had a chance to call them."

"Okay."

"I thought maybe I'd hit the Little Bighorn Battlefield along the way or on the way back."

She stood as I gathered the books, relieved that this research portion of the investigation was over. "It's on the way?"

Starting out, I paused at the front desk to hand the stack over to the nice young woman there. "Sort of."

"Is Henry going?"

"Why?"

"Henry always goes when it's a sort-of deal."

I nodded as we exited the building and climbed into my truck. "I've always found it best to keep the Indian scouts close in Custer country."

She reached back and petted Dog. "Amen to that."

The Busy Bee was pretty packed, but we were able to snag a spot at the counter. I slipped off my jacket, draped it on the stool, and studied the light reflecting off Clear Creek. "Custer was a teetotaler."

Vic slid onto the stool beside me. "Maybe he should've drank."

"But it's funny, don't you think, that a lot of his fame is due in part to a poster printed by a brewery?"

"You really are into this shit, aren't you?"

I shrugged. "Among other things, I'm interested in what Lucian said about the commercial value of the dead and the ability of corporations to give everlasting life to individuals who might've otherwise faded into obscurity."

"Walt, I read about Custer in grade school back in Philadelphia."

"Yep, but would you have if that painting hadn't existed?"

"I thought you and Lucian agreed it was his wife who mounted that campaign to make him famous?"

"She did, but she couldn't be in every bar in America spreading the word. I mean there are towns, counties, state parks, motels, restaurants, souvenir shops . . ."

"Walt, you can't credit all that to a single painting."

"Maybe not, but it certainly helped."

"Baloney." We turned to find the owner and operator of the Busy Bee Cafe standing before us with an order pad in hand. "I've decided to just tell you what the special is before you ask—thick-cut baloney sandwiches with fried green tomatoes and mayo with fries, only four dollars and ninety-nine cents."

I thought about it. "Is the special the usual?"

"No."

"I'll have the usual."

"Me too." Vic nodded. "And a cup of coffee."

Propping both elbows onto the counter, I stared at the two of us in the bar-back mirror. "I just can't help but think that it was perfect timing what with the merging of advertising and big business in the late 1800s. Plus the advent of inexpensive printing processes that allowed for a relatively new innovation . . ."

"Which was?"

"Color."

"Oh."

Tipping my hat back, I postulated. "I wonder how many of those lithographs were handed out?"

"Call Budweiser, I'm sure they have somebody in charge of their advertising archives—you could even fly to Saint Louis and check it out."

"I could."

"I was joking."

Dorothy reappeared with glasses of water, and I thanked her and took a couple of sips. "There were two very different types of establishments in those days, saloons and barrooms—barrooms had sawdust on the floors and spittoons while saloons had more refined tastes, and I can see beer salesmen coming in and telling barroom owners that they could sure class-up the place by putting one of these swell lithographs behind the bar."

"Swell?"

"It was a term, back in the day." Lowering my glass, I thought about it. "Art as a conversation starter—something to keep people bellied up against the bar, talking and more important drinking."

With a groan, she leaned in and spoke in a low voice. "In the final analysis, what are you getting at?"

Turning my head, I watched as she studied the scar that darted across the skin around my left eye. "Given the sociocultural importance, what would that painting be worth today?"

She thought about it and then slowly smiled the little corner of the mouth grin I found so entrancing. "Enough hundred-dollar bills to fill a Florsheim shoebox?"

"That's what I was thinking."

Dumping her customary five sugars into her coffee, she

took a sip. "You were also thinking that those people over at the COW would know?"

"COW?"

"Center of the West—COW."

"Please don't call it that while we're over there."

She went back to drinking her coffee just as the usual arrived, a grilled chicken sandwich with a side of fries. "I get to go?"

"I didn't figure there was any way to stop you."

Lowering her mug, she adjusted her plate and continued to smile.

"No Post-its?"

"No, no one loves you today."

Studying the empty door facing that held all my square yellow-paper correspondence, Vic passed me and went toward her office as I sat on the dispatcher's desk, which always antagonized the dispatcher. "Where's Saizarbitoria?"

At the mention of our Basque deputy, Ruby looked up over her glasses at me as she reached down and petted Dog, who had settled in under her desk—or as much of him as the furniture would allow. "Out, taking care of the Post-its."

I guessed. "Lost dog."

Dog raised his head to look at me and then registered it as a false call and resettled.

Ruby shook her head. "Somebody found a set of engagement rings in the parking lot of the Baptist church, so he went over to pick them up for the Lost and Found. I'll notify the paper and get it up on our website."

"We have a website?"

She frowned at me.

"I'm willing to try the computer again, if you want."

Having tired of my dilettante behavior toward technology, Ruby had gotten me a computer; Saizarbitoria had assisted in getting it on my desk and up and running, but the complications of operating the thing had thwarted me at every turn, and the entire office had decided it was more trouble teaching me how to use it than it had been worth. Currently it was downstairs on the community desk, where I sometimes paused in passing to hit the spacebar to see the screensaver photo of my daughter and granddaughter. "I think we'll all pass."

"Roger that." I stood. "Anything need my attention?"

"Payroll checks need to be signed, and they're on your desk."

"You know, I'm starting to feel like a turnkey around here."

Dismissing me, she went back to her mound of papers. "Tell me about it."

Entering my office, I placed the artwork on my guest chair and stood there looking out the western window at the Bighorn Mountains, thinking how easy it would be to just get into the truck and head over to Cody, but realizing it wouldn't be particularly fair to my riding partners, or to the Buffalo Bill museum, which I hadn't contacted yet. Giving in to the inevitable, I sat and began signing as I flipped through the Rolodex Vic had threatened to sell on eBay, finally finding the number of the chief of staff of the venerable McCracken Research Library that lurked in the basement of the sprawling Center of the West.

"Mary Robinson."

"Hi Mary, it's Walt Longmire."

Adjusting the receiver in my ear, I listened as she smiled over the line. "Well, hello, Walt Longmire."

"Mary, do you guys have anything on Cassilly Adams?"

"*Custer's Last Fight* and *Moonlight on the Mississippi*?"

"That's him."

"I'm sure we have some information on him. What, exactly, are you looking for?"

"Mostly information on *Custer's Last Fight*."

"The Budweiser painting."

"For lack of a better name, yep."

"You know it burned."

"I was hoping that wasn't the case, but that's what I've read. I think I might have an artist study that Cassilly may or may not have done."

"Oh, my."

"Anyway, I've got the thing and thought I might drive over tomorrow and have you guys take a look at it and see if it's the real deal?"

"We'd be happy to—I'll just make sure our conservationist is here."

"Great." Not quite ready to hang up, I asked, "Hey, Mary? Let's say for the point of argument that the painting wasn't burned and had been found—what would it be worth?"

She laughed. "You do know the original painting was a triptych and that the two outer panels are at historical archives in Arizona."

"What are they of?"

"Custer as a child and then the aftermath of his death— they're in pretty rough shape, but worth seeing if you're really interested."

"What about the worth of the painting?"

"The one that burned?"

"Yep."

"You're not kidding?"

"Nope."

There was a pause. "Well, if it were being auctioned, it would certainly be a price-on-demand sort of thing . . ."

"That doesn't answer my question."

"Twenty-four, twenty-five . . ."

I swallowed. "Million?"

"Easily."

"So, if somebody were to buy it at, say, a million, it'd be the bargain of the century?"

There was another pause. "Walt, are you serious about this painting having been found, because if you are, we here at the Buffalo Bill would be interested . . ."

"No, no I haven't found the painting, but the artist study we discovered was accompanied by a million dollars in hundred-dollar bills, and I'm just trying to assemble where all that money could've come from."

"If, and it's a big if, that painting were still in existence and was procured for a million dollars, then somebody was horribly robbed."

"Well, that settles a few things. Do I need to make an appointment, or can I just drop in sometime tomorrow?"

"I'll be here all day—we've got a shindig tomorrow night."

"Anything you need from this side of the mountains?"

"If you run into any spectacular specimens of historic fine art that have been until lately presumed destroyed . . ."

"You're number one on my list." Hanging up the phone, I rested my eyes on the cardboard print in the folded cardboard frame, and then the smaller, more personal struggle going on in the left lower corner. "So much for that theory."

Picking up the phone again, I rang the number I knew by heart and waited.

After a few rings, he picked up. "It is another beautiful day here at the Red Pony Bar & Grill and continual soiree."

"Do you have Prince Albert in a can?"

"No, we have him in a pouch, but the results are much the same—and before you ask, yes our refrigerator is running and no, we are not going to go catch it."

"You want to come over tomorrow morning and ride in with me, and we'll pick up Vic and head over to Cody?"

"Certainly. I am assuming we are spending the night?"

"Do you still want to stop at the battlefield?"

"I do on the way back, along with another short stop in Billings, if you do not mind."

"Overnight it is."

The line went dead before I could ask what the other stop might be, so I hung up and raised my face to find Santiago Saizarbitoria standing in the doorway. "So, you want to get married?"

"I don't think you're my type."

He stepped in, handing me the small box. "Too bad, 'cause I've got a hell of a set of rings here."

Flipping the thing open, I gazed at the intertwined twenty-four caret gold rings encrusted with multiple diamonds and a large setting flanked on both sides. "Jeez, somebody robbed the ice plant."

"I know, right? The Baptists are taking in way too much money these days."

Turning the box in my hand, I watched as the light played off the stuff dreams were made of. "Any idea?"

"Close to twenty thousand, I'd say."

"Between this and the cool million I found, things are looking up here in the county."

He leaned against the wall. "So, I don't get to go to Cody?"

"Somebody's got to stay here and collect the riches." Handing him the rings, I eased back in my chair. "Get that in the safe before we lose it. Somebody out there is having a heart attack."

Looking at the box, he pushed off the wall. "If nobody collects it, can I have it?"

"I'm sure Marie would appreciate that, but no."

Going out the door, he stopped and then gave me a parting shot. "First you give away our million dollars and now this—you're not much fun these days."

"You're not the first to notice."

Ruby's voice sounded from the other room. "Walt, Isaac Bloomfield, line one."

Holding a finger up to Saizarbitoria, I punched line one and lifted the receiver, holding it to my ear. "What's the word on the autopsy?"

"Well, hello to you too. Heart attack."

"Hmm."

"You sound disappointed."

"No hint of foul play?"

"None that we can find other than a syringe mark where he must've had some sort of injection that night, but there's nothing in his medical chart that says he should've had one."

"Nothing in the toxicology?"

"No. We went through Charley Lee's medications, and he was taking an assortment of drugs that had to do with his heart, but sometimes it's just the mileage."

"Nothing else?"

"No, I'm afraid not."

"Thanks, Doc." I hung up the phone and looked at my deputy. "Anything else?"

"The transport service is going to be here this afternoon to collect the Gibson guy and haul him back to San Jose where he has a number of priors and a few outstanding warrants."

I'd forgotten about the would-be kidnapper and stood. "Is he ready to go?"

"No, I'm heading there now."

"I'll go with you just in case you want to get him out."

Passing through the main part of the office under Ruby's careful eye, we started down the steps to the landing and took a left toward the basement and the jail proper. The holding cells upstairs were comfy by comparison, and I slept in one on a regular basis, but very little about Gibson had recommended the man, so we'd incarcerated him in the windowless bowels of the old Carnegie building.

Saizarbitoria was just as glad to be rid of him, having tired of providing docent service for the last two nights, including shower break, when the guilty man had attempted to climb out the bathroom window only to be thwarted by the bars we'd anchored there after the last individual had escaped into the populace at large wearing only a bathrobe.

Walking by the communal table, I hit the spacebar and smiled back at my tiny, MIA family and thought about calling Cady before following the Basquo down the hallway, where a completely unclothed Dean Gibson stood in the middle of the cell.

"I'm not going."

Saizarbitoria glanced at me and then back at the naked man. "Excuse me?"

"I have no reason to go back there."

"Well, the state of California and Santa Clara County appear to have other opinions about that." I leaned against the bars. "You mind telling us why you don't have any clothes on, Mr. Gibson?"

"I'm not going to make this easy. I got a tub of Vaseline from the bathroom and I'm all greased up—so it's going to be a fight."

On closer inspection, he did have a kind of sheen to him. "To make it harder to get hold of you?"

"You got it."

"What, did you see that in a movie or something?"

"Yeah."

"Mr. Gibson, the only thing that's going to do is get you in either a straitjacket or a full-harness cufflink and leg irons with a belly chain, which can be very uncomfortable for traveling in a van for a thousand miles."

He made a face. "A van? I don't even get to fly?"

"It'll be a van, yep."

"Fuck that, I'll fight all of you." He readjusted, feet apart, and raised his fists in a boxing stance. "I was a Golden Gloves champion back in San Jose."

I stared at the man for a good while and then raised my hands. "Well, we'll just wait until the transport boys get here and see how they want to handle it."

"You're damn right!" He threw a few punches, shadowboxing the air between us.

Saizarbitoria followed me down the hallway, where I stopped to let him pass before he turned back to study me. "That's it, we're not going to secure him before they get here?"

Reaching beside him, I closed the heavy metal door to the cells and then continued on before stopping at the base of the steps and jacking the air-conditioning to its maximum setting.

"Do me a favor and close off all the ducts out in this part of the basement?"

He smiled. "Yes, boss."

I hung up with the manager of the IGA, confirming that yes, the bag that had been used as a liner in the million-dollar shoebox was, indeed, the current version the grocery chain was using. After that I called Wes over at the bank and confirmed that yes, the serial numbers were not consecutive, and the bills ranged in date from 1952 to a year ago.

"No large-size bills?"

"Not since 1927."

"No silver certificates?"

"No, and no confederate money either."

I repositioned the phone in my ear. "Anything on the bands?"

"They're a strange color, unlike any I've ever seen. Blank with white borders as opposed to ours, which are white with colored borders."

"I thought they were all blank?"

"No, definitely two-tone, lighter than the ones we use for one-dollar bills in a fifty-bill count. You see, when the Federal Reserve gave up counting bills by hand in the late seventies, the American Bankers Association set a standard for both the value and color of currency bands."

"I had no idea."

"All bills larger than one dollar come in currency 'straps' of one hundred and the color allows for quick accounting even when the bills are stacked, say in a vault. Striped bands are only used on straps for star notes."

"Okay, you got me there—what's a star note?"

"A replica banknote that replaces a faulty one during regular production to account for the serial listing but with a notation, usually a five-point star."

"Well, you learn something every day." I heard some noise out front and assumed the transport contractors were here for Gibson. "So, you're telling me that every denomination has a color code . . . What did you call it?"

"Currency strap: those used to wrap ones come in a number of colors, but fives are red, tens are yellow, twenties are violet, fifties are brown, and one hundreds like the ones you have here are usually mustard colored."

"But these are white with white borders."

I listened to the silence on the line connecting me to the man across the street. "Yes, and one other thing. They're overlapped by quite a bit, which leads me to believe that they're foreign."

"Why?"

"Most foreign bills are wider than ours, hence longer currency straps."

"No way to tell what country?"

"I've made some inquiries, but at this point, nada."

"Anything else?"

"There was a receipt for the shoes in the bottom of the box, under a flap. They were bought in El Paso, Texas, in 1963 for nine bucks."

"Interesting."

"I know, shoes used to be cheap. Did you get a warrant for the security box, just in case there happens to be one, from Verne?"

"Not yet, but I think I'll go up and bug him."

He laughed. "Good luck with that."

Alone and bereft, I hung up the phone and studied the surface of my desk, the front page of this week's *Durant Courant* tempting me to open it up and read Charley Lee Stillwater's obituary. "What'd you do, Charley Lee, rob a South American bank?"

Vic appeared in the doorway. "Hey, the transport guys are here, and there's a lot of banging coming from down in the jail and every time I ask Sancho about it, he just laughs and says to ask you."

"Tell him to go see if Gibson's got his clothes back on yet."

"He took his clothes off?"

"Yep, and then he oiled up like he was competing in a greased pig contest."

"Oh, boy."

Standing, I followed her into the main office where two fidgety men in uniforms and ball caps were standing in front of Ruby's desk. The older one with the ubiquitous cop mustache stuck out a hand. "Rick Pritchard, Security Prisoner Services." I took the sweaty hand, and he gestured to the other man. "Jim Brewer, second-in-command."

"Nice to meet you. You have your paperwork?" Ruby handed it to me, and I studied the transport-for-hire forms. "Where are you guys coming from?"

The younger one answered, his voice a little strained. "We're on a loop out of Oakland and went as far as Chicago."

"Chicago?"

"Yeah."

"In a van?"

The older one nodded. "But we had stops in Minneapolis, Bismarck, and Rapid City on the way back."

I flipped through the papers, holding them and looking into his bloodshot eyes. "That's at least twenty hours of driving."

"Solid. So, if you could just sign those papers, we'll get your prisoner loaded and be on our way."

"You've been driving for twenty hours and are planning on driving another seventeen once you get my prisoner loaded?"

The older one volunteered. "Hotel rooms are out of pocket, so we like to just keep moving." He pointed at the papers I held. "If you don't mind . . ."

"How many prisoners do you have on board?"

"Eight, not including yours."

Handing the forms back to Ruby, I turned toward the two men. "I want to see them."

Confused, they both looked at me. "The prisoners?"

"Yep."

"Look, with all due respect, we don't have time for all this, really."

I faced him squarely and changed my tone. "You're in my county, and without any disrespect, I've asked to see your prisoners. Are you refusing?" I stepped in a little, making a point of looking very closely at their dilated pupils and flushed faces. "Because if you are, the first thing I'm going to do is arrest you and get a blood sample to see what you're on. I'm guessing some kind of amphetamine?"

They looked at each other, and the older one stammered. "We've just been drinking a lot of coffee, Sheriff."

"Let me see your prisoners."

They looked at each other again and then turned and started out as I followed, meeting Saizarbitoria on the landing as he came up from the jail. "He's got his clothes back on and appears to have lost some of his fight."

"Good, follow us."

We continued out the door to where a large van with a utility box sat in the parking lot, the only windows in the cargo area, small and up high. Pritchard unlocked the back doors and swung them open to reveal a set of metal cage doors with ventilation holes drilled into them.

Leaning forward, I could see that a Plexiglas blockade divided the inside, with two women sitting on one row of plastic seats and four men on the other. There was trash on the floor and the smell was horrible.

"When is the last time these prisoners were out of this van?"

He stared at me.

"When was the last time these prisoners were fed or allowed to use a toilet?"

He gestured toward the woman who sat closest, her head hanging down and her leg irons attached to the floor. "We picked her up in Rapid City, so she's only been in here for four hours."

"But at least one of these prisoners has been in here for seventeen?"

He didn't seem to have an answer for that.

"Sir?" I peered into the darkness and could make out a middle-aged man in a hoodie and sweatpants seated next-to-last away from me on the men's side. "The man sittin' next to me was supposed to be gettin' some kind of medication for diabetes but he hasn't and he's passed out and soiled himself somethin' awful."

I stepped back. "Get them out."

Pritchard looked at me in disbelief. "What?"

"Get them out of there right now. We'll put them in our jail till they can be fed and cleaned up, and we'll take the other one over to the hospital to be looked at—you have his medication?"

The younger one, Brewer, nodded. "Um, yeah." He disappeared around the corner, and I motioned for Saizarbitoria to follow as I confronted Pritchard. "Heard of the Jeanna's Act?"

"Nope."

"You're gonna; it set a lot of guidelines for what you can and can't do with prisoners in private transport situations."

Saizarbitoria, holding a Ziploc bag, arrived with the younger man in tow. He handed it to me. "This was on the dash."

I felt the warm bag. "Insulin—you know you're supposed to keep this stuff cold, like in a cooler?"

Brewer looked at me and blinked as I turned to Sancho. "Call the EMTs and get them over here with some fresh insulin and then get Vic and we'll start loading these people into our cells."

Pritchard made the mistake of laying a hand on my arm. "Look, you can't . . ."

I looked at the hand and then at him. "You have a medical emergency on your hands, not to mention the fact that you are in so many violations that it's going to take a legal pad to list all of them. Now, what's going to happen, is that you're going to help my staff unload your van and we're going to see to that man who is unconscious. Then you're going to go get a room in a motel and get some sleep while we feed and bathe your prisoners and get them a night's sleep before you head out tomorrow morning, and that's only if I decide to not charge the two of you with criminal negligence."

He stared at me.

I glanced at the hand on my arm. Again.

5

"Did you really threaten to beat him to death with his own arm?"

"Not a threat, really." Trying to keep my foot out of Lola, the Cheyenne Nation's pristine, Baltic Blue, 1959 Thunderbird convertible, I eased into Ten Sleep Canyon. "Actually, more of a promise."

Rolling her arm over her seat, she turned and looked at the Bear, shouting to be heard over the rushing wind. "What are you going to do about this?"

Henry, awakened from his nap, withdrew his hand from Dog's back, and lifted his Red Pony Bar & Grill cap, rubbing his eyes and looking at her. "What?"

"That's about a half-dozen people he's threatened to beat the shit out of in the last four months."

"Has he acted on any of them?"

"Not yet."

He pulled his cap back over his eyes, his long hair twirling around it as if it had a life of its own. "Then there is nothing to worry about."

She pushed back against the passenger side door, kicked off her flip-flops, and rested her feet in my lap. "I think you got some anxiety repressed anger here."

Negotiating the switchback in a spot I considered to be the most breathtaking in Wyoming, I glanced at her. "Look who's talking."

"Mine's not repressed—I give it free expression." She turned her head, adjusting her sunglasses, and lodged her fingers into the raven hair. "I like to think of myself as something of an anger performance artist."

The Bear snorted from the back seat. "So, what happened to the prisoners?"

"The diabetes patient was revived and stabilized but will remain here until the next transport. The others were given showers, fed dinner, had a night's sleep, breakfast, and then sent on their way with strict instructions to the attending security officers that they stop in Salt Lake City and Reno with documents of transference to be signed by the sheriffs in both locations or I'd be filing charges with the company."

"You really do not like those services, do you?"

"When they're run correctly, they're fine, but when they're not, they're a horror."

Henry nodded, and I watched in the rearview mirror as he looked off toward the fish hatchery below. "Mind if I ask why we are coming this way to go to Cody?"

"There's an individual in Ten Sleep who knows this Count von Lehman who is something of an expert on fine art and antiquities."

Vic lowered her sunglasses. "Count von Whosit?"

"Count von Lehman. Barbara Schuster over at the Brinton told me about him, says he's something of an expert on this type of thing, and that I should have him look at the canvas to see what he thinks. I don't know him, but there's a guy over here in Ten Sleep who does."

Henry leaned forward as we left the canyon and twisted our way into the small town that was lodged at its base on the west slope of the Bighorn Mountains. Ten Sleep is known for a number of things, but mostly for its unusual name that was derived from the belief that it was ten days travel from a number of destinations—it is supposedly ten days travel from either Fort Laramie to the southeast, the Yellowstone to the west, Old Sioux Camp on the site of what is now Casper to the east, or from north to a spot on the Clarks Fork River that is now Bridger, Montana. Whichever you choose, they are all ten days travel or ten sleeps—hence one of the best western titles this side of Meeteetse, Ten Sleep.

A rock-climbing mecca, the town is a curious place: part cowboy, part art and craft, and all bohemian. With only one gas station, a couple of motels, and the rodeo grounds anchoring the west edge of the village, it was easy to miss if you blinked, which we did as I edged toward the red rock cliffs just outside the small town.

"We aren't stopping?"

"Ahead just a little."

Making a right at the sign that read TEN SLEEP BREWING COMPANY TAP ROOM, I smiled as Vic sat up and announced, "I just want to go on record that in my experience this is the best investigation in which we've ever been involved."

Pulling up beside an oversize tour bus, I parked the Thunderbird and took the keys from the switch, tossing them to the owner in the cavernous back seat. "You coming in?"

"No, I spend enough time in a drinking establishment." Pulling his cap back over his face, he mumbled, "I will dog sit," and laid his arm on the beast to settle him from being overly interested in the chickens that appeared in the side yard.

Vic climbed out on the other side, and we made our way up the gravel path to the large building. "It looks like a barn."

"I think that's how it started out."

"You sure somebody's here?"

"The guy I'm looking for is always here." Swinging the door open, I allowed her to go first and watched as she walked past the large vats of beer fermenting in the front room to continue toward the bar.

Moving into the room, I took a left and walked between the sparkling, stainless steel containers of the mill—mash tun, kettle fermenter filter, and finally the serving tank—to where a pair of legs were sticking out, accompanied by metallic sounds of tinking and banging. "That's an awful lot of beer to try to shotgun."

He laughed, recognizing my voice. "What are you doing on this side of the mountain?"

"Oh, on our way west and thought I'd stop by—I'm looking for somebody."

More tinks emanated from under the giant container, but after a moment his head kicked sideways, and I could see the bright blue eyes under the grungy bill of a ball cap. "Uh oh."

"No, nothing like that. Have you ever heard of a Count Philippe von Lehman?"

He laughed. "He's part owner of the brewery, if you count his bar tab."

"Know where he lives?"

"Sure, he used to live out 434 toward the Red Reflet Ranch, but I heard he moved to Story, over on your side of the mountain. He do something wrong?"

"No, I have a piece of art I need to have looked at, and I thought he might be able to save me a trip to Cody."

"If you can catch him. From what I understand, people fly him in and out on their private jets over in Sheridan."

"To do what?"

He shook his head. "Couldn't say. Hey, give me two minutes, and I'll be out from under here."

"Meet you in the bar."

"Sounds good."

Vic was behind the counter, pulling a handle and filling a glass as I entered. "Starting early?"

"Sun's over the yardarm somewhere." She plucked another mug from the bar back. "What's your pleasure?"

"A small speed goat."

She looked through the handles, finally settling on one and expertly filled the tipped mug, not allowing the foam to inundate. "What's a speed goat?"

"Wyoming slang for antelope."

She shook her head. "Here, drink your beer."

Leaning against the counter, we sipped as the general manager entered, wiping his hands on a rag. I gestured toward the young man. "Vic, meet Justin Smith."

He finished wiping his hand and stuck it out to her. "Don't worry, it's just beer."

My undersheriff lowered her mug and shook. "Really good beer."

"Thanks, I made it from scratch."

I nodded toward the bus out front. "Somebody sleep over?"

"Jalan Crossland and his band. The fire department had a tap-takeover fundraiser last night and things kind of got out of hand."

Vic raised a quizzical eyebrow. "Why does the fire department need a fundraiser?"

"It burned down."

"Oh."

Justin glanced at his wristwatch and then out at the silent bus. "They've got a gig over in Salt Lake tonight, so I guess I'll go out there and bang on the side or they aren't going to make it."

"So, you know this Count von Lehman?"

He nodded. "He used to be a regular, and then when he moved over to Story, he had this big bash and asked me to run about a thousand gallons of beer over there."

"Can we find the Count's place pretty easy?"

"Yeah, it's a castle. No kidding, he had the thing shipped over. It's smaller than a real castle, but not by much."

"He owns a castle but can't pay his bar tab?"

"Oh, he rolls in here every couple of months, and I remind him, and he writes a check. He's good for it, just forgetful."

I took another sip of my beer. "So, he lives in Story now?"

"Big Horn and Bozeman before that, and Boston, Cambridge, Rheims, Zurich, and a bunch of other places too, but don't ask him to find his car keys."

"Think we can just go out to his place and knock on the door?"

"You can, but like I said, I'm not so sure he's there. I do happen to know where he'll be tonight though. Big fundraiser for the museum over in Cody, and he's providing some art for the auction, so I'd imagine he'll be there if you really want to track him down—I can call and get you tickets." Justin glanced at his watch. "And I've got to go beat on a bus."

After a brief pizza stop at the Burlington Place, we pulled into Cody in the afternoon, and I saw no reason to put off going over to the museum. Vic was asleep in the back with Dog, and Henry had taken her place in the passenger seat as we eased through town, busy with tourists headed for Yellowstone National Park to the west.

"Business or pleasure?"

I shrugged. "Business, I guess. I didn't happen to bring any fancy duds for a museum fundraiser, did you?"

"I always have fancy duds, as you call them, in the trunk for just such occasions."

"Of course you do." Wheeling in the parking lot beside the teepees, I drove along the lanes looking for a spot, finally finding some shade for the VIPs in the back. "Just leave them here."

"God help anyone who bothers them."

Concurring, I walked around the back, opened the cavernous trunk, and slipped out my files and the protected covering containing the canvas that was lying on top of the suitcases before handing the Cheyenne Nation his keys. "Let's go."

I went over to the security desk and asked for Mary Robinson while watching the holograph of William F. Cody talking to the tourists in the lobby. "If he were alive, what do you think he'd think about all this?"

The Bear smiled. "He was a showman—he would have loved it."

"You're probably right."

"I may go over to the Plains Indian section and walk around while you are doing this, if you do not mind—see if I can spot any family artifacts."

I nodded, and he disappeared as I walked toward the center of the lobby where a '63, split-window Corvette sat, gleaming red and bulging horsepower, which was being raffled off for the Patrons' Ball in September.

"You should buy some tickets; you'd look good in that thing."

I turned to find the chief of staff of the McCracken Research Library, a tall, silver-haired, handsome woman who oozed competence. "I'm not so sure I could fit."

She studied me and smiled. "You might be right, next year we'll auction off a forklift. How have you been, Walt?"

"Good." I gestured with the padded sleeve under my arm. "A little out of my depth with this stuff."

"Follow me."

Walking through the entrance and past a massive grizzly bear mount ravaging a life-size diorama, we took the stairs into the semi-bowels of the building and continued straight ahead toward the research library portion of the museum.

"There was a big article about you in the Billings paper a few months ago; something about Mexico?"

I nodded. "I was over my head in that too."

"You're getting over your head a lot these days." She studied me with a kindness in her eyes. "Is that because Martha isn't around to look after you?"

It seemed strange to hear my late wife's name, but she and Mary had been associates. "Maybe so."

Entering through the reading room portion of the Mc-Cracken, we took a private door to a hallway with a number of posters on the wall, the entirety of Buffalo Bill's Wild West shows in innumerable languages. "He got around, didn't he?"

She called over her shoulder. "In 1899 they logged eleven thousand miles and did three hundred forty-one performances in two hundred days."

"Wow."

Entering another room, she held the door for me. "That includes daily parades and two-hour performances."

I stood there, still looking at the posters. "These are all originals?"

"Yes."

"Can I have one?"

"You can order a copy."

"Ah, of course." I joined her in a very well-lit room with a number of workstations containing all kinds of devices and contraptions about which I knew practically nothing. Mary stopped at a cubicle in the corner. "This is the conservation lab, and this is Beverly Nadeen Perkins."

"Hello."

The woman was on the phone but turned to smile and wave at us as we continued toward a very large table not unlike the one at the Brinton Museum. "Let's see what you've got."

I unzipped the padded folder and withdrew the wax paper sleeve in an attempt to exude professionalism only to watch the thing slip out and land on the floor between us.

Mary stooped and picked it up, cradling it in the light while adjusting the overhead lamp a little closer, illuminating the intimate battle between the cavalryman and the Indian. "That's an odd little piece, isn't it?"

We both turned as the woman joined us, Mary handing her the canvas. "Anything fun on the phone?"

She took the partial painting and stepped in between us, adjusting it in the light. "No, just an angry patron who had been at one of our clinics who thought he had an original Remington, which turned out to be an original Klauzowski instead."

"Never heard of him."

She glanced up at me. "No reason you would. He lived in a second story apartment in Scottsdale in the seventies and sold his paintings on the sidewalk in Old Town for about seventy-five bucks a pop. He was sometimes known to borrow elements from more well-known artists."

"Like Remington?"

"Especially Remington."

She lowered the canvas and stuck out a hand. "Beverly Nadeen Perkins."

"Walt Longmire."

"No middle name?"

"Not for public consumption, no."

Turning the piece over, she studied the back, the edges, and everything except the painted part of the painting. "Interesting. It's not a real canvas—probably a sack of some kind that's had gesso applied as a primer; looks like Italian gesso, an animal glue, probably rabbit skin along with chalk, white pigment, probably mixed with linseed oil to allow for the flexibility of the canvas." She turned and looked at me. "It's in pretty rough shape."

"What period would you say?"

"I can guess, but I think I'll use the XRF."

She walked back toward her work area, picked up a device that looked like a ray gun, and brought it over. "It shoots out a beam into the sample, which excites the electrons in the elements—usually iron, zinc, or lead—and they respond, but sometimes other elements too. Take cadmium, it wasn't used until mid-nineteenth century; therefore, if it shows up in a Renaissance painting you know it's a fake or that some sort of conservation work has been done."

"So, you can shoot it with Buck Rogers here and tell me if it's the real deal?"

"I can give you an approximate age, but we can get more of

a sense of the artist by technique: how they use their brush and palette knife, what paints they used. If you've got a primary resource like we do with Remington, then you can just compare that to the paint on the painting."

"I don't suppose you've got Cassilly Adams' palette lying around here somewhere?"

"No, I'm afraid not. The Budweiser painting aside, he was something of a minor painter."

"Meaning he wasn't very good?"

"Adams was a relatively unknown artist and something of a victim of circumstance. The majority of his illustrations were done for publishers who didn't credit him for the work, and then the illustrations were borrowed for other books and not attributed to him. He painted a number of scenes depicting frontier life and illustrated the 1883 Frank Triplett book *Conquering the Wilderness*."

"Sounds like he did all right."

"Not really—he died in relative obscurity in Traders Point, Indiana, in 1921."

"The painting he's known for, the Custer painting, was destroyed?"

She nodded. "In 1946 when the headquarters of the Seventh Cavalry burned." She continued to study the painting portion of the thing under the light. "There is an amusing story connected with *Custer's Last Fight*. Just a bit after the first publication of the work, Adolphus Busch had a lithograph sent to the governor of Kansas, who, after he retired, gave it to the State Historical Society where it was put on display in the early 1900s. It created something of a stir when it was observed that the brewery's name was prominent underneath the painting in one of the state's public buildings. Things came to a boil when

Blanche Boies, a follower of the prohibitionist Carrie Nation, threw open the doors of the museum and entered with an ax in hand. Finding the litho she buried the ax in it before being carted away by the police. I guess Blanche was infamous for attacking taverns in Kansas. Of course, all the museum had to do was contact Anheuser-Busch, and they just sent them a new one."

"How many have they printed, back when they had it?"

"A hundred and fifty thousand of the large ones and who knows how many smaller ones between 1896 and 1942. At one point they were shipping out about two thousand a month to servicemen all over the world."

"Goodness."

"I think it's safe to say that it's been seen by more drunk, questionable art critics than any other picture in American history."

I shook my head. "When can you get me the results from the heebie-jeebie?"

"The XRF." She thought about it. "Nothing pressing this afternoon; I could get the results to you this evening?"

"Wonderful." I turned back to Mary. "Am I to understand you're having a party?"

"We are."

"Can I get three tickets?"

"Justin already called me, but do you mind if I ask why you want to come?"

"I understand that there's an individual, a Count Philippe von Lehman, who is to be in attendance?"

"You mean No Count?"

I shook my head. "Does everybody in the state call him that?"

"Not to his face. He's been very kind to the museum and donates a number of paintings each year for us to auction off."

"I'd like to meet him."

"I'm sure that can be arranged."

"I understand it is formal?"

"Well, Western formal."

"Which is?"

"Tie and jacket, preferably one from a tuxedo and then jeans and boots."

"And where does one rent a tux in this wonderful town?"

"The Village Shoppe on Main Street." She studied me up and down and then frowned.

"What?"

"I'm not sure if they're going to have your size."

"That, is a very well-dressed refrigerator." The two of them sat on the bench and snickered at me.

I turned in the three-way mirror and thought I didn't look that bad. "It's the biggest one they have on such short notice."

My undersheriff shook her head. "What size is it?"

"I'm not telling you."

Henry studied my boots. "You are going to have to polish those."

I looked down; at least the boots and jeans were mine. "I thought I'd just go across the street and buy a new pair."

"Tuxedo rental and a new pair of boots—Cody is receiving a financial bounty from your visit."

Straightening my slightly stained hat, I figured it was going to have to do. Besides, it gave me a rugged genuineness—at least that's what I liked to think. Turning to Cheryl, the nice lady at the Village Shoppe, I slipped off the jacket and handed it to her. "I'll take it, along with a shirt, tie . . ."

Vic stood and added. "And cummerbund and a stud and link set."

I turned to her as Cheryl hurried away. "What's a stud and link set?"

She reached up and straightened my collar. "No doubt, the tuxedo shirt will have French cuffs, so you'll need cuff links and studs for the buttonholes."

"Right."

"You need to get out more."

Henry stood and stretched in his sweatpants, Lame Deer Morning Stars t-shirt, and running shoes. "I think I will take your dog and go for a jaunt at the reservoir."

"You don't need anything for tonight?"

"No, I have it all in my room, already hung up and steamed."

I nodded. "Something I did not know about you."

"What?"

"That you drive around with a tuxedo in the trunk of your car."

Vic laughed. "Yeah, like what are you—Formal Man? If a prom breaks out you can get the outfit in your trunk?"

"In all honesty, I had it cleaned in Billings last month and forgot to get it out."

We watched him go, exiting through the glass door and climbing into the T-bird with Dog and driving west. "I think he was embarrassed to admit that he drives around with a tuxedo in the trunk of his car."

"I think you're right."

Cheryl arrived with all my worldly needs wrapped up in a garment bag on a hanger. "We open tomorrow at ten, but we've had people just leave them hanging on the rod by the back door."

"No one ever steals them?"

She handed me the outfit. "Not this one, they'll think a rogue grizzly returned it."

After buying a new pair of boots across the street, we walked back to our lodgings at the Irma Hotel and made it to the bar; we were soon sitting at a window on Main Street. "So, this is Buffalo Bill's hotel?"

"His town."

She sipped a dirty martini. "Really?"

I nodded and held up my glass, swirling the ice in the pristine liquid. "And this is what started it."

"Water?"

I nodded. "There were some businessmen, George Beck and Horace Alger, from over in Sheridan who had bought the water rights to irrigate land south of the Shoshone River where it comes tumbling out of the Absaroka Mountains."

"Pronounced differently from our county."

"Correct. Cody joined in with these fellows, lending his considerable name and money to the Shoshone Irrigation Company, and they began digging the Cody Canal back in 1895, an enterprise the Wyoming state engineer said could not fail."

"Uh oh."

"Cody didn't know squat about irrigation or anything else inherent to the project but thought he did and kept interfering. Beck and Alger weren't too much better and found themselves in over their heads. The canyon where they were trying to build the canal was solid rock, and pretty soon, they gave up on digging the thing and just made it above ground out of wood."

"Did it work?"

"For a while." I sipped my liquid. "Cody expected the project to attract settlers, but that never came to fruition, so the eastern bankers who had invested in the project started dropping out. Before the turn of the century, Cody was the chief stockholder in a leaking, wooden canal that got washed out by a torrential storm, and they decided that the only thing to do was sell it for the one hundred fifty thousand dollars they had in it."

"And?"

"Nobody wanted it."

"So, what happened?"

"The Carey Act of 1894 that gave each of the states in the west a million acres of public land to develop water resources along with the National Reclamation Act that put the federal government into the water business." I threw a thumb over my shoulder. "That four hundred sixty-five thousand acre-feet of water reservoir that Henry and Dog are running around right now irrigates ninety-three thousand acres, and the concrete arch dam that makes it possible was the highest in the world at its time. In 1946 the whole kit and caboodle was named for Cody."

She toasted. "God bless you, Buffalo Bill."

We touched the lips of our glasses. "A better businessman in building towns than irrigation ditches."

"He really did help build the town, then?"

"Yep." I glanced out onto Main. "You ever wonder why the streets are so wide? It's so you could turn an eight-horse team around, one of his many edicts. He owned the newspaper, livery stables, blacksmith shop, and a number of ranches. He may or may not have coaxed the B&M, but when the railroad finally arrived, he sank his stakes in this town in one fell swoop."

"And what was that?"

"You're sitting in it." I glanced around the hotel. "The only stone building in town, his buddy Frederic Remington lauded it as good a hotel as any in the west. He built a hunting lodge on the way to this newfangled national park west of here, Pahaska Teepee, that ushered in an age of Yellowstone tourism with a fleet of steam-powered cars, and he held Washington's feet to the fire in getting a circular road built through the park to the new, eastern entrance. He was still doing the Wild West shows in the summer, but then he'd come back here and have spectacular parties in the hotel."

She glanced around at the ornate interior. "Why Irma?"

"For his daughter." Leaning back in my chair, I thought about the old showman who was probably more responsible for the image of the romantic American West than anybody in history. "By the end of his life he was losing his shirt in gold mining speculation in Arizona and had to mortgage the hotel, deeding the place to his wife just to hang on to it."

"You said he died in Denver, right?"

"Yep."

"And was buried there."

I sipped my water.

"Are you ever going to tell me that story?"

"Maybe someday."

"C'mon, you've got an ancestor responsible for stealing the body of Buffalo Bill?" She studied me. "Let's fix up that cabin on the mountain."

I sighed. "It's in pretty rough shape; no electricity and an outhouse."

"What, you don't think I can rough it?"

"I don't know, can you?"

"I used to go to Camp Robin Hood back in Pennsylvania."

"Camp Robin Hood?"

She nodded. "I rode horses and was hell on the archery range."

"Why does that not surprise me?"

"It was supposed to make me a well-rounded young lady, but I suspect it was just to get me out from under foot for a few weeks each summer."

"Did your brothers go?"

"It was a girl's camp."

I pulled out my pocket watch and looked at it. "We've got about two hours before we need to be over at the museum, and I want plenty of time to take a shower and get this rigmarole on."

She shook her head, gulped down the rest of her drink, and stood. "I'll help you, that cuff link thing can get kind of tricky."

I draped the tux over my shoulder and picked up my new boots, and we threaded our way through the opulent dining room and then headed up the stairs to the second floor and down the hallway, where I fumbled getting the key from my pocket. Finally getting the door open, I pushed it aside and allowed her to enter and then closed it as she walked over to the window and looked down on the side street where they did gun fighting reenactments every day during tourist season.

I studied her. "You okay?"

"I sometimes feel like my life is like a TV show in season

five, when the writers are just throwing weird shit in to keep things interesting."

I laughed—that was the great thing about her; you never knew what was going to come out of her mouth next. "So, who gets the shower first?"

"Water reserves are still a big issue here in the west, right?"

"Yep."

She stepped in closer and clutched the lapel of my jacket and the smell of her was intoxicating. "What say we conserve precious resources?"

Boy howdy.

6

I did what I did best in just such situations—ate, drank, and stood against the wall like a totem pole. I didn't go to too many formal events, because we didn't have too many formal events in the county to go to, so if I did, I usually fell back on a threadbare, mothball-scented, brown-tweed blazer Martha had bought me at Lou Taubert's in Casper.

Reaching for a canapé on the buffet table, I had heard a ripping sound somewhere in the depths of my rented tux and stood very, very still.

"It's formal, not statuary."

I glanced down at my date. She had returned from the bar and was handing me a beer. She was dolled up in high-heeled boots, tight-fitting jeans, a silk top, a silver and turquoise necklace with matching earrings, and an extravagant DD Ranchwear leather jacket complete with fringe and conchos.

"I'm trying not to buy this tuxedo jacket. I'm afraid if I move, I'll rip it more than I already have."

"It looks good on you."

Carefully, I sipped the beer. "I can't breathe; besides, I don't have anywhere to wear it."

"We could have a Sheriff's Ball." She leaned in with a salacious grin. "I know you have them."

"All right kids, break it up." The Cheyenne Nation appeared to our right and sipped a glass of burgundy, looking like some kind of First-Persons-Indigenous-Peoples James Bond. "How is it going?"

"I can't breathe."

He touched the rim of his wineglass to the neck of my beer bottle. "Drink up, you'll be fine."

"Who are the chicks?"

The Cheyenne Nation glanced at my undersheriff. "Excuse me?"

She gestured to the room at large. "The tall blonde who was hanging all over you at the silent-auction exhibition table, the brunette who was attempting to dry hump your leg at the bar, or the audacious redhead who was trying to give you a tongue tonsillectomy by the ice sculpture."

The Bear was, indeed, cutting a wide swath through the upper end of female high society here in Park County.

"I have been exchanging in important cross-cultural references."

"As long as that's all you're exchanging."

He shrugged. "We will see."

"How do you not get diseases?"

"I lead a morally pure life. How about you?"

Lifting the rim of her martini, they touched glasses. "Here's to moral purity."

"Has anybody seen the count?"

Vic shook her head. "I have cased the entire joint, and there's not a single cape in the place."

Henry's black eyes glittered over the attendees. "There is supposedly a VIP reception upstairs in the boardroom, and I would imagine that is where he is along with the director, your friend Mary, and other assorted luminaries."

Spotting Beverly Nadeen Perkins, I nodded toward her. "That's the conservationist who is x-raying the painting."

"My painting?" The Bear cocked a head. "I have not met her."

Vic snorted. "She's the only one."

Ignoring her, he sipped his wine. "Did you say x-raying?"

"Yep, some kind of gadget that vibrates the electrons and gives you the age of the painting. I guess it also can tell from the elements in the paint as to whether it's a reproduction, an original that's been tampered with, or the real deal." I pushed off from the wall like a ship having sailed into view, acutely aware that I was moving like an inanimate object from the waist up. "I'm going to go ask her how it went before she disappears."

As I approached, Beverly was talking to some patrons and turned to smile at me and then suddenly looked concerned. "Are you all right?"

"What do you mean?"

"You're moving strangely."

"Um, I pulled my back a bit."

"You want to hear about your painting?"

"You read my mind."

She glanced around. "It's pretty interesting, but it might be best if I were to just show you back in the lab?"

"Sure, when?"

"After the auction? I'm off to Boston tomorrow, and I doubt I'll have much time. I was expecting you this afternoon."

"Sorry, I got busy."

"Nonetheless, after the auction tonight?"

"Deal."

"By the way, if you're looking for Count von Lehman, he's holding court over there with some of the other donors in the hallway by the stairs."

Looking that way, in a spot I could not have seen from where I'd been standing, there was a small gathering of individuals surrounding a large man wearing a dissolute, full-length velvet duster, an ascot, and wild hair that looked as if he might've driven in with his head stuck out the window the whole way.

"Thanks."

The conservationist made a face. "Wait till you meet him and then thank me."

As I drew nearer, I could see him gesticulating with an unlit cigarette and speaking in a vague accent. "The methodology requires the profundity of chaos, an ever-evolving cycle of destruction and resurrection, by turns exasperating and exhilarating, which defines the creative process. Do you honestly think that Picasso could have been half as productive without all those screaming wives and mistresses and untold amounts of legitimate and illegitimate children crawling around underfoot?"

A well-dressed man I knew, Barron Collier II, was bold enough to attempt a response. "Well, I think . . ."

"Of course not, in the greatest chaos is the clearest window to the human soul. As Cézanne once said, we live in a rainbow of chaos. And the desperate solitude of Van Gogh with his mysterious and innate ability to thrive in the sorrowful conflicts that comprised his burdensome life."

"He committed suicide." A woman on the fringes of the conversation ventured.

"Hogwash, he was murdered, likely by a teenager wearing a Buffalo Bill outfit, of all things."

The crowd grew silent at that one, but the woman persisted. "Surely, you're joking, he . . ."

"A young man whose family summered south of Paris—I don't recall the name . . ."

"René Secrétan."

He studied me, somewhat put off. "That's right, the pharmacist's son had seen the Wild West show the year before Van Gogh's death, and they say he modeled himself after Bill Cody, wearing a buckskin outfit with fringe, a cowboy hat, and an actual pistol that worked sometimes."

"Evidently it worked the morning he shot the Dutch painter."

Scratching his head, which did nothing to straighten his hair, he pointed toward me with the cigarette. "You seem sure."

"So do you."

"I'm sure of the theory, but you seem absolute in it." He studied me, unhappy that I'd taken some of his spotlight. "Are you some kind of art historian or something?"

"Um, no."

Barron took my elbow and spoke. "Count, this is Walt Longmire, the sheriff from over in Absaroka County."

He sniffed in disapproval. "A sheriff?"

"When I'm not on the lecture circuit."

There was a twitter of perfunctory laughter, but not from him. "And on what do you base your absolutist theory?"

"Forensic evidence of which there was a recent review that said there were no traces of powder burn even on the hands in a period when handgun cartridges were loaded with black powder, smokeless powder having only been introduced in 1884.

Black powder is extremely dirty and only burns about half its mass when fired, so there would have been a great deal of it evident if the artist had shot himself."

The count rested an elbow on a crossed arm, holding the cigarette from his mouth. "Really?"

"Also, the gun had been fired most likely from a range of two feet and at an oblique angle from the left."

Another man looked doubtful. "What does that . . ."

"Van Gogh was right-handed." I sipped my beer. "If it was suicide, as he himself claimed, why shoot yourself in the stomach with your off hand and then limp home and curl up in your bed to take twenty-nine hours to die? Why was the pistol never found, and why did his paint, easel, canvases, and other supplies never turn up?"

The count adjusted his glasses. "Then why do you suppose he told the gendarme when asked if he'd intended to commit suicide, that he thought he had?"

"He was covering for the young man who had shot him. Secrétan was a brat who had publicly tormented Van Gogh and only later in life admitted to loaning Vincent the gun, which, if he did, could be seen as a criminal act in itself considering the man's mental state. I think Vincent didn't want the boy to suffer and took the shooting as an opportunity to end a painful and tortured life."

"Death by Buffalo Bill." The count silently mimicked clapping. "Bravo, bravo."

I affected a slight bow and then watched as he took an extra moment to stare at me. Then he strolled off, pushing open a glass door and walking into the garden, where he dropped his head and cupped his hands, attempting to light his cigarette.

A chic brunette, with just a trace of silver in her hair, touched my arm, and I turned, happy to see Donna Johnson, a friend and ex-CIA analyst. "So, whatever happened to Secrétan?"

"He became a well-respected banker and businessman in France."

Her husband, Wally, laughed and slapped me on the shoulder. "Sounds like they needed Walt Longmire."

I shrugged and glanced outside where the count had disappeared. I smiled an apology. "Excuse me."

Moving through the crowd, I opened the door, relieved to be outside, especially in a garden. I'd just started to adjust my eyes and look around when a tall young man, impeccably dressed and with formidable blond hair, appeared to my right.

"Can I help you?"

"I was looking for Count von Lehman?"

"And this is concerning?"

I stared at him for a moment. "Who, exactly, are you?"

He stuck out a hand. "Conrad Westin, I'm the count's personal attaché."

We shook. "Walt Longmire, Absaroka County Sheriff."

There was a strange noise as if crickets were chirping, and he held up a long finger. "Excuse me for just a moment." He produced a small cell phone from an inside pocket and stepped away, speaking into it. "Yes?" He turned, and I couldn't make out the conversation, but after a moment he turned back, pocketing the device. "So, is there a problem?"

"Not if I can talk to the count."

He smiled a perfunctory grin. "Well, perhaps if you tell me what this is pertaining to?"

A voice called out from the darkness. "Who sold you that jacket?"

Nodding to the young man, I wedged off the jacket, laid it

over my arm, and moved toward a fountain to my right where the voice had come from.

Spotting the glow of his cigarette, I changed direction toward the bench where he sat. "It's a rental."

"It's a rental for someone two sizes smaller than you."

"It was spur of the moment, and they did the best with what they had in stock."

"I'm glad you took it off, I thought you were going to pass out."

"Me too." I stepped forward, extending a hand. "Walt Longmire."

"Count Phillip von Lehman." He glanced past me. "Thank you, Conrad, I'll take it from here."

The young man came over. "You're sure?"

"Quite."

Westin studied me for a bit longer and then entered the building as I turned back to the count. "I've heard a great deal about you."

"Oh, no."

"Most of it good."

He waved with the cigarette in a vague loop. "I can be an acquired taste." His face turned back to me. "Sorry about that— Conrad's on loan, and sometimes takes his responsibilities a little too seriously."

"An interesting young man."

He nodded. "Used to be quite an artist himself, until he discovered that arranging to sell paintings is actually more lucrative than simply painting."

I watched as the young man observed us from inside. "Barbara Schuster at the Brinton said you're gifted when it comes to ascertaining the credibility of period pieces of pigment-encrusted canvas."

He laughed to himself. "This is an odd conversation to be having with a Wyoming sheriff—come across something in a yard sale you want appraised?"

"You know what, *Count.*" I emphasized his title. "You and I will probably get along a lot better when you stop underestimating me."

He sat there for a moment, appraising me like one of those pigment-encrusted canvases. "You might be onto something there. I have a tendency to perform, and I imagine it's quite annoying."

"A bit."

He extended his hand this time. "Philippe."

"Walt." I sat on the bench with him. "What do you know about Cassily Adams?"

He stared at me for a moment. "That he was lucky Anheuser-Busch brewed beer."

"Anything else?"

He thought about it. "Busch had F. Otto Becker rework the famous painting I'm assuming we're discussing, brightening the somber tones to prepare it for the lithograph, and there were about three different versions produced." He inhaled the cigarette, raised his head, and exhaled. "Which is why you see the damned thing in every bar, saloon, rumpus room, man cave, and garage in America."

I nodded. "I did a little research and discovered that Busch donated the actual painting to Custer's old outfit, the Seventh Cavalry, in about 1895 when the unit was based in Fort Riley, Kansas."

"Later moved to Fort Grant in Arizona Territory while the Seventh was sent to Cuba in 1898 during the Spanish-American War. The painting languished, rolled up on a flagpole in the rafters of a forgotten building, until Brigadier General Robert W. Strong discovered it on maneuvers in 1929 and contacted then commander Schellie, who took it back to Fort Bliss, where it was placed on display in the officers' club." He took a puff of his cigarette. "God only knows what condition it was in at that point."

"Wasn't it sent to Boston during the Works Project Administration and repaired?"

"It was and then returned. It burned in 1946, along with the building in which it was housed." He studied me some more. "If you don't mind me asking, why so much interest in a minor artist who painted a mediocre painting that was destroyed more than a half century ago?"

"I think I may have an artist study."

"A study."

"Yep."

"Hmm." He smoked the last of the cigarette and then leaned down, crushing it out and depositing it into the pocket of the velvet duster that had seen better days. "May I see it?"

"I was hoping you'd ask."

He stood. "When?"

"After the auction? It's in the basement in the conservation lab being x-rayed. Supposedly, they'll have some information for me, but we think it might be bad form to abandon the fundraiser."

He shrugged and pulled another cigarette from a pack of Dunhills he produced from another of the myriad pockets. "I am the epitome of bad form, but since I have a few paintings that I own that I donated for the auction, I think it would be de rigueur to wait until after."

"Agreed."

He started toward the door but then stopped. "One last question."

"Yep?"

"Do you consider the gifts of a great artist to be a blessing or a curse?"

"It's according to the artist, and the art."

He slowly smiled and gestured with the unlit cigarette. "In the meantime, I have other performances to give and if you find them tiresome, imagine how I feel about them."

"Break a leg."

Walking over and opening the glass door, he ventured in where Conrad Westin waited. "One can only hope."

"Where the hell have you been?"

"Talking with Count von Lehman."

She reached up and fingered my collar. "Should I check you for bite marks?"

"You'd only find yours."

She grinned and sipped her third martini. "We appear to have lost the Bear."

"Probably got a better offer."

"So, how was the count? Any count at all?"

"An odd duck, as they say." I thought about it. "Kind of the absentminded professor type, but there might be more than meets the eye."

"He any help with your painting?"

"We'll see . . . we're all going to take a look at it after the auction."

"A private viewing?"

"So to speak."

We watched the auction commence. There were a few items I was tempted to bid on, but I'd neglected to get a number and was subsequently left in the cold. The pangs of non-purchase weren't so bad until a familiar artist came up with a dramatic depiction of the Bighorn Mountain foothills.

"Isn't that the artist you like from over in Big Horn?"

"Joel Ostlind, yep."

She peered toward the stage where the price of the painting was rising. "You like that one?"

"I like everything he does."

Her hand shot up with the card numbered 289. "Back here, you assholes!"

The auctioneer made a face but then laughed before committing to the fray as Vic battled it out with a matriarch in the front row, a well-heeled couple to our left, and a short-haired blonde sitting with Conrad Westin about halfway back in the same row as Count von Lehman.

My undersheriff was standing pat at four thousand dollars, and there was a momentary hesitation in the other buyers before the blonde struck again, setting off another round of bids that soon approached eight thousand.

"Isn't this getting a little rich for your blood?"

"Shut up." She raised her card again. "What did I get you for Christmas?"

"That's not the point."

"Your birthday?"

"I don't . . ."

"Shut up." She raised the bid, and there was another pause as the remaining buyers finally realized that bidding against Victoria Moretti was like swimming with sharks having been chummed to a state of frenzy. My father used to always say that when you bid on anything in an auction, be sure to set a price in your head as to what it's worth to you and not exceed it. Victoria Moretti had never heard that theory, and if she had she'd discarded it long ago.

"Ten thousand!"

The blonde in the middle row sat with her hands folded in her lap.

"Ten thousand, once!"

My undersheriff murmured under her breath. "That's right, bitch . . ."

"Ten thousand twice!"

The winning bidder scanned the ballroom with tarnished gold, daring anybody to take her on.

"Sold!"

She turned to me. "Gimme your checkbook."

Sighing, I handed it to her.

She disappeared, and I watched the remainder of the auction, enjoying the fact that the bidding was active and the museum would make a much-deserved profit. Still holding my jacket over my arm, I skirted the room, and stopped at the nearest bar to get a beer.

"Your friend, she must've wanted that painting badly."

Turning, I found the blonde from the bidding, the diminutive beauty with an undetermined accent, sipping what looked to be a vodka and tonic. "I think it's a gift for me."

"How very nice for you."

I extended a hand. "Walt Longmire."

"Katrina Dejean." We shook. "I know; I was on the out-skirts of your dissertation on Van Gogh."

I bent my lips in a smile that I hoped conveyed a little humility. "Dissertation, huh? I hope it didn't seem that way . . ."

"Oh, the count was being pompous, and it was fun watching him taken down a notch."

"You know him well?"

"Business partners—I've helped him with some acquisitions overseas."

"You, Conrad . . . He must have an entire team here."

"You met Conrad too?"

"He seemed concerned for the count's welfare."

She sighed. "The count has enemies."

"I guess he's a shaker and mover, huh?"

"He has the ability to spot things before the public, which gives him an advantage in artistic trends." She leaned in. "I don't mean to be nosy, but I noticed the two of you in conversation outside—what was that about?"

"An investigation concerning a piece of art; a study that may or may not be of significance."

"Historic?"

"Possibly."

"A sheriff concerned with a piece of artwork strikes me as fascinating. Can I see it?"

"I'm not so sure it would be worth your time. I'm having it looked at now to determine the age."

"Here at the museum?"

"Yep."

She smiled and shrugged. "Well, it must be of some worth if they're a part of your investigation."

"Not really—they're just doing it as a favor."

She turned back and smiled up at me. "One more question before I let you go, the really important one?"

"Sure."

"Who is that friend of yours, the Native American?"

"Henry Standing Bear, he's Northern Cheyenne."

"He's delectable, is what he is."

I nodded. "You're not the first woman to notice."

"I suppose not." She glanced around some more, looking for the Bear no doubt. "Is he available?"

"I think you need to take that up with him."

She eased away with a salacious smile. "I think I will."

I couldn't help but feel as if I'd just gotten the third degree, and then watched as she and Vic passed each other, both of them turning back for an appraising second look.

"They don't give you your painting until the auction is over, but I paid for it." She handed me my checkbook. "Well, you paid for it."

"Thanks."

"So, who's the chippy?"

"A patron of the arts, looking for access to the Cheyenne Nation."

"Access, is that what they're calling it these days?"

"Among other things." The bidding was continuing for the upper echelon, and I was just as glad that my depleted checkbook was back in my possession. "Want to head down toward the conservation area in the basement and get the final ruling on the find of the century?"

"No, I have to get your painting soon, and I want to be at the head of the line."

"I guess I'll go by myself then."

"Deal."

I watched as she drifted toward the tables to the right of the stage and then made my way along the wall, back into the main lobby, only to be cut off by Donna Johnson. "A word, Walt?"

"More than one if you'd like."

She smiled, an asset that came in second to the computer-like mind of hers that had led her to the upper reaches of the Central Intelligence Agency, a portion of her life she rarely mentioned. "If you don't mind my asking, what's the story with you and Lehman?"

"I have a piece of art that I'm hoping to get appraised for a citizen, and from what I'm to understand he's gifted in the field?"

"He is." She glanced around. "He's also as slippery as a lubricated eel."

"In what way?"

She leaned in closer. "He made his name filching unofficial art out of the Soviet Union back in the nineties, millions of dollars' worth of the stuff—Kharitonov, Leis, Mikhnov-Voitenko, Nemukhin, and Rukhins."

I shook my head. "He doesn't strike me as the covert type."

"Oh, he's not, that's just the problem. Back in the day he got picked up by the KGB a half-dozen times, so many times that we started thinking he must be working for them."

"Was he?"

"I'm still not completely sure, but I do know he was approached by the agency and he turned them down, saying it might compromise his attempts to liberate the art and artists."

"Liberate?"

"It was a period when art was severely controlled by the Russian government, and anyone who was doing anything modern or abstract was perceived as perverse and an enemy of the state. The artists were harassed, their paintings burned, some even died under peculiar circumstances."

"And Katrina Dejean?"

"An associate of his, French I believe, but I don't think she was around during that period. She's more of a conduit to Russian oligarchs who sometimes purchase art."

"Illegal Russian art returning to the motherland?"

"Coals to Newcastle, huh?"

"And Conrad Westin?"

"Who?"

I glanced around, trying to catch a glimpse of the tall young man. "He also appears to be attached to the count."

"Don't know him." She looked around again. "Anyway, she's not the one to be careful of; Lehman has a bodyguard of sorts, Serge Boshirov, who is rumored to be ex-KGB."

"You're kidding."

"No, when the wall came down and glasnost and the big thaw in the Cold War came, those guys were a dime a dozen, but don't underestimate him until I can do a little research."

"What, he's got a poisoned umbrella?"

She smiled up at me. "I just want you to know the lay of the land or steppes for that matter."

"Got it."

She patted my arm as she turned and drifted back into the crowd. "Be careful, big guy."

I watched her go and then moved along the wall, exiting through an archway and heading back into the main lobby. As I crossed toward the stairwell, the hologram of Buffalo Bill suddenly appeared again, like a ghostly apparition. "Ladies and gentlemen, permit me to introduce myself, I am William

F. Cody. I'll show you some of the stirring scenes of the frontier . . ."

I guess the thing was motion activated, but it didn't make it any less unsettling alone there in the darkened hall. Leaving Buffalo Bill to talk to himself, I walked down the hall and took the stairs leading below and then to the left.

There were lights but not much illumination as I went down the wide hallway past a number of displays and through the double doors that led to the research library. The door at the far end of the boardroom was open, and I could see lights on in there. I figured that Beverly Nadeen Perkins was probably still tied up upstairs, but that it wouldn't hurt anything for me to be there a little early. When I saw the door to the conservation area open, however, I got the feeling that something was wrong.

Hurrying in, I could see someone lying on the floor, a lamp and scattered papers forming a kind of halo beside the large table where we'd studied the partial painting. Reaching for my trusty Colt at my side, I discovered that I'd neglected to include it in my formal attire.

I kneeled by the table and could see that the conservator was still breathing, even with a pretty impressive bump at the back of her head. Rolling her to one side, I was relieved when she raised a hand to brush away my assistance. "Beverly, are you okay?"

"What the heck?"

"I think you must've fallen?"

She reached to the back of her head. "I guess. I was just coming down here to meet you, and I must have fainted or something."

Propping her up, I looked to the side and saw a small Chinese statue of one of the terra-cotta soldiers of the Qin Shi

Huang dynasty lying on the floor, broken. I held it up to her. "Did you knock this off the table when you fell?"

She looked at it, continuing to massage the back of her head. "No, that's from Margaret's desk in the next room."

Examining the thing, I could see a little blood and hair attached to the edge of one shoulder of the figurine. "Somebody hit you with this."

Mary Robinson appeared in the doorway behind us. "I'm sorry, but am I interrupting something?"

I slowly pulled Beverly up to a standing position. "I think your coworker has been attacked."

She came over and took the conservator's hand. "Are you all right?"

Beverly nodded carefully. "I think so, but why would anybody . . ." Her eyes darted toward the table. "It's gone."

"The Adams study?"

"Yes."

"How long have you been down here?"

Peering at her wristwatch, she glanced back up at me. "Less than ten minutes, I'd say."

I handed her to Mary. "Call 911 and get an ambulance to check her out. I came down the main entrance before you did, so I doubt anybody could've gotten through the way we came in." Looking around the room, I spotted the only other doorway. "Where does that go?"

Mary assisted Beverly to a chair. "It's a utility hallway— there's locked storage space and access to the auditorium and pretty much every room on this level that way."

"Great." Stepping toward it, I turned back. "Stay here but call security and have them send some people down to cover the exits."

"Where are you going?"

"I'm going to go look for that painting."

Pushing the heavy fire door open, I stepped into the hallway, lined with bays covered with security wire. The lights were on when I entered, evidently set off by motion, and I watched as they reflected along the concrete floor.

Feeling rather naked without my sidearm, I advanced, checking the bays as I went, but discovering they were all locked. Continuing on, I reached a crossroads with hallways going in opposite directions but then noticed the lights were only on in the one straight ahead. Testing my theory, I stepped in the one to the right and waited as it flickered on. Looking back at the one straight ahead, I returned to that course.

Reaching down, I opened the first door and found another storage area, this one for office supplies, which caused the lights to flicker on as I had supposed. Closing that door, I advanced and checked the next to my right, the lights not being on inside. I turned the knob, but it was locked, so I went on to the next to find a utility room full of breaker boxes and custodial supplies, my motion turning on the lights once again.

Moving to the next door, which was quite a bit farther, I discovered an entryway that met another—but in this one the lights were on. Pushing the door open the rest of the way and checking to make sure it wouldn't lock behind me, I entered what turned out to be an anteroom, and then pushed open the next door to find myself in the back of an auditorium, the steps to a light booth to my immediate right.

No automatic lights came on, and I surmised that the much larger room must've been on a separate system, the only illumination in the theater being warning lights at the foot of the rounded stage and small ones in the seat stanchions along the two carpeted aisles.

As the door quietly closed behind me, I waited and listened.

There was no sound, and I glanced around, seeing a set of doors to my left that must've been the main entrance and then another door to the far right marked as a fire exit.

I slowly began making my way down the aisle, checking the rows on both sides as I went. Getting to the front of the house and then center stage, I looked back at all the empty seats and the closed curtain behind me.

I found the opening in the curtain and pulled it aside to glance around. Finding a podium and an upright piano but nothing else, I dropped the curtain and was about to give up when I heard something.

It was the scuff of shoe leather on concrete unless I missed my guess.

Glancing down, I was pretty sure the entire auditorium was carpeted.

The anteroom was concrete, but that was on the other side of the heavy door, leaving the steps to the light booth as the only place from which the noise could've emanated.

Quietly moving back to my right, I got as far as the steps when there was a commotion at the doorway where I'd entered, a slab of light casting across the carpet.

Jumping from the low stage, I ran up the aisle toward the door and blew through it and the next, ending up in the empty hallway as footsteps slapped in a rapid retreat.

I ran toward the noise and found myself in the crossroads. I turned right where the lights had come on and ran forward and spotted a figure dart around a corner at the far end.

Charging down the hallway as fast as I could, I turned the corner and blew through another double set of doors and was confronted with a truck dock and dumpster. Circling the dock and following the sound of the footsteps, I turned at the corner of the building at a dead run into the parking lot, where hundreds of people were flowing toward their cars.

Standing still and breathless, I scanned the area trying to see if anybody was still running, but no one was. They all just looked like regular museum patrons heading home. It was at that moment I felt a hand on my shoulder and turned to find the Cheyenne Nation scanning the crowd along with me.

"Somebody stole my painting?"

7

"It was the real deal." Beverly nursed her head wound with a cold pack in the boardroom, with the rest of the staff, the Park County sheriff, Vic, and me as the medical technicians checked on her. "The study was period perfect with no pigmentation altered, and the style was consistent with Adams." She glanced up at me. "I am so sorry."

"Don't be silly. I'm just glad you're okay."

Vic shook her head. "Who in the world would go to these kinds of lengths to get that stupid portion of a painting?"

"Quite a few, I'm afraid." Having had enough, Beverly pushed the EMTs away. "I'm fine, really."

The young man in the blue jumpsuit wasn't deterred. "I'm afraid you're going to have to come with us back to the hospital for overnight observation."

She glanced up at him. "What?"

Jack Pharaoh, one of the new breed of Wyoming sheriffs, was seated next to Beverley, a handsome kid with his hat pushed back and a strong dollop of dark hair across his forehead, he was an ex-rodeo roughstock hand and tough as rawhide. "Routine with this type of injury, besides I'm sure they're going to want to x-ray your head."

"And find nothing?"

The young sheriff smiled as Mary got Beverley's coat and assisted her in putting it on as she stood. "It's the social implications of the piece and the fact that the missing painting is a national icon. There are plenty of private collectors who would be happy to pick up that artist proof on the black market and then keep it hidden for their own enjoyment."

I nodded. "Count von Lehman seemed interested in it and was supposed to meet us down here, but he hasn't shown?"

Mary shook her head. "No, I saw him leaving with an entourage."

"There was also a woman who was curious about the piece."

Vic turned to look at me. "What'd you do, send out a newsletter?"

Ignoring her, I continued. "A Katrina Dejean."

Mary and Beverley turned to each other—both of their faces blank. "Never heard of her."

Jack stood and watched the ladies go. "I'll do some checking."

Assisting Beverly in showing the medical staff out, Mary turned back. "As to the count, I wouldn't be too upset, he can be a little flaky."

Pharaoh nodded. "Roger that."

I stood, and Vic and I walked to the main room of the research library in time to see Henry reappear in the doorway of the boardroom. "She will be all right?"

"I think so, just knocked around a bit." I turned back to him as the Park County sheriff joined us. "Anything?"

Pulling a piece of paper he must've purloined from the staff, he unfolded it, revealing a flake of muddy blue about the size of a fingernail. "This must be a piece of pigment from the painting. I found it on the floor."

Jack sighed. "So, whoever hit Beverly definitely took it."

"I think it is safe to assume."

Vic studied the paint chip. "Someone who knew the building?"

"Maybe, but it's also possible that they heard me coming and just took the only other door that was available."

Jack rested a hand on his sidearm, a big Kimber semiautomatic, and pulled his hat down. "You didn't get a glimpse of them or anything?"

"Nope."

"I hate it when something like this happens in my county." The young sheriff shook his head. "A smash and grab."

"Oh, don't worry about it, Jack, it'll turn up." I nudged his shoulder. "Hey, how come you weren't at this shindig?"

"Too many old girlfriends at this thing, and I don't need that kind of drama in my life." He nodded and started off toward the stairs as we followed. "How long are you folks in town?"

"We head out tomorrow." I glanced back at Henry. "Heading home by way of where?"

"Billings." The Bear nodded. "Montana Girls Basketball Three-on-Three state championship."

Jack studied the two of us and then dropped his head. "Interesting."

We shook. "Let me know if anything pops up."

"Will do."

We watched him hurry off and entered the museum at large, where the hologram of Buffalo Bill continued to speak to the empty hall. Vic stopped and stared at the apparition. "Maybe he did it."

"Bill Cody?" The Bear gave it some thought and then shook his head.

Vic looked at him. "What?"

"A couple of weeks after the Battle of the Greasy Grass or the Little Bighorn, as the white populace called it . . ." Henry cocked his head as the hologram attempted to interrupt. "Cody rejoined the Fifth Cavalry still wearing his red fireman's shirt and velvet pants with jingle bells attached, which was ridiculed as being a preposterous outfit for a scout whose number one resource, by the way, was stealth. Anyway, Cody encountered a group of seven Cheyenne warriors, at which point he shot a young tribesman, Hey-o-wei, in the leg. Both men fired at each other, and the young warrior was killed. Cody then walked over, scalped his opponent, and proclaimed, "The first scalp for Custer."

"What, he was a buddy of Custer's?"

"As a matter of fact, yes." The Cheyenne Nation sighed. "Anyway, Cody sent the scalp home, where his wife opened the package expecting a gift and fainted dead away."

"Yuck."

"He immediately returned to the stages of the east where he reenacted the battle. As the run continued, the duel became more fantastic. Cody would end the show by holding the bloody relic aloft to the admiring throngs."

"I bet Philadelphia audiences loved that—you should see a Flyers game sometime." She yawned. "So, what happened to the scalp?"

"It is here at the museum, somewhere."

Henry glanced up at the hologram, which for once wasn't talking. "All is fair in love and show business."

Dog had not eaten the room but had made a sloppy mess when drinking from the toilet, which Vic reported on from behind the closed door. "Your dog had a water fight of epic scale in here."

"Sorry. I'm going to take him for a walk." I found the leash in my duffel, snapped the link onto his collar, and led him out, making sure I had the key to the room in my pocket. I walked us down the steps, turned the corner at the bar, and was surprised to see Count von Lehman entertaining a half-dozen revelers who obviously weren't quite ready to give up the night.

Circling around the stairway, I exited the hotel from the side entrance and walked to my right, noticing the missing newsstand and magazine shop that used to be there.

"Need some air?" Katrina Dejean, the blonde from the auction, lowered her head and peered out the passenger window of a silver Mercedes sedan gleaming in the partial moonlight of the velvety night. "Or just walking your grizzly bear?"

Stopping, I turned, and Dog ambled over and stuck his head in her window. Pulling his head back out, I apologized. "Sorry, I left him in the room while we were at the auction, and I think he got lonely."

She smiled. "Want a lift?"

"No, thank you. We'll just circle the block and then go back. I saw the count was entertaining in the bar."

"Yes, but I've heard all those stories before. How did it go with your painting?"

"It was stolen."

She stared at me and slipped the car into park. "You're kidding."

"I wish I was. While we were at the auction someone forcibly took it from the conservation area in the basement."

"Forcibly?"

"The conservator was hurt."

"Badly?"

"No, I think just her pride."

"But someone has your painting."

"Well, it's not really mine . . ."

"You should talk to Philippe about this."

"Why?"

"Hmm, how can I put it . . . especially to an officer of the law." She opened the door and got out, came around, and, leaning on her car, continued the conversation. "People who have questionable works sometimes see the count—he, um, has a somewhat malleable ethic concerning the ownership of art."

"He's a fence."

"Exactly." She smiled. "He has a habit of going from A to D by accidentally discovering C while forgetting B altogether."

"All right, now I have to ask—how did you two meet?"

"Nonconformist, unofficial art."

"Is that a major?"

"In Russia, yes." She folded her arms, covering the skin that was exposed by her dress to the cool of night. "Terms that were applied to certain artists in the period from Stalin to glasnost when, if their works were deemed as being dissident, they were likely to be shipped off to mental asylums or gulags."

"I've heard that."

"These artists constituted small, very insular groups who specialized in more modern styles that the government did not approve of, so they had to sell their wares on the black market. Unfortunately, there was little money being paid until Philippe arrived on the scene in the sixties." She shook her head. "He had all the charm of an unmade bed, but he could make his way around Kiev, Odessa, Moscow, and Saint Petersburg with hardly any trouble at all. By the time I met him he had a catalog of more than one thousand pieces of art."

"How did he get the stuff out of Russia?"

"Any way he could, stuffing them in the linings of his suitcases, down the legs of his trousers, and in the liners of his hats. Have you been to his home in Story?"

"No."

"It's amazing and horrifying all the same. I mean if the art had been left in the Soviet Union, it would have most certainly been destroyed."

"So he sells it?"

"A little at a time, and surprisingly back to Russians—oligarchs who are attempting to retrieve pieces from their national past."

"And these people come to him with other works of art."

"Yes, he knows the buyers." She turned and moved back toward the driver's side of her car and opened the door. "Let's go to the hotel, and we'll talk with him."

"All right. Dog and I will meet you in the bar."

Katrina met me at the entrance where we'd exited, her car parked at the curb. "C'mon."

I followed as Dog took in the surroundings: a little more upper class but a lot less comfortable when compared with our usual haunts back at the Red Pony. Count von Lehman was still there, and the numbers of the faithful had diminished only a little, leaving him, Conrad Westin, four other couples, and a very large man, who pocketed his cell phone and stood as we arrived. "I help you?"

Katrina motioned for the big guy to sit, but he ignored her and stepped between the count and us. Spotting the bulge in his suit jacket, I stopped, and Dog immediately growled.

"Serge, don't be tiresome." Katrina stepped around him and sat next to the count.

He was massive, certainly clocking in at over three hundred pounds, a power lifter kind of gone to seed, and his accent was thick although his voice was surprisingly high and fluttered through a very Rasputin-like beard. "Serge Boshirov?"

Staring at me, his small eyes looking a little unsettled. "I know you?"

"Depends." I smiled. "Are you armed?"

He smiled back. "Depends."

I think both Dog and I cocked our heads at that. "This is an establishment licensed to serve alcohol, and firearms aren't permitted."

He flexed his shoulders and chest, and I guessed his age to be somewhere around forty, forty-five. "Permitted and allowed are two different things, my friend."

"We'll see after I call over to the bartender, and he alerts my buddies over at the Park County Sheriff's Department."

He spread his hands. "We have barely met, and you already call for the backup?"

Katrina barked at the count. "Philippe, call off your eunuch."

After a moment, Lehman smiled. "Serge, sit down, or I'll put you on a leash like he does his dog."

I shook my head. "No, either the gun goes or he does."

The bodyguard didn't move.

"Serge, go."

He turned to look at the count but then did as he said and began to move toward us. But when Dog curled his lip, revealing some daggerlike ivories accompanied by a rumble that increased in his chest, Serge diverted to the other side, giving us the hard eye the entire way.

Frankly, I was relieved, because if he'd tripped and fallen on us he probably would've killed us. I sat, and Dog buried his head in Katrina's lap.

Conrad ran a hand through his blond locks. "I see he's friendly."

"Overly." I glanced around. "Actually, he's probably not supposed to be in here either, so Serge could've called it a draw." I stuck a hand out to the nearest couple, who looked a little uncomfortable. "Walt Longmire."

They relaxed a bit, the bald man indicating his companion. "Nadia, my girlfriend. I'm Klavdii Krovopuskov . . . nice to meet you."

I extended a hand to another couple. "Nice to meet you."

The tallish man, who was embellished with an extravagant mustache, nodded. "Patrick Monahan, and this is my wife, Monica."

I looked at the rest of the people—two blondes, a smaller man with thick glasses, and another man who looked as if he were ready to nod off at any instant. Giving a general wave, I smiled. "Hello, everyone."

The bald man leaned forward, cocking his head slightly and smiling, his Van Dyke to the side. "Philippe tells us you are a sheriff?"

I nodded. "Absaroka County, here in Wyoming."

"So, you are a *real* cowboy?"

Conrad laughed. "Define *real*."

Ignoring Westin, the bald man laughed, and he had perfect teeth. "You have the hat and gun, so you must be a real cowboy."

"Not necessarily, there isn't a cowboy I know who wouldn't take a rope over a gun any day."

"You can make a living with a rope?"

"Sure, you can hang people." Conrad settled into his chair with a smug look.

I also ignored Westin and continued. "A rope and a horse, yep."

"But surely, you can make a living with a gun also."

His friend leaned in and touched his arm. "Kiki . . ."

He shrugged. "Eh, we drop the guns for now . . . Which is more important, the rope or the horse?"

"Well, you're talking to a rancher's son, so I'd say the horse—you can work with a horse, and you can travel with one, and besides, they're good company."

Conrad once again studied me. "And you can eat them."

I made a face, just to let him know my feelings on the subject. "There have been instances, but most cowboys I know would rather eat their boots than their horse."

Kiki nodded. "Have you ever heard of the Tuva Cup, Sheriff? Tuva is a small province in Russia, Buddhist by nature, Turkic by language . . ."

"More Mongolian then?"

"Exactly, but they have a national race every five years, and it is spectacular." His companion, Nadia, touched his arm again, and he turned to look at her in annoyance. "What?"

"The plane, it leaves in an hour."

"It is my plane, it leaves when I say it leaves." Turning back to me, he continued. "In this fabulous race, they travel over a hundred miles a day . . ." She touched his arm once more, and he lowered his head, speaking quietly yet distinctively. "Do not touch me again."

She very carefully pulled her hand away.

He raised his head and sighed, looking around the table. "I am afraid that we must leave." He stood and extended his hand to me. "It was wonderful meeting you, Sheriff." He turned and clasped the count's hand in both of his. "Philippe, it has been glorious, and do remember what I said about that business we discussed."

"My pleasure, Kiki."

He turned to Conrad as the young man made to follow him. "You will assist the count in looking out for my interests?"

"Of course." He looked disappointed but then nodded and sat again.

The remainder of the group stood and followed him out the door onto the main street, but Krovopuskov paused before letting it close and studied me for a moment before disappearing.

"An interesting man."

The count turned to look at me and then laughed. "You could say that."

I motioned to the bartender who'd been studiously ignoring us, probably in hopes that we'd get out of there. As he approached, he looked down at Dog but said nothing. "Can I help you, sir?"

I gestured toward Katrina.

"Vodka tonic."

I looked at Westin, but he shook his head.

"And you, sir?"

"Got any Rainier?"

"Yes, sir." He didn't look very happy about it but headed back for the bar as I turned to the dwindling party and Dog sat.

"Someone stole your painting?"

"Boy, word travels fast in the art world."

He leaned back in his chair, running his hands through his hair, which did nothing to straighten it, actually making it look even more like a small gray bonfire on top of his head. "The local constabulary was present, so I made some inquiries."

Katrina took her drink as the bartender returned. "I told him you might be able to assist him."

"Because I know all the art thieves?"

I sipped my beer. "Something like that."

Conrad smiled and nodded toward Philippe. "How do you know he didn't steal it?"

I shrugged, turning to look at the count. "He doesn't seem like the type—he might take advantage, but I don't think he'd take private property."

The count turned to Katrina. "You've been telling stories out of school." He sighed. "I am something of an opportunist, yes." He shrugged and reached out for his glass. "It was stolen from the conservation room in the museum?"

"It was, and the conservationist was hit over the head to do it."

He seemed genuinely concerned. "Is she all right?"

I studied him. "Yes."

"Hmm . . . Then it is either someone intimate with the museum or someone who is desperate."

"I'm leaning toward desperation."

"Why?"

"As the local sheriff said, it just has a kind of smash-and-grab feel to it."

"Well then, perhaps I will hear from them." He set his wine back down. "Now, why would anybody be so desperate as to hurt someone over such a trivial thing?"

"As a Cassilly Adams study, what would you place as its value?"

"So, its validity was confirmed?"

"It was."

He thought about it. "Oh, perhaps a few thousand." He looked at Dog and then me. "Doesn't seem worth it, does it?"

"No, but there is a million dollars tucked away in a dead man's shoebox."

He sat forward. "Oh my, this is getting interesting."

"Now, as stated, I doubt the study itself is worth a million dollars—so where did the money come from?"

He lifted his glass of wine again and glanced at Katrina. "This individual had other resources?"

"Not that I'm aware of."

Conrad's voice was flat. "This individual, was he killed?"

"I'm still waiting to find out about that."

Count von Lehman sat back in his chair. "So, your investigation has more to do with the million dollars than it does the stolen study?"

"Overall, but I don't particularly care for people hitting people over the head and stealing things in my state."

Conrad chortled and drummed his fingers on the table in indication that he was ready to leave. "Understandable, but who would do such a thing?"

The bartender approached in a lingering fashion, perhaps in

hopes that we'd take the hint. "Would anybody like anything else? If not, I'll be closing the bar."

The count waved him away. "That's fine, my good man." He felt around in his pockets and then glanced at Katrina. "I seem to have left my wallet in my other pants, would you mind . . . ?"

She raised an eyebrow at him. "I have twelve dollars in my purse."

"I'll get this."

He smiled at me. "Thank you so much, Sheriff. I'll pay you back."

"No problem."

He inclined his head toward Katrina again. "Do you mind giving me a ride back to the hotel, dear?"

Before she responded to the count, she glanced at Conrad. "My hotel?"

"I'm embarrassed to say, but I really don't have anywhere else to stay."

Rolling her eyes, she stood and petted Dog and handed me a business card. "Here's my contact information—do you have one?"

I sighed. "I think I do in a drawer at my office, somewhere."

"Well, if we hear anything, I'm sure we'll be able to track you down."

"I'm sure." Shaking hands with the count, I watched them exit out the front onto Sheridan Avenue and walk toward the corner.

Conrad watched the two of them go and then turned to me. "I hope you find who did this, Sheriff."

His grip was sure, and I watched him depart through the front doorway. "Thanks, I do too."

The bartender arrived with the check.

$638.42.

No Count.

As I turned the corner at the landing at the top of the stairs, I was pretty sure there was a fight going on down the hall and slowed my pace, as it appeared to be coming from our wing.

Stopping in the hallway, I listened some more, but the noise had died down, so I drew the magnetic key card from my pocket and started to run it through the device on the lock just as the noise started up again from the room next door.

I stood there assuring myself that it wasn't the kind of altercation that needed any interference and then tripped the lock on our door and followed Dog into the darkened room with the television blaring.

Vic sat in the bed naked, the sheet tucked under both arms with the remote in her hand as Dog jumped up to join her.

Carefully placing my wrinkled rented jacket on the back of a chair, I turned it and sat, taking off my boots. "What're you watching?"

"*The Legend of Custer.*"

"Bad?"

"Very. The only person I think I recognize is the guy who rode the bomb in *Dr. Strangelove* . . . ?"

"Slim Pickens."

"Yeah—anyway, you can't watch anything for the bacchanalia going on next door."

I dropped a boot and pried off the next one, all the while listening to the noise. "How long has that been going on?"

"Forever."

"Well, how nice for them."

"How 'bout you go and pound on the door?"

"I don't really want to do that."

"How 'bout I do it?"

"I don't really want that either."

She flipped off the TV, and I had to admit there was an abundance of animallike noises emanating through the wall. "Then what?"

"If you can't fight 'em . . ." I dropped my second boot with a *thunk* and smiled at her. "Join 'em."

Jaya "Longbow" Long was truly impressive in an easy, nonchalant way, dribbling the ball on the outskirts of the game. As she passed it between her legs and then casually spun it on a finger like a rotating planet, I guessed her age to be seventeen going on thirty-five.

There were boys at the Montana Girls Basketball Three-on-Three state championship because, well, there were girls.

She was tall, like her aunt, Lolo Long, tribal police chief on the Northern Cheyenne Reservation, and the boys on the sideline waved to her, but she ignored them, instead watching the opponents from the Crow Reservation she would soon play. The Cheyenne and Crow had been adversaries for thousands of years, and the basketball competition did little to convince anyone that members of the two tribes had ever buried the hatchet, except into one another.

The girls were ferocious, using their feet to trip, and sabrelike elbows to crowd their way into the semifinals. The three young women from Lame Deer representing the Cheyenne stood by and watched the trio from Hardin as they attempted to put a lid on a Polson team from the Flathead Reservation.

"Are there any non-Indian girls who play basketball in Montana?"

The Cheyenne Nation turned to look at Vic. "Not as well as we do."

Glancing down the bleachers of the outdoor event, I was glad we'd gotten to Billings early—the place was packed. Granted, we were only an hour away from two of the biggest reservations in Montana, so the native presence was very strong, and you got the feeling that there was a lot of tribal pride on the line. There were four half-courts on North Broadway when the competition had started, but now that we were only one game away from the championship, the action had centered right in front of us.

One of the Crow girls faked a layup and then pivoted and passed the ball to another, who dropped a ten-footer with nothing but net. There was a thunderous cry from the assembled masses, and you knew that the majority of the audience was, indeed, Crow.

Jaya Long stood in the other court with the ball tucked under one elbow as she watched the Crow players congratulate one another, something I hadn't seen the Cheyenne women do after they had beaten the strong Hardin team earlier. They had simply walked off the court and stood together but not looking at one another, instead, watching the other teams the way red-tailed hawks sit on fence posts and watch field mice.

Predatory.

"They are going to take a thirty-minute break, so we can go down and you can meet her." Henry stood, but Vic remained seated.

"You're not going?"

She shrugged. "I'll save our seats."

I followed the Bear, and we squeezed out of the aisle, clanged down the aluminum steps, and moved through the crowd to stand at the curb. A breathtaking, tall woman with an interesting, scythelike scar saw us and approached, swinging her dark hair back.

"Coaches and contestants only, beyond this point."

Henry smiled. "How do you know I am not a coach?"

Chief Long didn't smile. "Because no one in their right mind would let you be responsible for youth."

"She's got a point."

Long stopped, and I found it amusing that she and her niece stood in exactly the same posture. "Hi, Walt."

"Hi, Lolo."

"Nice scar."

I gestured toward the young woman now shooting foul shots with the assistance of one of her teammates. "Another athlete in the family?"

"Extended family. She was having trouble at home, so I allowed her to stay in my basement but only if she lived by the rules."

"How's she doing?"

She turned to look at the young player. "Pretty well. She's got her senior year to go but there's already interest from the UConn, Duke, Stanford."

"So, she's smart too?"

The Northern Cheyenne Tribal Police Chief growled. "Too smart for her own good."

I glanced at Henry and then back to the chief. "So, there's a problem?"

"She's a teenager, so there are nothing but problems—you had one of those, didn't you?"

I thought of my daughter and granddaughter down in Chey-enne. "I did and another one to go someday."

"There's the stuff you normally have to contend with, but this is a little different." She sighed, running a hand through her hair. "Threats."

"What kind of threats?"

"Life-threatening threats."

Henry inclined his head and lip-pointed. "Show him the note, Lolo."

She reached into a pocket inside her jacket and produced a copy of a note that had been on the kind of paper you'd find in a school binder. She handed it to me and folded her arms.

I studied the typewritten words, which were pretty hor-rific, describing actions and making threats on par with the worst I'd ever seen. "Where was this given to her?"

"Here in Billings."

"At an event or game?"

"No, when she and some friends came up to see a movie, it was left under the windshield wiper of her car."

I flipped it over, looking for something that might resemble a clue. "Another student? I mean, it is notepaper from some-thing like a binder."

Long shook her head. "I don't think that's the language or idiom of a high school student, do you?"

"Not really, but I'm assuming you talked to her friends?"

"I have."

"And?"

"Nothing." She took the paper back. "You don't think this note has a racist slant?"

"It does."

"Ever heard of the Brotherhood of the North?"

"No."

She refolded the note and pocketed it. "It's a white supremacist hate group here in Montana—you might want to check them out."

"You think they're responsible for the threats?"

"It fits their MO."

"How many contacts has she received?"

"Twenty-three."

I sighed. "Since?"

"It all started with a feature article they did in the *Billings Gazette*, which got picked up on the AP wire, along with some TV and radio interviews."

"You contacted the local authorities?"

She cocked her head, the dark hair covering one eye. "I am the local authorities."

"Sounds like you need a bodyguard for her."

She glanced over her shoulder at insouciance personified with a basketball, still shooting foul shots. "Among other things."

I gestured toward the Bear. "You've got the best in the world right here."

She studied me. "I need an investigator."

"You are an investigator."

"I need a white investigator. Nobody is taking this seriously, but if I get you on board, then people might start paying attention—besides, as much as I hate admitting it, you're the best."

"Well, as much as I'd like to help, I don't see . . ."

"She's like a daughter to me, Walt. I don't think I could stand it if something happened to her."

"It's not even my state . . ."

"Things wouldn't heat up until late fall, early winter; months away."

"I don't know . . ."

"Just meet her." She turned and yelled. "Jaya!"

The young woman didn't respond and kept shooting, even though it was pretty obvious that she'd heard her aunt.

"Jaya Long!"

I watched as she finally turned, at the stiffness in her neck and the pride of her strut as she approached—and all I could think of was a kid I'd known years ago, a kid with too much muscle and not enough brains headed off to play offensive line for the University of Southern California. A crew-cut kid in a hand-me-down pickup truck who had never seen the ocean—a kid who thought he had the world by the tail and would soon come to figure out that that world's tail was something you'd do well to never, ever grab.

Jaya got close, and I could see she was about six feet tall, a smidge taller than her aunt, and that she made sure the older woman knew it. "Yeah?"

Giving her a good helping of silence, Lolo gestured toward us. "This is Henry Standing Bear and Sheriff Longmire."

There was a flicker of recognition as she glanced at the Bear, who had played in a Montana high school state championship himself back in the day and was a legend across the high-plains courts. Then she looked my way and immediately flicked me into the aged dustbin the way only a young woman's eyes can.

I extended a hand. "Walt Longmire, nice to meet you."

She ignored the hand and didn't make eye contact. "Sheriff, huh?"

"Yep."

Lolo crowded in, her face inches from her niece's. "You greet this man properly with the respect he deserves—he is meeting you as an act of consideration and you do not ignore another person's consideration."

The teen backed away a half step, gesturing toward the court. "I've got a game."

"If you don't behave properly, this game and any others will be put on ice until you can learn to control yourself."

She dropped her head with an exasperated sigh, and when her face came up with a dazzling grin, the transformation was pretty impressive. She extended her hand. "Jaya Long, so pleased to meet you."

I shook the hand. "Nice to meet you too."

The smile slammed shut like a door as she turned to her aunt. "Can I go now?"

Lolo stared at her for a moment and then gave a curt nod, and we watched as Jaya loped off to join her teammates.

I glanced at Lolo and leaned over to her ear. "Are you sure you're not the one who wrote those notes?"

8

Bits of ribbon fluttered from the budding branches of a stunted juniper, the National Forest Service having decided to allow the dancing prayer flags to have their day, and every other, since 1876.

"We don't know. We just come by here and there's another one tied to the branches, hundreds of them, actually." She leaned out the window of one of those elaborate golf carts the park rangers use to patrol the battlefield. "The Indians aren't as bad as the tourists. There was a man who wanted to know why we didn't plant grass and water the hill, since it was a gravesite after all."

"I guess they miss the point."

The older woman poked her Smokey Bear hat back on her silver locks. "Sand, rocks, and sagebrush; that's the way it was when they died, and it's the way it should stay. I swear if they had their druthers there'd be beer and hotdog stands and souvenir shops right here on the hill."

The history books say that there were no survivors at the Battle of the Little Bighorn, but there were thousands, thousands who waited after the battle for the other cavalry boot to drop. The combined nations of the Lakota and the Cheyenne, and even the five Arapaho who had fought, knew that a retribution was coming—they just didn't know when.

Vic slipped her thumbs into the back pockets of her jeans and looked down the ridge that had carried the Seventh to their doom. "I can't believe I've lived here all these years and never been here. I mean I saw it from the highway . . . But here, it's different."

I waved goodbye to the ranger and regarded the prayer tree one last time before stepping up with my friends. "In what way?"

"Fucking haunted."

It was a difficult statement to argue with, standing there above the winding river with the trees that had witnessed the battle and the mountains—our mountains—strung along the horizon, scraping the afternoon sky raw.

"Private Charles Windolph."

Vic looked back at me. "He one of those markers down there?"

"Nope, but he said that what he saw here would haunt him to his grave. Men staggering around in circles, confused and bleeding, wandering through the broken skirmish line at the ridge that looked down at the bloodstained grass and the waves of heat that distorted the vision of the dying men who lay there screaming for water while others farther down the slope were being hacked to bits by Lakota and Cheyenne warriors."

"This Windolph guy, he was here?"

"Yep. He had arrived in New York six years previously—had left Germany to avoid getting conscripted in the Franco-Prussian War, but he couldn't get a job, mostly because he couldn't speak English, and so he figured a great way to learn the language might be to join the army. Faulty logic. He was with Colonel Benteen, Company H, up here farther down the ridge, and he got a Medal of Honor for providing cover fire for the men who were attempting to get water."

Vic kneeled and plucked a piece of grass from the hillside and placed the stem into her mouth. "He survived?"

"Till 1950, buried over in the Black Hills."

"I thought there weren't any survivors?"

The Cheyenne Nation shook his head, turned, and walked past us. "None of Custer's personal command survived."

We watched as he continued across the roadway, dodging the tourist buses and quietly unaware of the looks he was receiving from the many tourists who were probably sure they were seeing the living embodiment of Crazy Horse or a distant relative of Sitting Bull.

"He gets emotional up here."

She smiled a sad smile. "I can understand that."

"His people may have won the battle, but in the end they lost the war—nomadic tribes with nowhere to be nomads.

We eventually followed Henry and entered a walkway on the other side where a large mound of earth rose up with the memorial to Wooden Leg and the Unknown Warrior, with red dirt at its center and wall panels for each of the tribes that fought there, and above them, the outlines of the Spirit Warriors, who stretched horizontally—ghostly figures.

The Bear stood there, looking through them at the high-plains sky, taut and threadbare blue; a few people walked around the place, giving him room. "Many Cheyenne children were born on the trail north from our imprisonment in Oklahoma; women would fall back in the hollows or clumps of sage to give birth to children whose mouths and noses were held shut to keep them from crying as the long knives . . ."

"Cavalry." I interpreted.

The Bear nodded and continued. "Would ride past. Then the women carrying their children would sneak through them in the night to rejoin the tribe. These children would learn the most important Cheyenne virtue first—silence." He smiled back at us. "There is a saying among my people that none are truly defeated until the hearts of their women are on the ground."

Vic attempted to get the chronology straight. "This is before the battle?"

"Yes, there were many things that led to this travesty, including the Battle of Washita River where Custer took his Cheyenne wife."

She turned to look at him. "You mentioned that back at the bar."

"Mo-na-see-tah, the fifteen-year-old daughter of Little Rock. After the battle in Oklahoma, some fifty-three women and children were used as human shields and then taken captive by the Seventh Cavalry. By all accounts, the young woman was beautiful, and Custer took her as his own. According to Benteen, Chief of Scouts Ben Clark, and the histories of my people, she bore him a son."

"Holy crap."

"There's some conjecture about that." They both looked at me. "Custer contracted syphilis while at West Point, which evidently left him sterile, leading some to believe that it was his brother, Thomas, who impregnated the girl."

"These guys were real charmers, huh?"

Henry shrugged. "A Custer is a Custer."

"She stared up at the sculpture and the skeletal figures on horseback. "Do you think they knew who was attacking them?"

The Bear shook his head. "No, I think not. They simply

knew that they were being attacked and that they needed to protect the women, children, and the aged."

"They didn't know that they'd killed Custer?"

"Eventually." He glanced at me and turned to look at her. "Do you know what the winter count is?"

"No."

"It is a pictorial account of a tribe's achievements painted on an animal hide, a sort of annual calendar of events of any great importance to the Cheyenne."

"So?"

"The Battle of the Greasy Grass appears in none of them; for my people it was a skirmish and a disorderly one at that." Watching his eyes, I saw them travel past Vic and me.

Turning, we found about a hundred and twenty people standing behind us with their sunglasses and ball caps, the tour buses having just disgorged their contents. Everyone was silent, held in thrall as they recorded the Bear on their cell phones, held aloft.

The Cheyenne Nation nodded solemnly and raised his hands. "The next show is at two o'clock."

Under the watchful eyes of Cassilly Adams's print of *Custer's Last Fight*, we ate our Big Crow Indian tacos, sipped iced tea, and looked out from under the eaves of the outdoor dining room at the teepees along the edge of the Custer Battlefield Trading Post parking lot. "So, when does the guest of honor arrive?"

The Bear smiled. "Who knows, he is a chief and works on Indian time."

"Has he always been that way?"

"Um hmm, yes, it is so."

We both smiled into our empty plates as Vic continued eating like a civilized person. "So, what are we going to do about your stolen painting?"

"It wasn't really a painting, and it wasn't really mine."

Taking another bite, she chewed on that and swallowed. "What was it worth?"

"Not much, according to the experts."

She turned to Henry, who had already finished his mammoth lunch. "What would you do if you had a million dollars?"

"Buy a heater for my bar that worked."

"And a sump pump for the basement during irrigation season."

He sipped his iced tea. "I could afford both?"

"I think so."

She gestured toward me. "My lamebrain boss just gave away a cool million."

The Bear shrugged. "It is his nature."

Vic made a face. "What's that?"

"Honesty."

She turned back to me. "I want a new truck."

"Go buy one."

"I don't have any money."

"The county does."

She slumped back in her chair. "They do?"

"The Department hasn't bought a vehicle in more than twelve years, so we're probably due."

"You're kidding."

"Nope."

She sat forward, studying me. "Don't you want a new truck?"

"No."

She thought about it. "How come you don't ever tell me these things?"

"You never asked. It's like the computer I got: you just put in a requisition and the county commissioners say yay or nay."

Henry leaned in and stuck a hand out to stall the conversation. "Wait, you have a computer?"

I nodded and gestured toward my second-in-command. "Yep, but they made me give it back."

He turned to Vic, who shrugged. "Wasn't me. Ruby decided it was more trouble teaching him how to use it than it was just doing the shit herself."

"*É-peve-ešeeva!*" The Chief of the Cheyenne Nation and Tribal Elder Lonnie Littlebird was rolled forward to our table, a muscular young man who looked familiar steering him over and smiling down at us as the chief displayed a mock anger. "You have eaten without me?" Glancing up at the young man, he shook his fist. "Gone are the days when the younger generation paid tribute and treated their elders with the respect they richly deserved. Um hmm, yes, it is so."

Barrett Long, Police Chief Lolo Long's little brother, extended a hand to Vic, then to Henry, and finally to me before glancing back at Lonnie. "You wanna Coke, old man?"

The indignity disappeared. "Yes, with ice, please." He turned back to us once the young man was safely out of ear reach. "He is a very good boy."

The Bear placed a hand on the old Indian's arm, slender with pronounced veins. "How are you, Lonnie?"

"My legs hurt."

"You do not have any legs."

"That is probably why they hurt." He glanced at Vic. "*Haaahe.*"

She smiled. "Hi."

"Have we met?"

"Yes."

He leaned in toward her. "Did we sleep together?"

"I don't think so."

"Well, hopefully we will get another chance. Um hmm, yes it is so." He turned back to me. "Someone has stolen your painting?"

I gave out with my rote response. "It wasn't really a painting, and it wasn't really mine."

Ignoring me, he threw the lock on his wheelchair and leaned back like a self-satisfied potentate. "When was the last time we worked on a case together?"

I glanced at Henry and cleared my throat. "I don't think we've ever worked on a case together, Lonnie . . ."

"The time we caught that guy who robbed the Blue Cow Cafe and then the other one a year and a half ago." He reached out and patted my hand. "That was a good case, the one with the girl who fell. We broke that one wide open, didn't we?"

I glanced at Henry, who shrugged. "Um, yep, we did."

"You should be looking for a white person. They steal things." He glanced around. "They stole a whole country from us."

Attempting to distract him, Henry inquired as to the subject of late. "They were asking about the Battle of the Greasy Grass, Lonnie."

Lost in thought for a moment, he pursed his lips and began speaking. "My grandfather fought in this battle, but he never talked about it; he never talked about anything. There was a time when I was growing up that I thought he didn't know how to talk. One time when we were sitting under a tree reading, he farted and closed his book and said, '*Excuse me,*' and I remember looking around and thinking the tree had spoken."

Barrett arrived with the Coke and sat it in front of Lonnie.

"No straw?"

"You said ice, you didn't say anything about a straw, old man."

"Get me a straw before I run over your big feet with my chair." Watching him go, he turned back to us. "He is a very good boy." Puzzled, he stared at the soda. "Where was I?"

The Bear quietly urged. "Your grandfather."

"What about him?"

"The Battle of the Greasy Grass."

"My grandfather, he was there."

Henry nodded patiently. "Tell us some more?"

Lonnie gave out with a tiny gasp, struck with recommencing his story. "I was going through his dresser drawer one time looking for his pocketknife, something that I wasn't supposed to be doing, and I found something strange in with his socks, a totem or charm. It was shaped like a bird but with this funny tuft of hair on top of its head."

Barrett arrived with the straw and unwrapped it, placing it in the chief's glass and pulling up the chair he'd moved for Lonnie. "You still telling that same story, *má'haeso*?" Seeing Vic make a face, the young man explained. "He had another guy who rolled him around and said yes-sir and no-sir, but he got bored and fired him." He whispered. "You might think I'm being disrespectful, but it's just job security."

Lonnie waved a hand at him. "Hush up and learn something." He turned back to us. "So, I found this tiny stuffed bird made of deerskin and took it out in the yard and was playing with it when he came over and snatched it away from me." Lonnie thought back. "He was very angry, and I'd never seen him that way. He held the totem up to me and said that this was the true Littlebird in battle and that he had worn it since his first combat experience when he was thirteen years old— that he would tie the charm to himself and that it gave him protective powers so long as the charm was never hit."

Vic smiled, never one to be taken in by spirituality. "And he tried this out, did he?"

Lonnie nodded. "The second time at the Battle of the Greasy Grass he was maybe seventeen years of age and said that he was old enough to notice a great many things and see the reasons for them. He said the Cheyenne had been on the camp by the Little Bighorn for only one night. He said the next day around noon, the troopers charged down Reno Creek and drove all the people out of the northern camp and set fire to the lodges, but the people from the lower camp heard the noise and rushed north. The troopers retreated as the people surrounded them. My grandfather said the soldiers seemed drunk, but I think he meant panic-stricken, and that they couldn't shoot straight."

The Bear rested a chin in his palm. "This would be Reno's detachment?"

Lonnie nodded. "Um hmm, yes, it is so."

"Perhaps they were drunk."

Lonnie shrugged. "Perhaps. If I had been there surrounded by that many hostiles, I would have wished to be stinko too." His eyes went past me to the hill on the other side of the road where the battle had actually taken place. "The soldiers could have stayed in the cover of the trees but instead crossed the river and rode to the high bluff where my grandfather said they were left alone because the men wished to return to the village to check on their loved ones. As they returned, they heard more noise and realized it was another assault. My grandfather said there was a woman who grabbed at his foot and told him that the soldiers were attacking from the north, so my grandfather turned and rode toward them. He said that the Long Hair and his men were at the level space at the bottom of the dry creek, and that the men on both sides fought valiantly, and that a man tried to shoot him from his pony when he charged him, but the soldier's carbine misfired, and so he knocked the man down with the butt of his pistol. When he turned his horse, the cavalryman was getting up and clearing his weapon and reloading. Raising the gun toward my grandfather, he fired."

Lonnie lifted the straw to his mouth as we all waited.

Tasting the soda, he made a face and looked at Barrett. "Did you get me a Diet Coke?"

"I got you a Coke, old man."

Lonnie made a face, licking his lips. "This tastes like Diet Coke."

Barrett made an agonizing cry in the back of his throat. *"Ayeegah* . . . Finish your story."

"What story?"

"The story you're going to tell before I strangle you to death."

He nudged the glass toward the young man with his fingertips. "Go get me a real Coke."

Barrett folded his tan arms. "Finish the story before I roll you into traffic."

Lonnie turned back to us, leaning in confidentially. "Have I spoken of the lack of respect that these young ones have for their elders these days?"

The Cheyenne Nation blew his breath out from pursed lips. "You have mentioned it, yes."

Lonnie glanced around. "Where was I?"

"The cavalryman at the Battle of the Greasy Grass who shot your grandfather," I ventured.

"Which time?"

"The second, I think."

Placing his hands on the table, he reared back. "Misfire, the soldier's rifle misfired again, and my grandfather shot him in the chest." He touched a spot at his sternum. "Here." The hand dropped to his lap. "My grandfather used to say that there were many kinds of men before a battle, but only two kinds after— the living and the dead."

He turned to Barrett. "Go get me a proper Coke."

"What are you going to do with Lonnie?"

"I don't know, put him on the case, I guess. He's bound to have more luck than I'm having." I thought about it as I drove across the Montana-Wyoming border, the light fading behind the Bighorn Mountains in a stringent purple that refused to turn black. "I was surprised to see Lolo Long's brother still around. I figured he would've moved on by now."

Henry looked out the window. "Did you know that most deer are born, live, and die within one square mile?"

"Barrett's not a deer."

"No, but he is also not very adventurous."

"Okay."

"He wants to be a police officer, but he does not want to work for his sister, which limits his options."

"I seem to remember that."

"Perhaps you should offer him a job."

I glanced at him. "Are you joking?"

"No." He turned to look back at me. "Why would you think that?"

"You just said he didn't want to leave the Rez."

"Absaroka County is not that far—besides, he could visit his family on weekends. He has a degree in law enforcement and speaks fluent Cheyenne and Crow. He could be an asset to you."

I continued to drive into the darkness, aware that I was not the first white man to be bushwhacked in this territory. "You've put some thought into this."

"I would like to see him out from under his sister, and I think he is capable of more than simply pushing Lonnie around."

Vic took a break from petting Dog and leaned forward between the seats. "You really don't like her, do you?"

"Immaterial." The Bear pivoted to glance at her. "She is a dominating personality, and I think it is difficult for her brother, as a family member, to overcome that and find his own path."

"What's his sister going to think about all this?"

"I do not see it as being any of her business."

"Have you spoken to him?"

He turned back to me. "In a general sense; I mentioned that perhaps he should be looking elsewhere for a job, but I did not mention your department specifically."

"He'd have to go down to Douglas for two months if we did hire him." I thought about it. "We are an officer short, but I have to confer with my undersheriff on all matters concerning staff."

"You know my theory, if he's got a pulse and a pecker we put him on patrol." The voice from the back confirmed. "Besides, he can have my old unit after you buy me my new one."

"Car shopping on a Sunday night?"

"There aren't any crowds, or salespeople for that matter."
She sashayed up and down the rows of vehicles at the dealership in Sheridan. "Do I have to go with silver or black and white? What if I want red?"

I called after her, "Join the fire department."

Henry leaned on the hood of a freshly minted pickup and watched her. "I think you have created a monster."

"You may be right." I called out to her again, "White, black or silver, or combinations of all of the above."

"Will the county actually pay for a new vehicle?"

"It'll have to go through the commissioners, but I don't see them saying no. Heck, I'm about to return a two-thousand-dollar computer."

"I thought it was downstairs?"

"Yep, but nobody uses it."

"Barrett would."

I laughed. "You're really pushing this kid."

"I think he is deserving."

"That's it?"

He turned to look at me. "Meaning?"

"You're not just trying to get under Lolo Long's skin?"

"I never have to try very hard to do that."

I nodded as a security guard exited the main building of the dealership and walked toward us with a flashlight in hand. "Which is why it surprises me that she's willing to ask us for help with this situation with her niece."

"That tells you how desperate she is. I think she is correct in having you involved in an investigation, and she knows I can provide a measure of security."

The guard arrived, an elderly man with a more salt than pepper mustache and a black operational dress uniform complete with ball cap and tactical shoes. He glanced at my truck, emblazoned with the Absaroka County Sheriff stars, emergency lights, and Dog's head hanging out the side window. "Walt?"

I stared at the man, finally recognizing him as security from the Soldiers' and Sailors' Home. "Gene?"

"Yeah, hey how are you guys doin'?"

"You work here too?"

"Gotta make ends meet after retirin'." He glanced at Henry and then back to me. "I saw your truck and thought there might be a problem."

I gestured toward Vic, who was now standing in front of a tricked-out half-ton with all the scoops, wheels, bells, and whistles. "My undersheriff needs a new unit."

"Oh." He glanced at Henry again. "I thought there might be something wrong."

"Nope, just shopping."

"Okay." He started backing away and then waved as he turned and walked by Vic, who ignored him.

Henry watched him go. "Conscientious worker."

"Maybe we can get Barrett a job here." I pushed off and moved over to where Vic studied her potential truck. "So?"

"I want this one."

"Why?"

"It has a ten-speed transmission and close to five hundred horsepower."

"No."

She turned to look at me. "What do you mean, no?"

"No, because you'd be dead in a week."

Placing her fists on her hips, she swiveled back and forth. "You said I could have anything I wanted."

"Within reason."

"Why is this not within reason?"

The Bear joined us as I leaned forward, reading the window sticker. "It costs as much as your house."

"Half as much."

"That's a lot of money for a truck." I stepped back to look at it. "Then we'd have to send it over to Jim at Michelena's to get all the emergency equipment put on the thing . . ."

"I want it."

I glanced at Henry, who was smiling and shrugged. "We'd have to put in a requisition with the county commissioners . . ."

"I want it."

I sighed. "On one condition."

"What?"

"We put a roll bar on it."

"And a brick under the accelerator," the Bear muttered.

Rezdawg wouldn't start.

"What, she's tired?" The Bear ignored me, and I glanced across the street at the T-bird. "Remind me again why you brought both vehicles into town?"

"Lola needed an oil change."

The Bear continued staring at the engine bay of the old three-quarter ton as I held the flashlight, doing my best to illuminate the crosshatch of wiring that I myself had helped re-configure at least four times. "How do you know which wire is which?"

"The yellow wire becomes brown at the firewall."

"And what color does the brown wire become?"

"Yellow, I think."

"That's convenient."

Vic appeared at the other side of the decrepit truck with three cans of Rainier that she'd retrieved from her refrigerator. She opened them and handed them to us in turn. "My neighbors called and wanted to know if this truck was abandoned and needed to be towed."

Henry pulled a wayward wire up into the flashlight beam with the remnants of twisted electrical tape. "I wonder where this one goes?"

I sipped my beer. "How 'bout I just give you a ride and you can come back and get it in the morning?"

He continued to study the maverick wire. "Black."

"What does black become at the firewall?"

"Black."

"You're kidding."

"No, I had an extra spool of wire, so all the extra wires became black."

"Extra."

"Yes."

I glanced around the interior of the dark engine bay and the leaking Y-block. "I don't think there's supposed to be extra."

"When you are as old as we are—there is always extra." Pushing my hand down, he redirected the beam toward the distributor. "Is that a loose electrical wire on the base?"

I peered under his arm to see what he was talking about. "How the heck should I know, I haven't really looked under the hood of one of these things since 1972."

Deftly twisting the wires and rewrapping the electrical tape, the Cheyenne Nation stepped back from the grille like a surgeon abandoning the operating table and sipped his beer. "I am going to attempt to start it, so if I were you I would step away—she can sometimes react unpredictably."

I joined Vic on the opposite side of the street. "Explosion?"

Vic shook her head, sipping her beer. "I'm thinking the engine will just drop onto the pavement."

Henry cracked the door, slid in on the bungee-corded shower curtain that served as a seat cover, and hit the starter. We listened as the solenoid engaged and cranked the remaining teeth of the flywheel, sometimes slipping and forcing the Bear to hit it again. He ground it a few more times, and I was about to step forward when the engine caught and blew out a dark plume of blue-black smoke, hiccupped, caught, and belched into an uneven idle, or what passed for an idle with Rezdawg.

Walking over as he reached across and wound down the passenger window, I took the half-empty can from him. "Heading out?"

He nodded. "I better."

"Before she gets tired?"

He said nothing and popped the clutch, allowing the refugee from a salvage yard to lay about six inches of rubber and then motored down Vic's street. He took a left at the end of the block with only one taillight aglow.

"I hope he makes it."

"Me too." Placing an arm over her shoulders, I walked her up the steps and across the sidewalk that bisected her small yard, stopping at the bottom as she mounted the first two steps and turned to look at me. "What is it about men and their vehicles?"

"I don't know, we get attached to things."

She draped her arms around my neck, taking advantage of the fact that we were momentarily the same height. "Just so you know." She glanced at the weather-beaten unit in her driveway that she'd been driving since I hired her. "I'm not attached to that piece of shit."

Wheeling my own vintage unit back onto Main Street, I drifted through the quiet town, and rolled the windows all the way down for both Dog and me. He let his enormous head hang in the breeze, causing the heavy lips of his muzzle to flap.

You had to take advantage of the decent weather on the high plains or you missed it. I slid an elbow up onto the sill of my truck, took a deep breath, and slowly exhaled, luxuriating in the warmth of the night.

I was about to pass the intersection that led up the mountain when I saw a strange car in our parking lot and somebody lying on the front steps.

Thinking about how tired I was, I was tempted to keep driving and continue on home, but that wasn't part of the job, so I turned and drove toward the entrance. Circling around, I paused behind the only vehicle in the lot, a silver import with California plates.

Turning once more, I circled back in front of the old Carnegie library we called the Sheriff's Office, stopped, and called out to the man who appeared to be asleep on our stairs, using a rucksack as a pillow. "Hello."

He didn't answer, so I switched off the ignition and climbed out, walking over and standing above him.

He was dressed a little strangely for Wyoming, with patent leather shoes, checkered socks, a bright colored shirt, an old leather jacket, and a porkpie hat, which covered his face.

Kneeling down, I tapped his arm with the back of my hand. "Hey."

He moved this time, grunted, and readjusted on the marble steps.

Tapping him again, I spoke a little louder. "Hey."

"What the fuck . . . ?" His hand came up and swiped the hat away, and I was surprised to see he was wearing sunglasses. He, on the other hand, was even more surprised to see me. "Oh, shit . . ."

"Howdy."

Moving slowly, he rolled to one side and removed the shades.

"Can I help you?"

"You the sheriff?"

"I am."

"I'm Bass Townsend." He stuck out a hand. "My grandfather was Charley Lee Stillwater."

9

"You look like him."

"I do?" He added sugar to his coffee, taking a pinch and throwing it over his shoulder.

"I thought that was only for salt?"

"I'm what you might call overly superstitious." Smiling into the mug as he stroked Dog's wide back, he took a sip. "My mother used to say superstition is the poetry of life."

"That was Charley Lee's daughter, Ella. She was a nurse?"

"Yes, sir, that was her."

"And your father's name was Townsend?"

"Yes. They met when my mother was on a vacation in California. He was a commercial artist in Pasadena and did some work for Disney at one time. She always felt guilty about leaving my grandfather, but he said he was living the life of Riley up at the Soldiers' and Sailors' Home after my grandmother died and that there wasn't anything she could do that they weren't already doing."

"Did you ever meet him?"

"Three times. Back when I was a kid I actually spent a summer with him, and we went to Texas where he'd soldiered a bit the first time around. When my momma died, we kind of drifted away from each other, and I never saw him again." He sipped his coffee and looked up at me as we sat there on the bottom steps of the office that led to the jail proper. "Did he suffer?"

I laughed. "Charley Lee Stillwater never suffered a day in his life. The jury's not in until we get the autopsy and toxicology reports, but as far as I can tell, your grandfather died teasing a Texan during a bingo game."

"I thought he was born in Texas?"

It always felt odd, telling people what they didn't know about the simple facts of their deceased relatives' lives. "He was born in Saint Louis, but I guess he assumed the guise of a Texan after being there."

"He's responsible for my name."

"Bass?"

"Yeah, everybody in California thought I was named after a fish, but I believe I was really named after Bass Reeves, deputy US marshal and model for *The Lone Ranger*—not too bad for a black man during that time."

"Three thousand arrests and only had to kill about a dozen as I recall—not bad for any man in any period. Maybe that's why Charley Lee wanted to be a Texan."

He raised his head and glanced around the room and sighed. "I always figured my grandfather was born at the wrong time. I think what he really wanted to be was a Buffalo Soldier. My father even did a painting of him as he might have looked like one, but I don't know what happened to it."

"I do—it's on his wall up at the Veterans' Home."

"Really?"

"I'm pretty sure."

He sighed a quick laugh. "I guess it meant more to him than he showed."

"Not a good relationship between your father and your grandfather?"

"Not really. Well, I mean my father was a quiet, soft-spoken man, and well . . . You know how Charley Lee was."

"A little." I sipped my own coffee. "How did you find out about his passing?"

"Got a call from the Veterans' Home."

I thought that odd considering no one knew of any living relatives. "Carol Williams?"

"No, it was some kind of strange voice that said Charley Lee had passed away and then just hung up—really weird shit."

"Do you remember the name?"

"No, no, they left a message on my answering machine and didn't leave a name, just the regular number of the Home." He thought about it. "Had a strange voice though."

"Strange how?"

"Computer generated, I suppose."

"And you drove all the way here on that?"

He laughed more openly this time. "I've never seen this part of the world as an adult—the last time I was here I was seven years old."

"If you don't mind my asking, Mr. Townsend, what do you do?"

"I'm a musician, blues guitar, but don't be too impressed, every third person you meet in L.A. is a musician of some kind."

"What are the other two?"

"Actors and lawyers." He finished his coffee. "I do the club circuits and a little studio backup stuff. I played on a Blind Boy Paxton album, an Eddie Daniels, a John Bishop, and one with Bonnie Raitt."

"Impressive company."

"Yeah, and I've got the most impressive, un-air-conditioned, four-story walk-up, studio apartment in East L.A., with private parking in the alley by the dumpster out back." He pet Dog one last time and then stood, stretching and yawning, and returned his mug to the sink by the coffee maker. "As near as I can figure it, I've got just enough gas money to get me back to L.A. and maybe buy a few drive-through meals along the way." He glanced around the dank dayroom and hallway leading to the jail cells. "I hate to be an inconvenience, but you wouldn't happen to have a spare bed around here, would you?"

"I do, but I can also call Jim down at the Blue Gables Motel and Coffee Bar and get you a room for the night—they're music lovers, are reasonable, and I can spot you."

He turned to look at me. "Now, why in the world would you do that?"

"I think you should probably be getting this information from a more official source, but I think you're about to come into some serious money, Mr. Townsend."

He looked a little uncertain and then laughed at the absurdity of my statement. "Oh, I know my grandfather never had a pot to piss in . . . I just thought that if there were any family items or photographs . . ."

"Well, there are a lot of things to go through in his room up at the Home, and I mean a lot of things."

"Hey, and if there's enough money to buy a few sit-down meals on the way back, that'd be great."

I nodded. "I think there's enough to cover that, yep."

"I still want a new truck."

"I wasn't going to use Charley Lee's money for that anyway."

She stuck her boots up on the edge of my desk and sipped her coffee. "Ruby gave me all the forms, and I called up the dealership this morning to run the numbers. They said they would come down on the price a little, but only a little."

"Did you identify yourself as law enforcement?"

"About six times."

I looked at the Post-its in my hand, a mild domestic dispute, a sideswiped car—must be Monday. "Well, the county commissioners will either come back with a yes or a no."

"If they come back with a no, I'm going to the next meeting armed."

"I'll write them a memo." I glanced around. "Where's my dog?"

She tossed her head in the direction of the main part of the office. "With Ruby." She yawned. "So, what's the millionaire like?"

"Superstitious." I couldn't help but smile. "He doesn't know he's a millionaire yet."

"You didn't tell him?"

"I didn't think it was my place, but I did tell him that he was probably going to need a lawyer."

"What'd he say to that?"

"That he couldn't afford one."

"Oh, boy."

"He's a musician, and I guess he's pretty good—maybe a little down on his luck."

"Maybe he can do a benefit concert for himself." She dropped her boots to the floor. "In the meantime, I'm ordering up the emergency equipment for my new truck."

"Are you sure you don't want to wait till the commissioners have a vote?"

"Fuck that."

"I'll put that in the memo too."

"You do that." She stood, stretched like a panther, and exited.

Ruby appeared in her stead. "You've got a call on line one, Mary from Buffalo Bill Center of the West. My, aren't we all hoity-toity."

"I'm attempting to rise from my hoi polloi beginnings." Picking up the phone, I punched line one. "How's the patient?"

"Embarrassed, but she's fine and already back at work this morning and then flying to Boston in the afternoon."

"Catch the attacker?"

"I'm afraid not."

"Nobody found a dropped wallet or anything in the conservation area?"

"Nope."

"My painting rolled up in the dumpster out back?"

She sighed an exhale of embarrassment, and there was a long pause. "No, but I did want to call and apologize—we've never had anything like that happen here at the museum."

"Probably my fault . . . There seems to be a lot of the criminal element in my proximity."

"Was it insured?"

"I doubt it. The man who would've eventually owned it is here to settle his grandfather's estate, and with the amount of money we're talking about, I don't think he's going to be concerned about an odd little partial painting like that one."

"It still bothers you though, doesn't it? I can tell from your tone of voice."

I leaned back in my chair as far as I dared without flipping over, listening to it cry out in submission. "That obvious, is it?"

"A little. It bothers me too. Why in the world would any-body go to those lengths to steal that particular piece? I mean, if they were going to steal something, there are far more valu-able pieces right there in the conservation area."

"The thought did cross my mind."

"Come up with any ideas?"

"Not yet."

"Yet?"

"Yet." Leaning forward, I sighed. "Tell Beverly that I'm glad she's feeling better."

"I will, Walt." There was another pause, and her voice took on a concerned tone. "You be careful out there with all that criminal element."

"You bet, and you be careful with that artistic element."

She laughed. "I'm not sure which one is more worrisome."

I hung up the phone and thought about it. Why in the world would somebody go to all the trouble of taking such an oddity? Even in the best of conditions it was worth less than a thou-sand dollars. I mean, I would understand if it was the actual painting, which, as the history books say, was destroyed in the fire in Texas.

Fort Bliss, Texas.

Fort Bliss.

There are times when thoughts finally rub up against each other enough that they provide a spark, a spark that should've ignited much sooner. Charley Lee Stillwater had told me his first tour of duty with the army had been in Texas, and he'd been discharged in '46, the year of the commissary fire that had destroyed the painting.

Had Charley Lee taken that painting before it burned or even caused the fire to cover his tracks?

It just didn't seem like the man.

"Three-thousand four-hundred dollars for the lights, spot-light, and siren."

I looked up at my undersheriff, framed in the doorway. "What?"

"My new unit that you're going to buy me."

"Oh, sorry." I glanced up at the Seth Thomas on the wall. "I'm supposed to meet Bass Townsend over at the bank at ten. Do you want to go?"

"Sure, maybe I can get a loan from him."

If you could imagine the response of a person who had just learned they'd inherited a million dollars, Bass Townsend's wouldn't disappoint. I thought for a moment that the man had swallowed his tongue, but then he'd finally spoken, and it was what I myself might've said.

"You're . . . You're shitting me."

Well, maybe not exactly what I would've said. Wes Haskins seemed to be enjoying it too. I mean, how many times do you get the opportunity to effectively give somebody a cool mil?

"It's a million dollars in unmarked United States currency, and unless Walt here uncovers some reason why the money shouldn't be your grandfather's, you're quite a bit richer, Mr. Townsend."

We all listened to the clock on the bank president's office wall.

"You're shitting me."

"Nope, and then there's the question of the security box he left that's in our protection." Wes smiled in spite of himself and the greater banking industry. "Of course, there will be probate and tax responsibilities—your grandfather could've done a better job in delivering the money to you than cash in a boot box."

Townsend said nothing more, probably because he was afraid he might repeat himself again.

I sat forward in my chair as Vic leaned against the wall, preferring to stand and cover the smile on her face with a hand. "Are you all right, Mr. Townsend?"

He still said nothing.

"I said, are you all right?"

"I um . . . I think I'm going to be sick."

Wes was up in an instant, taking Townsend by the shoulder and helping him as we both led the man out of the office. "The restroom is down there on the right."

We watched as he moved carefully down the hallway and disappeared through the appropriate door as Vic joined us. "Think he still thinks you're shitting him?"

"It's not unusual, that kind of response."

"I've seen what a couple thousand dollars can do to people, but I've never actually told anyone about an amount as large as this in cash." He waited a moment and then glanced at me. "Think he's okay?"

"I'll give him a minute and then check on him."

"So, Wes, can I get a car loan if the county commissioners turn me down?"

He glanced at Vic and then at me again.

"She wants a new unit, and they've got one of those pursuit half-tons over on a lot in Sheridan."

"One of those five-hundred horsepower jobs?" He looked at her. "You'll be dead in a week."

She folded her arms. "Shut up, Wes."

"I told you, you drive too fast."

She glared at me. "You shut up too."

Excusing myself, I headed down the hallway to the men's room and, pausing at the door, tapped lightly. "Mr. Townsend?" There was a noise inside, but he didn't say anything. "Mr. Townsend."

The knob turned, and he opened the door a few inches and looked at me, his face covered with sweat. "Um, yeah?"

"Are you okay?"

"Yeah, I just need another minute or two." I started to turn away, but he added, "Is this really happening?"

"What's that?"

"Is this real? I mean is there really a million dollars that's really mine?"

"As near as we can tell, yes."

"I'm honestly not feeling very well." He studied me for a moment more and then added, "I just need a few more minutes."

I nodded. "Well, whenever you're ready but take as much time as you need." He closed the door, and I walked back down the hallway and rejoined the conversation. "I told her she could have it if it had a complete roll cage."

"Shit, I forgot about the roll cage." She stared at me for a moment and then turned and started out of the bank, I assume to cross the street to our offices to order a roll bar.

Wes watched her go and then turned back to me. "You realize you're creating a public menace?"

"I don't have final say, that's up to the county commissioners."

"They're not going to tell you no, Walt."

"They tell me no all the time." I glanced toward the restroom again. "Ever had this big of a response?"

He glanced at his wristwatch. "No, not this much."

"You think I should check on him again?"

He adjusted his glasses and shrugged. "Like I said, I've never had anyone have this long of a reaction."

We both walked down the hallway, and I knocked again. "Mr. Townsend?" No response. "Bass, are you all right in there?"

Wes and I looked at each other, and then I tried the door, which was locked. "Mr. Townsend, if you don't answer, I'm going to have to break the door down." I listened but then looked at the banker. "Do you have a passkey?"

"No."

I put my shoulder into it and felt the jam break apart. Townsend was lying on the floor, gasping for breath. I kneeled and felt the pulse at his throat and watched as his eyes fluttered.

He looked up at me. "I was sick, but then my chest started hurting, and I couldn't catch my breath . . ."

"Does your chest still hurt?" He nodded, and I turned to Wes, standing in the doorway. "Get us an ambulance."

"He's fine. It was a mild coronary blockage aggravated by the agitation, which might've caused an arrhythmia."

Standing with Isaac Bloomfield in the hallway of Durant Memorial Hospital, I was holding my hat and feeling a little guilty. "I guess we didn't think that telling someone that they'd just inherited a million dollars would give them a heart attack."

The old concentration camp survivor smiled, pinching his lower lip with an extended thumb and forefinger. "Medically, it was bound to happen; unfortunately for you, perhaps, but fortunately for him, it happened on your watch. He's resting peacefully, and we have him on a mild sedation to allow him to regain his footing. Do you know of anyone we should notify?"

"Not that I'm aware. When will I be able to speak with him?"

He shrugged one shoulder. "Possibly an hour, possibly a day."

"But he's in no danger?"

"Not at this point, I don't think. I mean, he had an episode, but I think he'll be fine."

David Nickerson came out of the room and approached us. "He's asleep, and all his EKG readings are good. Does he have any genetic propensity?"

Isaac nodded. "His grandfather, the one we did the autopsy on, was a victim of cardiac arrest, but there were mitigating factors, such as his age."

"Anything more on that?"

"Not really, as I said, it appears that he had some sort of injection the night of his death but the toxicology report came back negative. There are some elements that might remain in urine or blood samples, but I suppose we'll never know because such samples don't exist."

"What kind of elements?"

"Oh, speaking hypothetically . . . Sux, for example."

"Sux?"

"Suxamethonium chloride, part of the rapid sequence intubation protocol, which would include respiratory support, but it's been used by some clever murderers in the past."

Nickerson snapped his fingers. "The guy in New Jersey?"

Isaac nodded. "And Florida. They now have acquired the

detection abilities in tissues and biological fluids to pick the stuff up, but you would need a urine or blood sample prior to death, which we don't have."

The younger doctor glanced back at the door where Bass Townsend was comfortably resting. "Perhaps we should do a little further testing, just to be on the safe side?"

"Possibly."

They both looked at me. "You're going to have to take that up with Mr. Townsend." Slipping my hat back on, I turned to head toward the emergency entrance. "You'll let me know if there are any changes in his condition?"

They both called out the ubiquitous Wyoming response. "You bet."

When I got to the curb, Vic was waiting for me in her soon-to-be-retired unit. "Get in."

I leaned against the door. "If you're going to show me why you need a new unit I'm not getting in this vehicle."

"No, we got an emergency call from the Soldiers' and Sailors' Home."

I climbed into the nest she called a vehicle, pushing empty soda bottles, notepads, books, and fast-food wrappers to the floor mat. "What's going on?"

Vic jetted out of the parking lot, took a right, and then made the next right onto Fort Street, winding through cars with her siren wailing and lights flashing a Morse code of *get the hell out of my way.* "What's up?"

"Somebody broke into Charley Lee's room."

"Good grief." Buckling my belt, I braced a hand against the

dash in hopes of mitigating the impending crash. "Why are we in such a hurry?"

Passing two cars on the left, she rocketed back into our lane barely avoiding an oncoming semi whose horn rattled my fillings. "Police business."

"When did this happen?"

"How should I know? Carol Williams called and said that the room had been broken into and that you might want to come up and take a look."

Once we'd barreled past the edge of town, I watched as she swerved around a slow-moving pickup and veered into the entryway of the Veterans' Home, the four men in their wheelchairs waving as if this were an everyday occurrence.

Roaring past the first parking lot and the administrative offices, she turned the corner and slid sideways to a stop in the no-parking area in front. I glanced up at the bumper-sticker-covered window on the second floor and could have sworn I could see someone's shadow quickly disappear. Vic threw open the glass doors and charged in as Country Joe McDonald strummed his guitar and warbled "I Feel Like I'm Fixin' to Die" from the speakers above.

"Are you coming?"

Breaking from my reverie, I turned and glanced at Vic and rushed after her as Carol intercepted us in the lobby. "It's okay, it's okay. I've got the room blocked off."

"When did it happen?"

She walked along ahead of us. "Must've been very early in the morning; the night man made his rounds at around three and didn't see anything, but the morning man spotted the door on his first pass." We arrived at room 124, and it was obvious somebody had used a crowbar or something similar to pry open the heavy door. "Looks like a professional job."

"Hmm . . ."

Vic slipped on a pair of plastic gloves that she had taken from the kit in her unit and pulled the door open, which revealed an even greater mess than the one that had been there before. "Cripes."

Looking over her shoulder, I could see that all the piles of books and magazines had been toppled over and the artifacts had been swept from the shelves. "Somebody was looking for something."

I glanced around the room at the walls, but none of the hanging art was damaged. "Nobody could have done this quietly."

Carol peeked in. "The men on either side are medicated at night, and the rest in the area are pretty heavy sleepers."

"Was Charley Lee medicated?"

She entered and made her way to one side, standing by the door to the bathroom, where the stack of books still sat on the toilet. "No."

"Isaac says he might've had an injection the night he died?"

She waved her hand before her nose. "He mentioned it, but there was nothing on the charts."

"Did you have all the books cataloged?"

"I can't be sure, but it doesn't look as if anything has been taken." She glanced in the bathroom. "God, that smell. I'm going to have to let housekeeping get in here."

I scanned the room. "Why in the world would somebody come in here and dump the books over and . . ." My eye caught something that appeared to be out of place.

Stepping over the collapsed stacks, I found an empty section of floor where the built-in elongated closet door hung partially open. Taking a pen from my pocket, I slipped it through the handle and pulled the door the rest of the way open.

There were a few items hanging there, including Charley Lee's dress uniform, topped by a shelf for his hat and a remarkable ball-cap collection, mostly military themed. There were a few dress shirts that had been knocked to the floor of the cabinet, but what caught my eye was the back of the closet, where a faux-wood panel had been pulled away.

Curious, I reached in, took the items that were still hanging from the support rod and handed them back to Vic. I gripped the panel, which popped away with ease, and then carefully turned it sideways in order to remove it from the closet.

Reaching my hand back to Vic, I stuck my head inside. "Give me your Maglite?"

She did as I requested and then leaned in to watch as I shined the beam onto the open back where the drywall was chipped away to reveal a space about fourteen inches between the studs in the wall. Turning the beam upward, I could see that there was a hidden compartment that broke through the ceiling where the sill wood had been carefully chiseled away in a circle that continued upward.

"What do you think is up there?"

I turned to look at my undersheriff. "Nothing."

"Nothing?"

"Nothing now, but I'd be willing to guess that if you rolled up a nine-and-a-half-foot by fourteen-and-a-half-foot canvas, it would fit in this little cubby perfectly."

She looked back at Carol, who stood near the bathroom door. "Are you telling me there was a twenty-four-million-dollar painting propped up in this closet the whole time?"

"Possibly."

I watched as she stepped into the bathroom and reached for the toilet handle.

"Don't flush that."

"So, who took it?"

"I wish I knew." As she drove away from the Veterans' Home, I thought about it. "As near as I can figure, Charley Lee had only one thing in his life that could've been worth a million dollars."

"A twenty-four-million-dollar painting?"

"Yep."

"So, you think he sold it?"

"Possibly." I thought about it. "Selling a twenty-four-million-dollar painting for a million? Of course, it's difficult to sell one that was presumed destroyed and in possession of the Seventh Cavalry headquarters, a branch of the United States military, and in proxy the United States federal government."

"They have a lot of lawyers."

"Yep, they do." Watching the rolling scenery go by I was momentarily mesmerized by the glimmering sun reflecting through the quaking leaves of the trees like vibrating million-dollar bills. I looked past the brick sign and the chiseled marble that made up the entryway to Fort McKinney and at the four wheelchairs parked by the road. "Stop."

She glanced at me. "What?"

"Stop!"

She locked the brakes, and the aged SUV slid to a halt as I flung open the door, circled around the hood, crossed the sidewalk, and stood in front of the Wavers.

The old servicemen looked up at me in mild surprise as I stood there and studied each of them in turn. Army Command Sergeant Major Clifton Coffman was going light today with an outlandish Hawaiian shirt, but the ubiquitous boonie hat still covered his crown. Kenny Cade, chief petty officer, was wearing a blue t-shirt with a blue-nose polar bear emblem I recognized from my time in Alaska. Air Force Master Sergeant Ray Purdue was still peering at me from under his cap with the scrambled eggs on the bill, and Delmar Pettigrew, the oversize sergeant major of the marines, was still holding down the far right with the everyday attire of satin jacket and red cap.

I continued to study them and gave them a moment to study me as I slowly took off my sunglasses, summoning as much of my former commissioned officer as I could muster.

Kenny was the first to clear his throat. "Can we help you, Lieutenant?"

I waited another moment and then delivered the words slowly. *"Custer's Last Fight."*

They stared at me, their eyes collectively widening a bit.

Clifton had a coughing fit, and now they were looking at one another before allowing their eyes to come back to me.

We stood or sat like that for a few more moments before Navy summarily pivoted in his electric wheelchair and drove off down the miniature rolling highway that led back toward the Home. Army followed suit along with Air Force, which left me staring at my comrade in service, Marine Corps, when he suddenly turned and followed after the others.

Watching the diminutive convoy disappear over the hillocks, I became aware of Vic standing beside me. "So, you want me to shoot out their tires?"

10

I can't see, but in a way I can see more clearly than ever before. There are small swirls and swipes, muted patterns, brushstrokes of mostly browns and greens with figures darting from all sides under a flat sky with waves of heat on a July, high-plains day. There is dust, and there are noises, screaming high and loud, not all of it human.

I've got my hand around another man's arm where a cuff of some kind embraces his bicep, and some sort of bone breastplate strains across his chest. Dark with dark features, he's wearing some sort of headdress, but it's a strange one and the orange feathers on top make it look like his head is blooming.

The heat, the dust, and the noise are so oppressive that I feel like dropping back and resting in the high grass that overlooks the river in the valley below. But he's moving, and I watch his other hand as it rises up, blocking out the sun for just a moment, and I'm almost glad for the shade. He hesitates, and our eyes meet, joined in disbelief. There is a stone club in his hand, the clear tawny sinew, the red paint on the river rock, and the delicate feathers that flitter a rainbow of color in the sun.

Then.

With all his might.

He brings it down into my face.

"Earth to Walt, come in, Walt."

Hearing her voice in the distance, I turned in what seemed like slow motion as the images faded and disappeared. "What?"

She leaned back on the bench that rests on the bridge spanning Clear Creek. She sipped her soda, her unfinished grilled cheese sandwich lying on the wrapper in her lap. "I'm so glad you're not having those spells anymore."

Taking a deep breath, I stretched my neck muscles and listened to the popping noises. "How long?"

"About two minutes—I'm sitting here chattering away, and I look over and you're staring off into the ozone. Did Doc Bloomfield say if this was supposed to go away?"

"He didn't."

"Well, at least they're getting shorter." She continued to study me. "So, what was this one?"

"I think I was at the Little Bighorn, or in a painting of the Little Bighorn."

She nodded. "Were you an Indian?"

"I don't think so."

"Well, then this one ends badly . . ." She sighed and stared at me. "So, I'll repeat my most recent question—did Charley Lee sell the painting and did the purchaser come back to retrieve it? And if so, why trash the place?"

"Huh?"

"For the third time—did Charley Lee sell the painting and did the purchaser come back to retrieve it? And if so, why trash the place?"

I tried to concentrate; it was so hard these days. "A warning?"

"To who? Charley Lee is dead."

I leaned forward, rested my elbows on my knees, and listened to the rushing sound of the water beneath us as the twilight shouldered the sun to the west. We sometimes got our dinner to go from the Busy Bee Cafe only twenty yards away and then ate it on the bench to avoid the summer crowds. "Maybe they were frustrated when they couldn't find it."

"Or maybe they were frustrated and then they did." Dog sat beside her, or more important beside the remains of her sandwich, adjusting his weight as she regarded him. "I'm going to give you some, but you have to wait."

"Who in the world has a million dollars in cash to throw around?"

"The federal government."

"It's their painting, so they don't have to buy it."

She picked up her sandwich but then paused mid bite to look at me. "Are you going to call in DCI to dust the place?"

"I'm trying to decide if they have better things to do."

"A million dollars' worth of better things?"

"I know, I know."

"How long are you going to sweat the Joint Chiefs of Wheelchairs up at the Home?"

"I haven't decided yet, probably till tomorrow."

"They're going to be trying to get their story straight."

"Yep."

"Hey, how come there aren't any coast guard guys up there?"

"Most are under six feet tall and drown when their ship sinks and they try and walk to shore . . ." She stared at me. "Sorry, old marine joke."

"So, the next time there's something really important, I'd rather not have you or Wes tell it to me—*capisce*?"

"I thought we were relatively gentle in the delivery of the information."

"He had a heart attack, Walt."

"Bloomfield and Nickerson said he was heading in that direction anyway and that we just exacerbated the condition a bit."

"No way he was up at the Home looking around?" I turned to glance at her. "Hey, everybody's a suspect until we catch someone."

I leaned back on the bench and smiled at some tourists on their way to the bandstand for Dave Stewart's bluegrass night. "No, he was waiting on the steps of the office when I got there and then slept over at the Blue Gables."

"You're sure?"

"I called Jim at the office. He said Bass checked in, went to his cabin, and didn't appear till morning, when he came out and ordered a cappuccino."

"Lucky for him he's staying in the only place in the state of Wyoming that has such a device." She handed the rest of her sandwich to Dog, and we watched as he swallowed it in one great, snapping gulp. "Jesus . . ." She checked her fingers to make sure she hadn't lost any. "It's like the shark tank at Sea-World."

"He doesn't have very good manners."

She stood and took a few steps toward my truck. "So, what's the game plan?"

"I guess I have to call DCI. We haven't got much to work with since I let the most important piece of evidence be stolen."

"Well, we know it was the real deal, that's something."

I stood up and we walked along Main Street until we got to

the truck, where I opened the rear door so that the beast could jump in. He sat on the sidewalk looking at me, just to make sure I wasn't fooling him by uttering the word *ham*.

"Get in, it's not a trick." I glanced at Vic. "He's got a memory like an elephant."

She reached out and batted his nose. "Get in, you moron."

With the possible exception of Henry and Ruby, I figured Vic was the only one who could get away with that and then watched as he jumped in. I closed the door and had started around the truck when I noticed she wasn't getting in. I stopped at the front fender and rested an elbow on the hood between us. "What, I have to beg you to get in too?"

"Are you happy?"

I laughed until I saw the seriousness in the tarnished gold eyes. "What?"

"Are you happy?"

"What are you talking about?"

She rested both forearms on the hood and placed a chin there, studying me. "Are you happy? It's a simple question."

"What is this all about?"

She set her eyes on me for a good, long while and looked very serious—it was more than a little unsettling. "These fits that you're having where you just go away, are you sure it's not something simple like maybe you actually want to be somewhere else?"

I thought about it. "I don't think so, I mean it's usually not a pleasant experience."

She looked down the street. "You'd tell me, right?"

"Tell you what?"

"If something was wrong."

I studied her until she finally turned to look at me. "Yes, I would."

"Cool." She pushed off the truck and started down the block at a saunter.

"Hey, you don't want a ride?"

"Nah, I'll walk." She paused and considered the goods behind the plate-glass of one of the stores as I studied her reflection.

"You'd do the same for me, right?"

She stood without moving and then finally turned just enough for me to see the side of her face. "Have you ever known me to hold my feelings in check?" The sly smile held for a few seconds and then she walked off, the Glock bouncing on her hip as she checked the door of every shop on Main Street to make sure they were locked.

Watching her until she turned the corner at the end of the block, I finally opened the door and climbed in, turning to look at my companion. "Next time, just get in the truck, okay?"

Doubling back, I took the left and then another left, parking in our lot and letting Dog out. I unlocked the door to the office and allowed the beast to go up the stairs to Ruby's chair first. I didn't bother to turn on the light but picked up her phone, called DCI in Cheyenne, got an answering machine, and, after telling a shortened version of the situation, requested its assistance in fingerprinting a room at the Soldiers' and Sailors' Home.

It was about then that someone picked up the phone, and I recognized the voice of Steve "Woody" Woodson, the director. "You're kidding."

"I wish I were." Stuffing the phone into the crook of my

neck, I glanced around. "What, you get the Big Dog if you call DCI during off-hours?"

"Nobody else is here, and I was walking by the reception desk when I heard a familiar voice. Did you say a million dollars?"

"I did."

"And something about a Custer painting?"

"I did."

"I'm getting in my car and heading up there right now."

"Woody, wait . . . I mean you can wait till tomorrow."

"This is the most interesting case I've heard of in years, and I'm not letting anyone else have it. Whatever you do, don't call the field office in Sheridan or Gillette . . ."

"I'm not calling anybody else, Woody."

"How's the fishing up there this season?"

"I knew there was an ulterior motive in all this."

"No, but if I'm driving all that way I might bring a rod and wet a fly or two."

"I'll call the Ferg and get you the lowdown."

"He still working for you?"

"Retired. I think law enforcement was getting in the way of his fishing."

"I understand perfectly."

I hung up the phone and glanced around at the graceful cursive writing on the assorted notes, forms, and papers that made up my dispatcher's desk. I'd heard that they were going to stop teaching cursive in schools, which was fine with me, because then all us old people would have a secret code.

I was about to get up when I noticed that Dog had walked to the end of the counter and was looking toward the main entrance. He stood there a moment more and then approached the edge.

There was a gasp from the entryway and then a voice. "Oh, my God."

I stood and walked to the end of the counter and grazed my fingers on his back to let him know I was there and then peered over the edge to where what appeared to be a woman in a hoodie stood, plastered against the glass door. "Howdy?"

Pulling the hood down to reveal her blonde hair, Katrina Dejean looked up at me and sighed. "I thought I was a goner, there for a moment."

"Only if you were a ham. Can I help you?"

She smiled. "Katrina Dejean, from the Buffalo Bill Gala?"

Taking a few more steps, I sat on the edge and Dog went down to greet her properly with his tail in full wag. "I know. Is there something wrong?"

She petted Dog and came up the steps, stopping a few down to look me in the eye.

"What, a girl can't just stop by to see the sheriff?"

"Sure, but it's after hours."

"I saw your truck and thought I'd try your door."

"Well, we're here. Is there something I can help you with?"

"This is going to sound odd . . ."

"Okay."

"There was a notice on one of the social media marketplace sites about a lost set of rings that were found?"

I thought about the report Saizarbitoria had given me a few days ago, and I was sure that as tech savvy as he was, he was the one who had posted it. "An engagement set."

"I think they're mine."

"Really?"

"I came through Durant a few days ago on my way to Cody

and stopped in a parking lot on the way up the mountain and I think I lost them there."

"Can you describe them?"

"Better. I can show you a picture." She held out her phone, turning the screen to show the selfsame rings on her own hand, or at least a hand similar to her own with the same fingernail polish.

"Sure looks like the ones that were found."

"Oh, thank goodness. From what I am to understand, they were quite remarkable—almost thirty thousand dollars' worth."

"That's remarkable, that's for sure. Mind telling me how it happened?"

"I threw them away. I was angry."

"Thirty thousand dollars' worth?"

She crossed to the side, resting her back against the railing and spreading her hands on the steel. "I don't suppose you've ever done anything stupid like that?"

"Daily, actually."

"I was mad at the individual who gave them to me."

"A natural response to a very expensive gift."

She sighed, smiling and looking down at her tennis shoes. "I've been trying to get this person to ask me to marry him for years, and he finally did but the timing was wrong." She looked up at me. "I'm interested in somebody else, and he thought the rings would bring me back."

"It didn't work?"

"No, but I felt bad about throwing them while on the phone with him and even worse when I couldn't find them."

"Sounds like a stormy relationship."

"To say the least." She continued studying her shoes.

I studied her. "It sounds like you want to tell me about it."

Her eyes came up. "I guess I just want to talk to someone, and sometimes a relative stranger is best because they're not involved."

Dog realized from our tone of voice that the conversation was going to be a lengthier one, so he sidled up the steps and collapsed beside me with one great heaving breath and closed his eyes. She looked alarmed, and I assured her. "If we aren't talking about meat products, he gets bored." She didn't look any less puzzled. But I continued. "It sounds like more than a personal problem. Tell me, has the count gotten himself into some kind of trouble I should know about?"

She stared at me. "Possibly."

"I'm all ears." I reached up and stroked the missing portion. "Except for the small part of one I lost a few years ago."

"You're a funny man to be a sheriff."

"You're not the first person to say that. Now, about the count?"

"There are people, and mind you Philippe knows many of them, who will pay for the things they want badly no matter what the price."

"I've heard of such people."

"They are in the habit of getting the things they want."

"Yep."

"Philippe is in the business of getting those types of things for those types of people."

"I see."

"Sometimes things that aren't supposed to exist."

"Things like *Custer's Last Fight*?"

She was silent for a moment, then spoke to her feet. "I'm feeling bad about being involved in all this."

"Involved in what, exactly?"

She practically whispered. "I feel as if I've already said too much."

"Actually, as the man who is the investigator in a case involving a missing, legendary painting, a million dollars in cash, and a man's death, I don't think you've said nearly enough."

"A man's death?"

"Charley Lee Stillwater."

"I thought his death was accidental?"

I smiled and shook my head. "So, you know the man?"

It took her awhile to respond. "I never said that."

"Katrina, your accent is very good, but I can still detect just a touch of far-western Russia in there somewhere—possibly Saint Petersburg? You see, I had a friend while I was working in Alaska years ago who was from that same region and you sound remarkably like him."

Her voice, along with the Russian umlaut, took on a defensive tone. "And what does that have to do with anything?"

I threw a thumb over my shoulder. "I've got four guys who sit out in front of the Soldiers' and Sailors' Home who say they've had dealings with people they referred to as 'the Russians' and as near as I can tell, you, Serge, and Philippe are the only ones who fit that bill."

"I've said too much."

"Possibly, but this conversation took a professional turn for me, and now I'm going to need you to answer some more questions."

She looked toward the door but didn't move, only folding her arms. "I don't really know more than what I've told you—you need to talk to Philippe."

I stood, aware that I was towering over her. "I guess I do."

"Am I under arrest?"

"No, but I think I'll have you accompany me over to the count's house for a little chat and to get things straightened out."

"Now?"

"No time like the present."

"I really don't want to go over there, for personal reasons."

"I really don't care. You come in here and open this can of worms and now you want to just turn around and walk away? I'm afraid I can't allow that. Right now, the only thing I've got you on would be conspiracy and collusion to the tune of grand larceny, but that's certainly enough to detain you if you continue to not cooperate."

"You know what I said about you being a funny man to be a sheriff—I take that back."

"Okay, but in the meantime let's just be two folks taking a twenty-minute ride to a guy's house and having a conversation about what the heck is going on around here."

"Okay."

One more thing?"

She turned to look at me. "Yes?"

"Do you still want your rings?"

Story is on the frontier of two counties, Sheridan and mine. A picturesque western community, it boasts of a couple of supper clubs and inns, along with a gas station and a guesthouse known as the Waldorf A'Story. Having long been a haven for the independently minded along the foothills of the Bighorn Mountains, it is popular with the artistic set.

Taking the exit near the fishery, I glanced over to see her admiring the engagement ring that she'd been reacquainted with as she turned to look at me. "That woman who was with you the other night, I understand she's your second-in-command?"

"She is my undersheriff."

"And is she more than that?"

I gave her a sidelong glance. "I'm sorry, but that's really none of your business."

She laughed. "Oh, come on now, Sheriff. I've been dumping all my personal problems out for you, don't you think turnabout is fair play?"

"What leads you to believe my personal situation is any problem?"

"Oh, they all are, aren't they?"

"Not really."

"Hmm . . . I must be doing something wrong."

I turned left into Story proper, past the manicured lawns and small log cabins, passing the town sign and firehouse. "Where to?"

"Keep going straight, then right on Loucks and left on Route 2 toward Penrose Trailhead."

I did as she said, and we followed North Piney Creek west to where the road turned to gravel. "I never even knew there were houses out here."

"Only one . . . do you know the story?"

"I heard it's a castle."

She shook her head. "Actually the barn of a small abbey in Ireland that the count had disassembled, brought over, and reconstructed."

"At a reasonable price, I'm sure."

She sighed, scrunching into the seat. "Like I said, Philippe knows people who if they want something, they get it and a little of that might've rubbed off."

Making a long left, we brushed near the creek where there was an opening in the trees with an expansive lawn, and in the glow of the half moon, a genuine, old-world building of large stones. The main entrance was at the center with a portico, and the roof appeared to be rounded tile.

Easing to a stop, I could see where two wings shot from the back, obviously a more modern design with glass walls and multiple floors and exposed circular staircases where some lights were on. The workmanship was remarkable, and the entire building, even though from different centuries, worked together to give a breathtaking appearance.

As I stopped, she cracked open her door. "He had more native stone shipped over from Ireland to match the original tithe barn."

Closing the door and enclosing Dog, I looked at the main structure. "That's some barn."

She shrugged. "He got it cheap."

"Why?"

"It's haunted." I turned and looked at her. "Really."

"By what, unpaid contractors?"

"The Spanish Lady." As we walked toward the front entrance, she started to tell the story. "After the sinking of the Spanish Armada off the coast of Ireland, the British navy seized a number of the ships that were still floating and ran them aground, taking the crew prisoners. Since there were no proper prisons, they housed the Spanish where they could, putting them up in barns and other such buildings."

"And this was one of them?"

"Close to a hundred men were kept in this very building as valuable trading commodities, but the locals were none too happy about them and neither were the local Catholic sympathizers. There was a woman who fell in love with one of the sailors and brought him food, only to be caught and hanged as a traitor." We stopped at the front door. "She's been described as the Spanish Lady and can be seen gliding along the lane, shrouded in a flowing mantilla, a ghostly specter in the moonlight."

"Does she answer doorbells?"

"Let's find out." She pushed the illuminated button, and we listened to the chimes inside.

Pulling out my pocket watch, I noted the time. "Only nine o'clock—does he go to bed early?"

"Never." Reaching out, she pressed the heavy lever and swung the door open. "Philippe, you have guests!"

We stood there for a moment more, and then she entered, and I followed. "He does, though, take naps, or work in his library at the far back of the building."

Entering the front room, I glanced around, taking in what looked like the main hall of a hunting lodge, complete with flags and a staggering amount of taxidermy mounts. "He hunts?"

Continuing on, she headed toward an opening to the left. "Antique shops and estate sales."

I stopped to thumb through the stacks of canvases leaning against every wall, then followed her through a formal dining room. She flipped on the lights and entered a commercial-grade kitchen with stainless steel counters, appliances, and a wall-size wine cooler. There was a half-eaten sandwich on a plate and an empty wine glass along with a burned-out cigarette in a marble ashtray on the center island next to a soap-stone sink.

Gesturing toward the repast, I glanced around. "Well, he's here, or was recently."

"He eats all the time and never gains a pound." Continuing toward the back, she called out again. "Philippe!"

She rounded the center island and pulled up short. Her hand came to her mouth, and she backed away.

"Is there something wrong?" She stopped, and I continued forward where I could see a large pool of blood and bloody handprints sliding down the shiny surface of a massive refrigerator. There was a large Japanese cooking knife lying on the floor, also covered in blood.

I pulled out my Colt and turned off the safety on the large-frame semiautomatic, the metallic snap being the only sound in the room. "C'mon." Rushing her back through the dining room and entry hall, I pushed open the door and ushered her to my truck to place her inside.

Grabbing the mic from my dash, I keyed it and called in to the Sheridan County Sheriff's Department and spoke to a nice young woman who promised to send the entire personnel along with any armed janitorial staff they might have there in the building. I handed the mic to Katrina, telling her to give the address to the dispatcher and to lock the doors, stay in the truck, and assist them in getting here if they needed it.

Holding the mic as if she might crush it, she nodded. "Right."

"Whatever you do, don't get out of the truck."

"Right."

Shutting the door and locking it, I headed back in, allowing the beam from my Maglite to lead the way. I switched on all the lights as I went until finally arriving back in the kitchen area where it still looked as if a pig had been butchered.

As I stared at the scene, I was pretty sure we weren't going to find him in the bathroom unless someone had hauled him there to cut him the rest of the way up in the tub.

Glancing around, I could see no other signs of blood, no splatter or drag mark to show where the body might've been moved . . . nothing. I continued down the hallway into a sitting area. I kept looking for blood, but once again didn't see anything.

I stepped into the next room and reached over and turned on the lights. There was a space that was even larger than the others we had been in, with tables, desks, and rows and rows of large art and research books. When it was in order, I'm sure that it was breathtakingly beautiful with the stone floors, glass walls, and rough-hewn rafters, but at the moment—it was a disaster.

Bookshelves had been overturned, desks cleared, and most of the furniture was scattered and upset, much in the same way Charley Lee's room had been destroyed up at the Home.

Trailing the Colt across the room, I could hear no noise and nothing moved, so I stepped in closer to the large oak library table and peered down at the books that remained there. I saw what I'd expected—Custer, Custer, and more Custer. There were the usual history books, some nonfiction, and even a few novels along with tome after tome of Western art books mostly from the nineteenth century, and, at the center of the table, a few enlargements of portions of the Adams's piece.

I picked up the one where the cavalryman was fighting for

his life against the determined Zulu warrior and then flipped it back onto the flat surface.

I started toward the other wing, pausing to take in the carefully planted trees, bushes, and flowerbeds under a huge skylight at the center of the house. No wonder Philippe had felt more at home in the garden at the museum.

There was another hallway, and I entered with the .45 at the ready, then moved along the wall and spotted one of the stairwells that circled to the second floor, which must've been a hayloft back when the abbey barn held horses and incarcerated Spaniards. The treads were metal and clanged, no matter how carefully I climbed, but I finally made it.

It was another large room with a king-size bed and French furniture and a picture window overlooking the garden below. The room was in general disarray, but nothing like the ones downstairs. The bed covers were pulled back, and it looked like there might've been some activity in there recently. Clothes littered the floor, and there were plates and glasses strewn on every surface, but nothing that spoke to anything other than the owner being a wealthy slob.

There was some movement to the left, and I swung around to take aim at a startled black and white cat, or what my grandparents used to refer to as tuxedo, that froze coming out of the bathroom.

Lowering my weapon, I took a breath. "Howdy, Jellicle Cat, are you one of the Practical Cats from *Old Possum's Book?*"

The feline leapt from the floor onto the bed and stared at me.

"If you killed him or T. S. Eliot, you might as well come clean."

She continued to regard me and finally meowed.

"I should warn you that anything you say can and will be used against you in a court of law."

She licked a paw.

Holstering my Colt, I glanced around and sighed. "Yep, that's the response I usually get."

11

"Well, at least you were already making the trip."

He sighed, stretching the cuffs of his plastic gloves. "This is cutting into my fishing time."

Sitting on one of the already dusted stools, I watched as Woody Woodson applied some sort of adhesive pad to the refrigerator over the handprint and stood, looking at his wristwatch. "So, what are you thinking?"

He glanced at the floor and shook his head. "I'm thinking the same thing you're thinking—nobody loses this much blood and lives."

"How long was the blood here?"

"As near as we can tell from tactility analysis, about three hours before you arrived."

He glanced at me, reading my expression as I looked toward the glass ceiling. "Where did he go? There are no drag marks, spatter off-scene, drops . . . Nothing."

"I know." He stroked his beard. "It's a puzzler."

"Did you look in the refrigerator?" His face took on a panicked expression, but I assured him. "Don't worry, I did."

"You know, you keep treating me like this and you're going

to stop getting jiffy service." He glanced around. "As near as we can tell there's no way you could clean up in that amount of time, so the body had to be put in something, but like you said, there's no drag marks, nothing." A young man in a blue windbreaker with the large DCI lettering on the back came in and took the print that Woody peeled off the refrigerator. "Sample that, then scan it and get me the results."

The young man disappeared as Woody went back to working the floor.

"The knife?"

"Bagged, but from preliminary analysis it had no tissue remnants."

"Prints?"

"Loud and clear."

"Chances?"

"Actually, pretty good. He was a world traveler and was printed by at least four other countries, along with artistic conservation groups of which he was a member—if it's him, we'll know in no time." He glanced around at the extravagant home. "Art collector, huh?"

"I think he sold more than he collected."

He smiled and shook his head. "You know what the most-watched television show down at the State Penitentiary happens to be?"

"Prison Break?"

"Antiques Road Show."

"You're kidding?"

"Nope. We're breeding a more knowledgeable crop of thieves."

I stood, stretching my shoulder muscles. "You need me?"

"For what, play-by-play?"

"I've got to go do some fence-mending with one of my fellow sheriffs."

Turning, he studied me. "How are you doing, Walt?"

I stopped. "In what sense?"

"In the I-heard-you-went-to-Mexico-a-couple-of-months-ago-and-killed-a-bunch-of-people sense."

"Yep, well . . ." I sighed, which flattened my lungs like a punctured tire. "They didn't give me much choice on that."

He nodded and continued to look at me before changing the subject. "I saw your daughter at one of the attorney general's functions over in Cheyenne."

"How did she look?"

"Breathtaking." He paused for just an instant. "Reminded me a lot of Martha."

"Tell her I said hi, the next time you see her." Before he could respond, I turned and headed out, but his muffled voice rose up from the floor. "I'll let you know if I find the body."

Walking back into the main room past the temporary tables that DCI had set up, I spotted Sheridan County Sheriff Carson Brandes standing near the door with another individual I recognized. The young sheriff glanced up at me, gesturing toward Conrad Westin. "You know this jaybird?"

"Informally, yes."

Westin turned to me. "Philippe is dead?"

"There's some blood and the Division of Criminal Investigation's crime lab is here."

"Blood?"

"Yep."

"How much blood?"

"How can I help you, Mr. Westin?"

Sheriff Brandes yawned. "He says he's got some personal items in there that he needs."

"Well, I'm afraid at the moment this house is a crime scene and we can't have anything disturbed."

He stared at me. "The entire house?"

"For now, yes." I studied him back. "Do you mind telling me when the last time was you saw the count?"

Brandes interrupted. "Excuse me, the what?"

"He was a count, supposedly."

Westin crossed his arms. "Are you accusing me of something?"

"As a known associate and employee, it's possible that you may have been the last person to see Philippe Lehman."

"Alive? So, he is dead."

"Mr. Westin, so far there is no body, but considering the circumstances alive or dead, we are concerned as to his whereabouts—I'm sure you understand."

He weighed his response. "I saw him early yesterday evening when I brought some papers over, contracts for some artwork he'd sold."

"How did he seem at the time?"

He thought about it. "Distracted, maybe a little worried."

"About?"

"These were big contracts. There was a lot of money involved."

"Can you think of anyone who might want to do Mr. Lehman harm?"

"No, I mean . . . No."

"You were going to mention someone?"

"Well, you met him the other night, Serge?"

"The bodyguard."

"Yes. Philippe owed him some money, and Serge made the remark that he was going to get the money from him the hard way if he had to."

"The hard way."

"Yes."

"Any idea where Serge was last night?"

"No."

"Any idea where he is now?"

"He was in Sheridan. He has a room there somewhere."

I glanced at Brandes, who pulled out his cell phone and walked away as I turned back to Westin. "Hard to be a bodyguard from twenty miles away."

"Philippe didn't allow him on the premises full time—he said he was oafish."

"And yourself?"

He barked a laugh. "Myself what?"

"Where did you go after you dropped off the papers last night?"

"So, now I am a suspect?"

"Just covering all the bases. If you have a reasonable alibi, we don't have to trouble you again."

"I was at a party in the clubhouse at the Powder Horn by six p.m."

"Any witnesses?"

"About seventy of them."

"Well, there you go."

"Can I get my papers now?"

"No. As I explained, nothing can be disturbed until DCI is finished." Adjusting my hat back, I looked at him. "If you don't mind my saying so, you don't seem particularly upset."

"Sheriff, you say there's blood but no body, and you refuse to surmise as to whether the man is dead, so Philippe might turn the corner and come walking in, right?"

"We can hope."

"Well, indeed, there you go. Am I free to leave?"

"Yep."

He started to but then turned and leaned in. "Just so you know, Sheriff. Philippe was a real piece of shit, although he didn't warrant killing. Even so, you'd have a hard time finding enough people to mourn him to play a rubber of bridge."

I watched him go out through the open door and then turned to my fellow sheriff. "Hey, Sheriff."

He hung up his phone, his face lined with fatigue. "Hey, Sheriff."

"Wanna talk sheriff stuff?"

"Sure."

I pulled up a chair, and he sat in the one opposite. "It was just a social call."

The tall, lean young man laughed a response; it seemed like all the sheriffs in Wyoming were younger than I was. "Do all your social calls end like this?"

"Not generally."

"Hey, I've got a county jurisdictional deal for you—you take Story, and we'll take Clearmont."

"Clearmont is already one of your towns."

"I knew you wouldn't go for it." He looked at me. "There are a lot of people in this state that think you're kind of a pain in the ass, Walt."

"Are you one of them?"

"As a matter of fact, I'm not, but the next time something like this comes up I'd appreciate a call."

"It wasn't business."

"It's always business with you, Walt." He shook his head. "If you come over here to go to the grocery store, I'm gonna send people out to scour the frozen food section for a body."

It was a small lecture, but a lecture nonetheless. "You want it?"

"No, what I want is the courtesy of a phone call—is that too much to ask?"

I pulled in my horns. "No, no it's not."

He studied me for a moment more. "I'm glad to hear that."

I nodded and studied my boots. "Do you remember Sundown Pierce?"

"Hell yeah, he locked me and my brother up in that ancient, historic jail during Clearmont Days one time and then forgot about us—came out the next morning and took us into Sheridan and bought us breakfast at the Palace."

"He and Lucian had a turf war one time."

"Really? I'd have paid to see that."

"Lucian ran over his foot and broke three toes, and Sundown shot out the back window of Lucian's old Nash."

He laughed and shook his head. "Crazy ol' bastards."

"Yep."

He studied me. "And you're the last one."

"I'm not crazy."

"You know the first sign of crazy?"

"Saying you're not?"

He grinned a consummate political smile, and it was easy to see how he'd been elected. "You got it."

I studied him back and then looked through the open doorway at the lawn outside and the assemblage of vehicles. "Yep, well . . . How's Katrina?"

"Out in the truck—hey, she's cute. Are you going to get in trouble with Vic?"

"No, she's usually with me when the bodies turn up."

"Katrina Dejean—French?"

"By way of Russia."

His face twisted. "We picked up a Russian very late last night—kicked some guy in the head at the Mint Bar."

"His name wouldn't be Serge Boshirov?"

"Might be."

"Can you hold him?"

"As long as you'd like—the victim is still unconscious."

"Do it—he might be involved with all this."

He glanced around. "Oh my, like one of those Russian nesting dolls, two crimes for the price of one?"

"Might be." I looked at the younger version of myself and thought about how many times I'd wished someone had given me the advice I was about to give to Carson Brandes. "Why don't you go home?"

"I'm thinking about it."

"Don't think—go." I smiled and set out for the parking lot where Dejean was, indeed, sitting on the tailgate of a Sheridan County Sheriff's Department pickup. She was sipping a cup of what I assumed was coffee with Dog sitting at her feet.

"Your dog is begging coffee."

"That's because I only give him decaf."

Lori Saunders, the silver-haired chief detective over in Sheridan County, laughed the way she always did at my jokes, one of the many reasons I really liked her. "I let your dog out."

"I figured."

"Can I have him?"

"No."

"I'll treat him better than you do."

"Everybody treats him better than I do, that's why I don't have to."

Lori stood. "You will make sure this nice lady and your dog get home?"

"No more questions?"

"No more questions for now. Get her home."

I saluted. "Will do." Helping Katrina off the tailgate, I closed it, and we watched as Lori fired up her Suburban and drove off into the burgeoning dawn. "Where is home, anyway?"

She glanced toward the ostentatious house.

"Oh." Woody Woodson appeared in the doorway of said house and waved at me as I turned back to Katrina. "Take Dog and climb into my truck, and I'll find you someplace to stay when I get done here."

She called Dog, and the two of them headed toward the Bullet as I walked back toward the house. "What's up?"

Woody peeled off the plastic gloves, punching them in his shirt pocket where they hung like a dead flower arrangement. "You want the good news or the bad?"

"Why not the good?"

"We have a positive ID, down to prints and blood type."

"The bad?"

"It's the Count."

After dropping Katrina off at the Blue Gables at dawn, I swung around to the office and unlocked the door, climbed the steps, careened off the walls to the holding cells, and collapsed on one of the cots as Dog curled up on the floor. In two minutes, we were asleep, or I exaggerate and it was one and a quarter.

"Late night?"

Ruby was always the first in, unless I slept at the office, which I seemed to do more and more these days. "Go away."

"I made coffee, you grouchy old bear."

"Okay."

"I'll leave your mug on my counter to lure you out of your lair."

"Okay."

"Get up, or it'll get cold."

"Yes, ma'am." She'd been treating me a lot nicer since giving up on teaching me how to use a computer, something that had severely tested our relationship.

Groaning, I rolled up to a sitting position and scrubbed my hands across my face to get some circulation going. Then I gathered my hat from the floor and sat it on my head to capture my wayward hair. Dog was gone, having better recuperative powers than I did, and had evidently joined my dispatcher in the main office.

I stood and stretched my broken parts that woke up slower than the other ones and steadied myself in an attempt to start walking toward coffee, the only thing that would save me from the desperation of coma.

When I got there, she had already pulled a stool up for me. I stared at it.

She sipped from her own mug, peering at me with the ferocious blue eyes over the lip of her drinkware. "What?"

"I might fall off."

She reached down and petted Dog. "You'll have to risk it—I'm not hauling a chair in from your office."

"Is this going to be a long lecture?"

"Maybe."

"I already had one from the Sheridan County sheriff last night . . ." I thought about it. "Maybe it was this morning."

"Sit."

"Yes, ma'am." I did as instructed and then, satisfied I wasn't going to topple over onto her, reached out and took the mug and held it under my face, allowing the steam to help open my eyelids that felt as if somebody had glued them together. "At the risk of sounding like an eighties' action movie, I think I'm getting a little old for this."

She nodded. "Surprisingly, among other things, that's the title of today's lecture."

I sipped my coffee. "Go ahead."

"You were in Sheridan County?"

"I was."

"Running and shooting?"

"No, more like detecting and analyzing."

"Well, that's a relief and certainly more age appropriate."

Nodding, I tried to smile. "I don't usually look this good after a night of running and shooting."

She continued to study me. "You are under the mistaken impression that you are looking good this morning?"

I shrugged, straightening my shirt that looked as if it had been slept in for a week. "Questionably representable?"

"Did it ever occur to you to call for some backup from a staff that is considerably younger than you are?"

"It was an impromptu situation."

"With you it always is." She lowered her mug. "Did you think of handing this situation over to the proper authorities in Sheridan County?"

"It was discussed."

"And?"

"They didn't want it. Besides, it might pertain to the case I've been working on."

Her voice changed tone, and I was pretty sure about thirty-seven percent of the oxygen had just left the room. "And which case is that?"

I muttered. "The missing painting."

"Walter . . ."

"It's taken a turn."

She sighed, more than audibly. "In what way?"

"Someone may have been murdered."

"You're not thinking Charley Lee Stillwater?"

"Possibly, but this is someone else."

She sat forward a little. "So, who may have been murdered?"

"Philippe Lehman."

"No Count?"

I sipped my coffee, the siren song of caffeine whispering to the dormant portion of my reptilian brain stem. "Proprieties for the dead, please."

"Habeas corpus?"

"There's a lot of blood and prints."

"But no body?"

"Woody Woodson is working on that."

She nodded. "He stopped in yesterday with his fishing pole."

"That turned out to be wishful thinking."

"On everybody's part." She glanced at the mass of Post-its on her own desk, and I casually wondered if she had stock in the company. "The grandson, Bass Townsend, is ready to be released from the hospital, but Isaac wanted to just give you a heads-up."

"Hmm . . . Do you think we can get Jim over at the Blue

Gables to just hold a cabin for us in perpetuity?" I sipped my coffee. "Did Isaac mention if the patient was capable of driving two days back to Los Angeles?"

"He did not."

"But he's doing better?"

"Apparently." She studied me some more. "Isn't that a glimmer of light in this particular part of this wide-reaching investigation?"

I reflected, which was what she wanted anyway. "Here's my line of supposition, and you can correct me if you spot any errors in my logic."

"Of course."

"A local veteran dies under questionable conditions and leaves a box containing a million dollars' worth of unmarked, nonserialized, hundred-dollar bills; an individual with an impressive layman's interest in not only western art but in one piece of artwork in particular that was destroyed in a fire in a military facility in Texas at a time when and where he happened to be stationed."

"Okay."

"A study of said painting is discovered that matches the historic work of art exactly and after violence is perpetrated, it is stolen."

"Granted."

"Further investigation reveals a hidden cubby in the veteran's ransacked room that could have contained said oversize, historic painting."

"A painting no one has actually seen."

"Granted, but Philippe Lehman, noted art historian and collector, is discovered missing with prints and an inordinate amount of blood saturating his kitchen floor."

"But no body."

I shrugged. "No."

"So, once again, no painting and also no body."

"Yes." I drained my coffee cup. "There is one aspect you may or may not be aware of."

"And that is?"

"There is an ex-KGB arm-breaker over in the Sheridan jail by the name of Serge Boshirov who might be mixed up in all of this."

She looked at me, one tick past incredulous. "KGB arm-breaker?"

"Ex . . . Well, maybe a head-kicker—at least that's why he's in the Sheridan jail. Anyway, my next trip is over there to have a word with him as long as Carson Brandes and I are still on speaking terms."

She sat her mug down. "Well, before you go, I have something serious to talk about with you."

"This hasn't been serious?"

"You need to call your daughter."

"She could call me."

"That's not how parenting works, and you know it." She studied me. "How long has it been?"

"Seventeen days, eight hours, and forty-three minutes."

"Call your daughter."

"Okay." My turn to study her. "Something else?"

"I'm thinking of retiring."

I felt my stomach flip. "Don't say that."

"I just did."

"I'm going to pretend like you didn't." I sat my own mug down. "Look, if this is about the computer thing . . ."

"It's not. Walter, I only have so many years for all this in me, and I need to know if you're going to stand in the next election, because if you are, I'm going to start training a replacement and then retire."

I stared at her. "And if I'm not?"

"Then I'll ride out the rest of your tenure and assist in the transition of whoever comes in to dispatch for the next sheriff."

"Meaning Saizarbitoria."

"Whoever, I really don't care—I'm just not going to leave all this to the next person that comes in to do the job. I've got another year in me, but I can stretch it to one and a half if I have to."

"Either way, you're leaving?"

"Yes."

"You know, not all good things have to come to an end."

"Yes, they do, it's the nature of all good things."

"I don't think I want to be here without you. I'm not even sure I can." I leaned in and took her hand. "When the whole computer thing was going on, I was sure you were going to quit. I told Cady, and she said to do whatever it took to make you happy."

"She's a good girl." She waited a polite moment before continuing. "So, you're not going to stand?"

"I honestly don't know."

I snorted out something that resembled a laugh.

"It's not like I haven't been thinking about it myself."

"And?"

"I'm not sure what else I would do."

"You and I both know that's not a good enough reason to have this job."

"Yep, well . . ." I looked at the floor. "I go up to the home for assisted living and look at Lucian, and I'm not so sure I can do that. I mean even working full time I can barely stay out of Cady's and Lola's hair." I sighed. "Not that that's been a problem lately."

Her voice took on yet another tone. "Why haven't you called her?"

"I need to tell her about Charley Lee, but was calling her too much, so I stopped."

She shook her head at me. "All or nothing, huh?"

"Something like that."

"Tough guy."

"Not at all."

"Why don't you take a sabbatical?"

"I told you, I have been."

"I mean from the job."

"In case it missed your notice I was gone for two weeks in Mexico a few months ago."

"That was hardly a vacation."

"You think I need time off?"

"It's better than just quitting—you could try having some time to yourself and see how it goes." Her eyes stayed steady on me but then flicked over my shoulder where I heard someone coming up the steps from the main entrance. "Can I help you?"

I turned to see the last person I expected, Lolo Long's little brother, Barrett, who had stopped at the top of the steps and waved. "Hi."

"Howdy."

"Is there any other way up here?"

Ruby and I looked at each other. "What do you mean?"

"Lonnie is down here, and he wants to come up."

———

"I need a job."

I studied the résumé and looked up at the chief of the Northern Cheyenne and the little brother of the tribal police chief, figuring there wasn't any way out of this in the political sense. "How come you don't work with your sister?"

He glanced at Lonnie and then back at me. "You're kidding, right?"

"Yep, I kind of was."

"He is a very good boy—um hmm, yes, it is so."

Lonnie nodded, and I wondered how old he was. I figured he had to be at least approaching a hundred. "You sure you want to lose him?"

The older man glanced at the younger one and nodded. "He is not a good driver."

"With a car?"

"No, with my wheelchair. He runs me into things."

Barrett interrupted. "*Áahta . . .*"

"*Áahmomoto . . .*" The older man looked back at me. "He also has trouble keeping his mouth shut, but I don't think that has ever kept anyone from being a police officer."

I studied the recommendations, which did not include Lolo. "What does your sister think about all this?"

"Nothing, she's my sister, not my mother."

"You understand, I'd prefer to have good relations with her department."

"Me too, but I don't belong to her." He slumped back in the chair pushing a handful of thick hair from his face. "I've got two more semesters, and then I can work full time."

"So, we're talking about a part-time job for now?"

"Weekends and then the better part of a month during the holidays."

"You worked security at the tribal headquarters, but you haven't listed your sister as a previous employer."

He gestured toward Lonnie. "He was my previous employer."

"As I recall, you weren't armed."

"No, but I can be."

"Not without six weeks down at the Law Enforcement Academy in Douglas."

"Okay."

The idea that had been evolving in my mind was bubbling to the surface, and I was thinking maybe I could kill two birds with one stone. "How are your radio skills?"

"My what?"

"Ever done any dispatching work?"

"No."

"Want to?"

"No."

"Then I can't hire you—the opening I've got is part-time dispatcher on weekends."

He looked at the chief, who nodded. "Nothing else?"

"Nope."

He thought about it as he looked at the cardboard Budweiser version of the Adams painting propped up on top of my filing cabinet. "Do I get a uniform?"

"Sure, if you want one."

"A gun?"

I shook my head. "Not till after the six weeks in Douglas."

"So, two semesters working part time as a dispatcher, and then in the spring you'll send me to the academy and give me a job as a real deputy?"

"We'll see how you do and then go from there."

"Really?"

"Really." I stood. "That gives you nine months to impress me."

He also stood. "Deal."

"Not yet. Not till you meet your real boss for the next nine months."

I walked out of my office, and Barrett turned Lonnie's chair and pushed him out after me. Ruby was talking to Vic and Saizarbitoria, but the conversation broke up when we arrived at her counter. "Ruby, this is Barrett Long. I just hired him as a part-time, weekend dispatcher."

It was hard to read all the emotions that played across her face, but she entertained an honest smile and held out the second hand that had been offered to him and they shook. She glanced at me. "Does he know what he's getting into?"

"He'll eventually figure it out." Allowing the two to get acquainted, I took the handlebars of Lonnie's wheelchair and moved past the rest of the staff, who were waiting at the top of the stairs.

"New dispatcher?"

"Yep."

She tilted her head to look past me. "Since when?"

"Since this morning."

"Those are big shoes to fill."

"Yep." I glanced at Sancho. "Questions?"

He held up his hands in compliance. "Not a one." Walking past, he introduced himself to Barrett as Vic studied me. "What about Double-Tough?"

"What about him?"

"Isn't it the usual practice to bump the Powder Junction

deputy up here and put the low man on the totem pole down there?"

"Yep."

She glanced past me at the young man again. "He know that?"

I shrugged. "He's got nine months to find out."

She looked down at Lonnie. "Kind of quiet down there in Powder Junction."

He nodded and smiled. "Kind of quiet up in Lame Deer too . . . Um hmm, yes, it is so."

Reaching out, I touched her arm to get her attention. "I'm headed over to Sheridan to talk with the KGB. You can read the file on him as I drive?"

"The who?"

"Serge the arm-breaker, kind of like Ivan the Terrible but without the charm."

"How can I turn that down?"

I glanced at Lonnie. "Want me to get you out of here?"

The chief glanced at his mode of locomotion. "No, I will wait on him—he is mine until Friday, right?"

"Right." I started down the steps with Vic. Dog didn't join us but rather had planted himself in front of Barrett and was now getting an ear massage from the new hire.

Smiling, I pushed open the door, and we walked across the parking lot toward my truck. "So, No Count is dead?"

Opening the door, I climbed in; she did the same on the other side. "So it would appear."

"And the woman is at the motel?"

"Yep, along with the grandson, Bass, later this afternoon."

"Are we bailing out the KGB guy and putting him at the Blue Gables too?"

"Probably not."

"We could do it like an Agatha Christie—I suppose you're all wondering why I've called you here today . . ."

I started my truck and headed north. "You miss a lot when you go home to bed."

"Didn't miss a night's sleep." She turned to gaze at me. "You look like shit."

Negotiating the ramp at the edge of town, I eased onto I-90. "Thanks."

She lodged her boots up on my dash. "No, you really do."

I slipped on my sunglasses in an attempt at creditable appearance. "Really, thanks."

She watched the early morning scenery whiz by as the sun rose, illuminating the mountains to my left and highlighting the small remainder of snow at their tops.

After a while, I asked. "You okay?"

"Yeah." She turned, looking straight ahead at the road. "So, Ruby's calling it quits? We'd spoken about it a few times."

I passed a group of lingering minivans in the right-hand lane. "I think she's just tired."

"Yeah."

I glanced at her again. "Are you sure you're all right?"

"Yeah, I just liked having at least one other woman on the force."

I drove on. "Me too."

12

The Sheridan County sheriff was kind enough to loan us his interrogation room, so we did not have to look at Serge through Plexiglas. Vic was enjoying posing in front of the two-way mirror. "So, this is what a real sheriff's department looks like?"

"Big sheriff's department."

She vogued some more and then turned to look at me, her hand on her hip.

"So, Serge kicked some guy in the head in a bar fight?"

"Just a little old-fashioned fun—some nineteen-year-old. I guess there was an altercation, and the kid swung at Serge, missed, slipped, and then fell on the ground. Boshirov kicked him and unfortunately connected with the kid's head—knocked him out cold. From what Branden told me, the kid woke up about three hours ago and decided not to press charges. So, unless we discover something, Serge goes free after he talks to us."

"Does he know that?"

"I don't think Carson has relayed that to him, no."

The door jostled and then opened, revealing Serge Boshirov and the Sheridan County sheriff, Carson Brandes, himself. The massive prisoner smirked upon seeing me and then held his belly-chain handcuffs out to Carson. "You want him loose?"

"Sure."

As Brandes uncuffed him, Boshirov smirked some more and then spoke in his adenoidal voice. "You are sure you handle me?"

I turned to Vic. "You got the rubber hose?"

She patted herself, coming up empty. "I thought we were just going to kneecap him, but they took our weapons."

He sat in the plastic chair across the metal desk from us and straightened his orange jumpsuit, and I had to wonder where Brandes had gotten one that big—the Big & Tall Prisoner shop? "That would be violation of my Geneva Convention rights."

"You're not involved in an armed conflict, so the convention doesn't pertain to you."

He looked uncertain.

"I know that because I was actually in the military."

He looked even more uncertain.

"Unlike you." I glanced up at Carson. "I bet you've got better things to do."

He backed away, twirling the cuffs in one hand. "I did, but this is getting interesting."

I stared at the prisoner. "I hear you've been doing a little head-kicking."

He smirked. "I am bad man."

"I heard the victim is nineteen years old and half your size?"

He opened his hands in absolution. "My training, it kick in."

I shook my head and rolled my eyes for effect. "Look, we can do this one of two ways . . ."

"Serge Boshirov, Militsiya VDV Spetsnaz, Spetsial'nyy Otryad Bystrogo Reagirovaniya, special attaché to OMON units, SOBR Terek—and of course, KGB." He sat there, crossing his arms and looking supremely satisfied with himself and his knowledge of the alphabet.

I turned to Vic. "Sounds pretty impressive, huh?"

She snorted, and he glanced at her and then back at me, perhaps not quite so sure of himself. "Serge ol' buddy, I have good friends in the intelligence community, and I had them do a little digging on your background, and it wasn't too difficult in that everybody was willing to tell us what a piece of crap you are." Pulling a manila folder from under my leg, I tossed it onto the table between us.

He stared at it like it was a bowl of poisonous borscht and then ran a hand through his hair. "What is you think you know?"

Vic laughed. "Enough to know that you are one major bull-shit artist." She reached out and flipped open the folder, revealing his youthful arrest photo and reams of printed material. "First off, you're not even Russian, you're Chechen. You were a driver for Ivan Gorinsky in Urus-Martan where he made a fortune for himself working meat import scams with the Russians and starving his own people. From there you graduated to working for Mikhial Kodorkovsky, who made his fortune by taking over the energy giant Yukos during the 'Wild East' period in the nineties, but then you got caught screwing his housekeeper and had to run for your life." She looked at him. "Showing up in Bulgaria, where you were arrested for stealing women's lingerie."

He looked a little uncomfortable. "Underwears in great demand at that time."

She continued reading. "Then, for some reason, you were released and made your way to Napoli, where you were once again detained for not paying import taxes on outgoing shipments . . ."

"It was drug charge."

Vic made a sound like a buzzer in a game show. "The detector test determined that is a lie, goombah; says here it was sex toys."

Carson chuckled.

Looking a lot less sure of himself, Boshirov mumbled, "Must be mistake."

"I don't think so. The next time you surfaced in an official capacity was because of a child pornography ring in London . . ."

"My, you are one greasy, slimy, worldly thug, aren't you?"

"Look . . ."

"Finally coming to rest in Baltimore, as if that city doesn't have enough problems. And got yourself associated with Philippe Lehman as a driver and bodyguard by passing yourself off as ex-KGB."

"You think what you wish."

"Look, fuckwit, the Committee for State Security, or KGB, as the direct successor of Cheka, NKGB, NKVD, and MGB, was dissolved in 1991—what, you worked for all these agencies when you were twelve?"

"Assassins can do trade any age."

"Evidently, so can bullshit artists." She sat and then leaned back in her chair. "You're a small-time driver and child pornographer who sells neon dildos, and I wouldn't touch you with a proverbial ten-foot pole." She leaned forward and stared at him. "So, are you going to play ball or are we going to ship you off to one of the multiple global organizations that would gladly hang you up by your gonads and use you for guard dog practice?"

He studied her for a good long while and then stammered, "What . . . what you want to know?"

I stated it with as much matter-of-fact as I could. "Who killed Philippe Lehman?"

He stared at me, his eyes finally growing wide.

"If that's who you think was going to sweep in and get you out of this mess, then you've got some rethinking to do."

His voice wasn't much above a whisper. "Philippe is dead?"

Vic glanced at me. "That was pretty good, really."

"It was."

"Stanislavski-like, almost."

Serge glanced at Carson, who nodded, and then looked back at the two of us. "He is dead for true?"

"It would appear."

"But who kill him?"

I stood and walked over to the mirror but quickly turned to avoid the view. "We had a chat about that, and funny enough your name came up—at least until we dug up your past, which, as tawdry as it might be, hasn't included any acts of violence until now."

Serge sprang up. "That cowboy boy, he crazy . . . I bump into him, and he swing at me. He slip and fall and as I was try to get away, I happen to step on head, but I not mean to kick him."

Carson stepped over and put a hand on Serge's shoulder, carefully but firmly placing him back in the plastic chair.

Boshirov placed his head in his hands and sobbed suddenly. "I try so hard to live good life, but I getting with bad people." Raising his face, he shook his head. "I not mean to hurt boy."

"Tell me about your relationship with Philippe Lehman."

Wiping his eyes, he sniffed. "What?"

"Philippe Lehman?"

"The count, I drive for him. Sometimes I stand around and look tough, but he never ask me hurt anybody, just be there so look like I hurt people. Difficult situation in Russia long time ago, there was period when I help him get into certain places and help with certain things."

"Like Katrina Dejean?"

His face suddenly took on a look of concern. "She all right?"

"She's fine, a little shaken up, but fine." I sighed, studying the concrete floor. "What about Conrad Westin?"

He wiped his face some more. "The things I help with? Different. People I deal with, not so fancy, but full of power."

"Was it someone like that who was trying to buy the Custer painting?"

He stared at me.

"Cassilly Adams's *Custer's Last Fight*; bigger than a bread box?"

He snarled out the next words. "That fucking painting, I think it not exist."

"Really?"

"Philippe pay the man, but we no see painting."

"The count paid a million dollars in cash for a painting without seeing it?"

Serge nodded. "He see photographs, but competition so great that he pay man before seeing."

"And just for the record that man would be Charley Lee Stillwater?"

Boshirov shrugged. "Black man in soldier home, yes?"

"Yes." I placed my elbows on the table, palming my face with both hands and speaking through my fingers. "Okay, just so I get this straight . . . Charley Lee gets the word out that this painting is in existence and available for sale, correct?"

"Correct."

"How?"

He looked confused. "How what?"

"How do you sell a legendary painting, which supposedly no longer exists, on the black market, if you don't mind my asking?"

For the first time he smiled, I'm sure at my naivete. "Very simple to do on internet. In this time, nobody believe old man actually have painting, but the count, he research and find man and speak to him since he is living local."

"So, Philippe and Katrina talked to the old guys in front of the Soldiers' and Sailors' Home?"

"Yes, funny old mans in wheelchairs with flags."

"And finally Charley Lee."

"Yes."

"So, walk me through this. Charley Lee shows the count the photos, and Philippe gives him the million dollars in the boot box . . ."

"No, was in IGA grocery bag."

I uncovered my face and looked at him. "Well, I'm glad it was something secure."

"Yes."

Apparently, irony was not one of the languages he spoke. "So, what happened then?"

"We meet old black man at soldier home late one night, but he not show up."

I sat back in the chair and sighed. "Bingo."

Vic snorted. "Oh, shit."

"Next thing we know, old man is dead. So, no painting."

"Who took the proof?"

He looked genuinely confused. "Proof of what?"

I stood and walked away, one of my old interviewing techniques. "The small painting that I had that was stolen at the Buffalo Bill Center for the West. I'm assuming that was you?"

"I no know what you talk about."

"You didn't knock the conservator on the head over in Cody and run off with a small painting of a cavalryman and Indian fighting?"

"No. Who says I do this?"

I leaned forward. "Nobody, but you were my number one suspect. Where were you the night of the ball? I didn't see you there."

"I was in hotel, watching football game; soccer."

"Anybody with you?"

"No, but I order room service three times." He patted his substantial stomach. "It was big match, and I get nervous, and when nervous I eat."

"Who trashed Charley Lee's room?"

"What room?"

I walked back over to the desk. "At the Soldiers' and Sailors' Home, somebody tore the place apart in an attempt to find the painting. Either they found it or found out where it might've been hidden."

"So, painting is true?"

"Well, the place where it might've been hidden exists."

He shook his head. "Not me."

"You're sure?"

"This not something the count tell me to do and only do what count tell me do."

"Wasn't he a little upset about losing the million dollars?"

He shrugged. "Saw it as reasonable business expense on

black market. I am sure would like million dollars back, but he dead, yes?"

"Possibly."

He folded his arms, sat back in his chair, and took on a different demeanor. "As legitimate business partner, I would to lay claim to million dollars."

I stared at him. "We'll get to that."

"I prefer original the cash, if please."

"Right . . . So, you mentioned that there were other people who might've been interested in the painting?"

"Yes, there is always market is interested." He smiled. "The heavy-lined pocket."

I sat back in my chair. "Were any of them actually here?"

"Here?"

"Physically, in Wyoming?"

"Yes, once other buyers realize the count is interested in painting, they think it is real."

"You know who 'they' are?"

He tossed off the next remark. "Some of them were in bar the night I meet you."

I thought back to the group of people who had been there, at first not so happy to see a sheriff in their midst. "Do you know their names?"

He cleared his throat and looked at the table, and I couldn't help but think that he was sorry he'd mentioned them. "No."

"Kiki." He looked at me, and the fear there was palpable. "A man named Kiki, Klavdii Krovopuskov, with a woman by the name of Nadia. Russians. You know them?"

"No."

"You're sure? They were at the table that night and leaving by private jet."

He was breathing funny, almost panting. "It is mistake."

"I don't think so. Besides, I can check with my sources and find out who he is."

His eyes widened a bit. "Do not do that."

"Why?"

He glanced around the locked room. "You be sorry if you do."

"Really? Well, now you've peaked my interest. Who is he?"

"Krovopuskov, it means . . ." He was literally sweating at this point. "What is translation? Bloodletter."

I glanced at Vic first and then Sheriff Brandes. "The Bloodletter?"

He shook his head, gesturing with his hands. "Bloodletter, as to bleed the persons."

I stared at the man. "Charming—and what does this bloodletter do?"

His hands froze there between us when he suddenly withdrew them and folded them, sticking them under his arms. "I say too much."

"You think this Krovopuskov might be the buyer of the painting in question?"

"I say nothing."

"Do you know where he is?"

He sat there with his arms folded, refusing to make eye contact.

"I said, do you know where he is?"

He still didn't answer but turned to Sheriff Brandes. "I will need the lawyer now."

The Sheridan County sheriff glanced at me, indicating that the jig was up and unless I could find some other reason to hold him, he is going to have to let Serge free as the proverbial Russian or Chechen bird.

Vic leaned in. "You're sure there's nothing else you want to tell us?"

"Lawyer." He stared at the surface of the table. "And I want cell phone."

"No one has ever heard of him, and that's what worries me."

I held the phone in the crook of my neck. "Nothing at all?"

"Nothing."

"He said the plane was his. Now how can he have a jet licensed in the US and not have his name pop up anywhere?"

Donna Johnson sounded as exasperated as I felt. "Corporate or group ownership . . . I'll have the logs checked in Cody, but like I said, he's a ghost, Walt."

"Do you think that's his real name?"

"Difficult to say, but the literal translation is bloodletter."

"Where do you get a name like that?"

"Oh, I can think of a number of places . . . So, Boshirov hit the bricks?"

"For now, but he seems to think he has a right to the million bucks the late count paid for the painting that may or may not exist."

"You're sure Lehman is dead?"

"I'm not sure of anything in this case, but like Woody said, nobody loses that much blood and lives . . ."

"The Bloodletter?"

"You tell me."

"I'll try."

"Thanks, Donna." I hung up the phone and stared at my undersheriff staring at me from across my desk. "Bass Townsend?"

"Still asleep in his room."

"Katrina Dejean?"

"Sitting in our office, waiting for you to finish playing Longmire, Secret Agent."

"We need to go to the Soldiers' and Sailors' Home."

"Do we finally get to use the rubber hose?"

"Maybe." I stood, and she followed me into the main office where Katrina sat, typing on a laptop. "Klavdii Krovopuskov."

She looked up at me. "Excuse me?"

"Klavdii Krovopuskov. Ever heard the name?"

"A friend of Philippe's."

I sat in the wooden chair beside her. "What do you know about him?"

"He collects art."

"He was there at the bar in Cody the other night."

"Yes."

"Could he be involved in all of this?"

She closed the laptop. "I don't know. I have only met him twice, there at the Irma and at an opening in San Francisco years ago."

"Could he be attempting to acquire the Adams painting?"

"It's possible—he has a fascination with the American West, and as I recall he was a patron of Philippe's."

"A patron?"

"Philippe procured art for a number of clients, and even if he was never referred to in that fashion, the relationship between the two at least gave the appearance of being close."

"Any reason Krovopuskov would want to do the count ill?"

"None that I know of, why?"

"Someone ran off with my study, someone ransacked Charley Lee's room, someone may have killed Philippe Lehman, and I'm fresh out of suspects. Did von Lehman have a million to spare in attempting to buy the Adams painting, or would he have needed backers?"

She laughed.

"Something funny?"

She opened the laptop again and turned it toward me. "Aside from being one of Philippe's personal assistants, I was also at least partially in charge of his finances." She tilted the screen back. "As you can see from this spreadsheet, he was about four million dollars in debt."

I scanned the screen, and what she said certainly appeared to be the case. "So, he wouldn't have had an extra million in cash lying around?"

"It's possible but highly unlikely."

"So, where can I find Klavdii Krovopuskov?"

She closed the computer. "I have no idea."

"You're not being helpful."

"I don't mean to be unhelpful, I simply don't know."

I nodded, turning to Ruby, the font of all knowledge. "See if you can get Sheridan County Detective Lori Saunders on her cell phone for me?" I turned back to Katrina. "Where would Philippe keep his contact information, address book, cell phone, computer files, Rolodex?"

Katrina thought. "He had a small black-leather book that he kept on him that he would refer to occasionally. He never put anything down on the computer or cell phone in that he didn't trust them."

"I know how he felt."

"Walt, Lori, line one."

I got up, approached the dispatcher's counter, and took the phone from the Font. "Hey?"

"Yeah?"

"Are you at Philippe Lehman's place?"

"Where else would I be?"

"Could you do me a favor and keep an eye out for a small black-leather book with names, addresses, and phone numbers?"

There was a jostling as she adjusted the phone. "Something like the one I'm holding in my hand as we speak?"

"Possibly."

"French manufacture with a small sterling-silver pen attached?"

I turned back to Katrina. "Does the leather book have a sterling-silver pen attached?"

She nodded.

"That's the one. Can you look and see if there's contact information for a Klavdii Krovopuskov?"

There was a pause. "You wanna spell that?"

"Like it sounds."

"Right." She rustled around, and I could hear the pages flipping. "You're never looking for a John Smith, you know?"

"Tell me about it."

There was another pause. "Nothing."

"At all?"

"Nothing as close as I can get to the spelling of that name, K-L-A-V-D-I?"

"Close enough. What about Kiki?"

"K-I-K-I?"

"Yep."

"Oh, he's got a whole page to himself—addresses, phone numbers, email addresses, even bank account and routing numbers."

Pulling a Post-it from Ruby's pad, I snatched a pen. "Cell phone, please."

"There are five of them."

"Is there a US one?"

"Yes."

"Give me that one." She read the number, and I scribbled it down. "Hey Lori, take a photo of all that information and text it over to Vic, would you?"

"You trying to catch my murderer?"

"Maybe."

"I want an executive producer credit."

"You got it." I gave the phone back to Ruby and turned, walking over and handing the number to Katrina. "Call him."

She stared at the number and then up at me. "Why me?"

"He sees this call is from the sheriff's department, then he may not answer."

She nodded, then punched the number, and held on to the phone for a bit before placing it to her ear. After a moment, she started and then spoke. "Hello?" There was another pause, and I could hear someone speaking on the line. Her response seemed strained. "I was hoping to speak with Mr. Krovopuskov?"

Extending my hand, I gestured for her to give me the phone, which she did. "This is Absaroka County Sheriff Walt Longmire, and I need to speak with Klavdii Krovopuskov."

"This is Mr. Krovopuskov's personal secretary, can I help you?"

The voice sounded familiar. "Mr. Westin?"

"Yes, can I help you, Sheriff?"

Convenient. "Is Mr. Krovopuskov there, wherever you are?"

"Sheridan, and no, he's not here."

"Do you have a number where he can be reached?"

"I can give you some numbers—all of which he most certainly will not answer—or I can contact him myself and have him get in touch with you, if that would suffice."

"I guess it'll have to."

"Is this the number you would like him to call?"

"No." I gave him the number of the office and then hung up, figuring if I ever heard back from anybody it would be a miracle.

"So, how long are you going to give him?"

I handed Katrina her phone and then turned to Vic and frowned. "About an hour, then I'll call Mr. Westin back and impress upon him the importance of the murder investigation in which we're involved."

I turned back to Ruby. "Bass Townsend?"

"Still resting in his cabin."

Katrina put her phone into her purse. "The grandson of the man who had the painting? The one in the cabin next to mine?"

"Yep."

"He seems like a nice man."

"A suddenly rich man, that's for sure." I studied her. "What are your plans?"

"I really don't know." She twisted the expensive rings on her finger. "I had no official standing with Philippe, so I suppose I'm out on the streets."

"You might want to contact the Sheridan Sheriff's Department to see when you can go back in the house for your belongings."

"I will."

"Did the count have any family?"

"No, I'm afraid the creditors will be the only ones picking the bones."

"Well, I'm sorry for your loss."

She gathered her things and headed down the steps. "I'd like to stay in touch? I'm curious as to how this is all going to play out."

"I've got your number, and I promise to keep you in the loop. If you decide to leave the state I'd appreciate a call."

She stared up at me. "I'm still a suspect?"

"Nope, just an interested personage."

She smiled. "I like the sound of that."

Watching her go, Vic leaned against the wall by the stairs. "Are we going to the Veterans' Home, 'cause if we're not, I'm going to go study the options catalog for my new truck."

"I'm going to the Home, but you don't have to."

"Are you kidding? I wouldn't miss this for the world—besides, it might be walleye and Tater Tots or pizza."

"We live in hope." We'd just started down the steps when the phone rang. Ruby picked up the receiver and simply handed it to me. "Absaroka County Sheriff Walt Longmire."

Sheriff Carson Brandes's voice rang in my ear with all the finality of the bell on a ten-round bout. "All right, get your ass over to aisle thirteen in frozen foods—your buddy Serge Boshirov was found dead up at the rest stop on I-90."

13

"This is the last time I'm ever letting you in my county."

I kneeled, studying the dead body as flies buzzed in the high grass around the mound of flesh that until recently had been Serge Boshirov. "It's not my fault."

"You should start your own funeral home." Sheriff Brandes kneeled beside me. "You know, keep it in-house."

"Shot?"

He nodded curtly. "9mm."

"Smallish caliber for a man this big."

"Not in the back of the head it's not."

Vic joined us and watched as Woodson and the DCI crew gridded the scene and gathered evidence into plastic bags. After seeing me, the director of DCI and thwarted fly-fisherman walked over in his yellow jumpsuit.

Vic looked him up and down. "Nice Tyvek."

Pulling his hood back, he lowered his glasses and mask and smiled through his beard at my undersheriff. "Thank you—DuPont Tychem."

"The yellow is a nice change."

He nodded. "Keeps us from getting run over sometimes."

Vic gestured toward the body. "So, he's dead?"

"Through deliberate and diligent detection, we've ascertained that he is, indeed, dead."

"Long dead?"

He looked at her. "I'd say about four hours."

"So, right after the interview at the Sheridan jail?"

"Couldn't have been too long after."

I got up and turned to Carson, who was still kneeling. "You've got security cameras in front of the jail?"

"Sure do."

"Anybody pick him up?"

"I haven't had a chance to look at the footage, but I'll check with the front desk." He glanced around. "Kind of isolated over here on the scenic loop. People sometimes walk their dogs, but unless you want a view of the Montana border there really isn't any reason to come this direction—all the services are down the other way."

"Close range?"

Woody turned to me. "Very. He's got powder burns all over the back of his head. Hell, part of his hair caught on fire, but that might just be because of the amount of hair product." He smiled. "Maybe it was Vic."

"She was with me."

Woody shrugged, his yellow hazmat suit crinkling. "Back to zero."

Looking at the pull-out, I could see the dry dirt and gravel ceding to the Johnson grass and thistle. "Vehicle tracks?"

"Plenty of passenger cars and pickup trucks, take your pick."

"He didn't walk here in that amount of time."

"No."

"So, somebody picks him up and drives him up here and gets him out of the car and then walks up behind him and shoots him in the head."

"Sounds like the most plausible of scenarios."

"I need tracks, all of them."

Woody nodded. "I was afraid you were going to say that." He called over part of his crew.

I turned back toward the body. "Cell phone?"

Woody shrugged. "Not yet."

"It should be around here, he was preoccupied with the thing." Turning back to Carson, I mended fences. "You don't mind if I take point on this?"

He gestured toward the dubious surroundings. "Be my guest, just keep me tight in the loop and credit me in the papers."

"Deal." Taking a few steps to the right, I placed my hands on my hips and stared at the recently departed. It was true that he wasn't a man I particularly liked, but fate had brought him in contact with me and now he was dead and that made me partially responsible.

Who did he know?

Who would he trust?

Who would kill him and why?

"Earth to Walt." I turned and looked at her as she smiled. "So, you're getting pissed, huh?" She stood beside me, toeing a tuft of grass. "There's always a point where you start taking it personally. I like that part because that's when shit starts happening, and I like when shit starts happening." She turned her face toward me, listening as I clenched my fists, like a cinch being tightened on a saddle. "So, is shit about to start happening?"

"I believe so."

She placed her hands on her hips and joined me in gazing at the dead man. "God, I love my chosen profession."

We were speeding across the ridge along the Bighorn Mountains that separated it from Lake Desmet, running through the potential suspects, but not coming up with much more than we already knew.

"So, if we find the painting we find the killer?"

"Possibly, but if you've got the painting, why kill Serge or the count for that matter?"

She lodged her boots on my dash like she always did. "Covering your tracks?"

"I always mean to tell you, if we were ever in a crash, the airbags on this thing expand at about a hundred miles an hour and are going to drive your kneecaps through your collarbones."

"I guess my new truck will have airbags, right?" She shrugged. "Anyway, not with my catlike reflexes." She turned back toward me, moving her legs and placing her feet in my lap. "Anything from DCI on the murder scene in Story?"

"Nope."

"Shit."

"My thoughts exactly."

"How the hell do you get rid of a body like that, roll it up in a priceless painting?"

I glanced at her.

"Just a thought." We were interrupted when her phone rang with the Philadelphia Eagles fight song. She fished around to her back pocket and answered. "What fresh hell is this?" There was a pause. "He's right here, hold on." She made an exaggerated look of shock and then covered the phone. "It's Klavdii Krovo-puskov."

"You're kidding."

"Sounds like him."

Luckily, there was a truck pull-off where the 18-wheelers could strap on their chains only a quarter mile ahead, and I took the phone as I eased into the parking area that had a marvelous view of Blacktooth Mountain. "Mr. Krovopuskov?"

"Hello, Sheriff, I hear there has been a terrible accident?"

I lowered the windows to let in a little air and switched off the engine. "Well, I'm not so sure it's an accident. Do you mind if I ask where you are?"

"Helsinki."

It was a surprisingly good line from about a quarter of the way around the world. "Finland."

"Yes."

"And how long have you been there?"

"Well, the flight was the night I left your company there in Wyoming."

"I see."

He laughed. "You sound disappointed."

"No, not particularly, but I'm sorry to tell you that two of your associates are possibly dead."

"Two?"

"Yes, Philippe Lehman and Serge Boshirov."

"Who?"

"The count's bodyguard and driver?"

"The fat one."

"He was rather large, yes."

"How was he killed?"

"Shot."

"Conrad Westin informed me Philippe had been killed . . . was he shot too?"

"We're not sure."

There was a silence on the crystal-clear line. "You think I had something to do with this?"

"Not necessarily, but you did know both victims."

"Not really. Philippe was a business associate, and I did not know this man Boshirov at all."

"Funny, he claimed to know you."

"A lot of people claim to know me, Sheriff." A moment passed, and I was acutely aware of the tenuous thread that connected me to this man, fully aware that all he had to do was hang up, and I would never have the opportunity to speak to him again. "This is a murder investigation, yes?"

"Yep."

"Would you like me to come back to Wyoming?"

I laughed. "I don't think that's necessary at this point . . ."

"I can be there in twelve hours, where is the nearest airport from your town?"

"Well, Durant has an airport."

"How long is the runway?"

"I . . . I honestly don't know."

"Never mind, I will find out."

The phone went transatlantic dead in my hand, and I gave it back to Vic. "What?"

"He'll be here in twelve hours."

"From Finland?"

I nodded, started the truck, and pulled back onto the highway as she postulated. "Do you ever get the feeling that there are people out there who are living lives that we know absolutely nothing about?"

"I'm pretty certain of it."

"So, he was flying to Helsinki when both of these individuals were killed and has an ironclad alibi?"

"So it would appear."

"Then why is he coming back?"

"I have no idea."

"The borscht thickens."

When we pulled into the Soldiers' and Sailors' Home, "Spooky," by the Classics IV, was blaring into the empty parking lot from the speakers above. Taking the closest parking spot, I got out and stretched my back, feeling a stitch in my side.

"You know, I might just start hanging around in this parking lot when I get my new truck."

I sighed.

"What, you don't like this music?"

I started toward the glass doors of the main building. "It reminds me of things."

"Like what?"

"Like the Tet Offensive."

Carol Williams was waiting for us in the entryway. "I've got them corralled in the library section of the recreation room, but they're restless."

"I'll try not to say anything that might touch them off—we don't want a stampede."

She smiled and led us into the interior of the building, where we wound our way down the corridors, finally making a left by the ramp next to the pool table, which led us into the open area where I'd been before.

The four flagships were in field presentation, the major

branches of the armed forces sitting in their wheelchairs with their arms collectively folded. They ignored me with Talmudic concentration.

"Gentlemen."

"We didn't do anything." Clifton unfolded his arms, but then with nothing else to do with them, adjusted his boonie hat.

"Well, for starters, what do you suppose I think you did?"

"Stole that painting." Delmar blurted it out before realizing what he'd said and then glanced at the others before slamming his mouth shut.

Kenny turned to him. "Damn it, Delmar."

Trying to hide a smile, I addressed all of them. "And what painting is that?" They tightened their folded arms in a collective wall of silence. "All right, guys, let me tell you what I think I know and then you better start filling in the blanks, or else."

"Or else what?" Ray fixed me with a defiant glare.

"I'll bust all of you. As near as I can tell the painting in question is the property of the United States government and theft thereof is in direct violation of federal law, which means I can charge all of you as accessories in a conspiratorial act on a federal level akin to terrorism. Now that means I'll be dishonorably discharging all of you, and you'll be relieved of your military benefits."

Vic, having walked past them to stare out the window, turned to glance at me with a wide-eyed look, fully aware that this was an inordinate and monumental display of horseshit.

Figuring I needed to ratchet it up yet another notch, I turned to Carol. "What's on the menu tonight?"

She fixed them with a hard stare. "Pizza."

The four horseman looked at one another, torn at the

thought of being deprived, Navy grumbling at Air Force. "I told you it wouldn't work."

"Shut up, Kenny."

"You shut up, Ray."

The airman grunted. "He was always talking about that damn painting, about how it was going to be his retirement." He gestured to the area around them. "Like he wasn't already retired here in God's Waiting Room."

"Tell me about the painting—you've seen it?"

Clifton grumbled a response. "Oh, we called bullshit on it so many times that he finally hauled it out and showed it to us."

Kenny added. "With some help."

"What do you mean?"

"That thing was huge, and with all of us in wheelchairs it was kind of unwieldy, if you catch my drift."

"So, who helped?"

None of them spoke.

"Gentlemen, if you don't cooperate with me on this, I will make sure that you never see another pizza as long as you live."

"Magic Mike Bursaw."

Semper fi.

I thought about the second floor window, plastered with stickers, and the speakers blaring 60's music over the parking lot. "The disc jockey?"

"Yeah, him. He's a big guy and could carry the thing." Delmar the marine rolled his chair backward and pointed toward a large event table. "Late one night, Charley Lee got Mike to wrestle the thing out here and unroll it on the table, rolled the damn thing right off the end of the table in fact, and started off down the hallway."

Navy nodded. "Mike's big, but he ain't real handy."

Army added his two cents. "Deaf as a post."

Air Force affirmed. "All that damn rock and roll music or working the decks on an aircraft carrier and didn't wear his ear protection."

I sighed as they collectively nodded. "When was this?"

"Vietnam."

I sighed. "No, when was the last time you saw the painting?"

"About a month ago, when the Russians showed up."

Navy added. "He's deaf-mute, now how the hell did working on an aircraft carrier rob him of speech?"

Ignoring him, I tried to get the conversation back on the rails. "Then what happened to the painting?"

Air Force shrugged. "Waddaya mean, 'then what'? Mike rolled it up and carried it back to Charley Lee's room."

"And that was the last you saw of it?"

"Yeah."

Marine Corps spoke up. "We tried to get him to cut it up."

Vic glanced at me again and then addressed the man. "What?"

"Well, it was a big ol' thing, so we thought he could cut it up and share it. You know, give us all a piece for our retirement."

I smiled and massaged the bridge of my nose with a thumb and forefinger. "Did he happen to tell you how he came into possession of the painting?"

Clifton took the lead. "Said he saved it from a fire in Texas."

"Fort Bliss in '46?"

"Something like that."

"So, he stole it?"

"No, he didn't." I said nothing and waited as the old soldier pulled at his lower lip. "He told me about it after he showed us the damn thing, about how he worked in the commissary connected to the officers' club, washing dishes in the kitchen when the place caught on fire. He said it was bad, an old wood building that went up like rice paper and kindling. The CO was a real asshole and ordered them into this thing to try and save the silverware and whatnot, but nobody said anything about the painting. Anyway, Charley Lee went back in three times, the next-to-last time hauling one of his buddies out by covering the two of them up with the only thing that was handy . . ."

"The painting."

Clifton nodded. "With the heat, whatever it was they glued the thing to the wall with let go and it was lying there on the floor. Charley Lee said that the rafters were falling and there was fire everywhere and that covering themselves up with the painting was the only thing that saved 'em."

"Go on."

"When they got out the CO started screaming at them for not getting the company loving cup or some nonsense, and Charley Lee started to tell him about the painting but the piece of shit tells him to shut up and get to policing the area, and Charley Lee does as he's told and hauled the painting away—rolling it up and throwing it in a trash bin. Later that night he was coming back from taking a shower and the damn thing was still there, so he took it. And I don't blame him one damn bit."

"He had it all these years?"

"In his closet."

"Where did the smaller painting come from, the proof?"

They looked at me blankly.

"Never mind about that. You gentlemen are aware that the painting is no longer in Charley Lee's room, right?"

They looked genuinely surprised. "It's not?"

"No, it's not." I looked at each of them, one by one. "Do any of you have even the slightest idea as to who might've taken it?"

Delmar looked at me like I was the fort idiot. "Told ya, Russians."

"Did any of you actually see Russians take it?"

They all looked at one another.

"I mean, physically see Russians in here taking it?" They were silent, for the first time. "Is there anything else you think you should tell me?"

They looked at one another once again and then agreed, Kenny the first to speak. "No."

"If you think of anything more, any of you, will you tell me?"

They nodded.

I turned and headed back into the main building. "Let's go."

Vic and Carol trailed after, Vic pulling up beside me. "Where?"

"To make a request, with a bullet."

"He can be difficult."

I paused. "Is he really deaf-mute?"

Carol nodded. "Pretty much."

"Then how do you communicate with him?"

"We have a staff member, Diane Morris, who knows sign language, but . . ."

"Is she around?"

"I doubt it, she generally works nights."

"I can sign." We both stopped on the landing between the stairs, and I turned to look at my undersheriff, who rested her hands on her hips. "What?"

"You can sign?"

"Yeah, I learned from the kid who worked the snack shack at the pool where I lifeguarded every summer back in Philly. I might be a little rusty, but I think I can get the thought across."

I shook my head. "Wonders never cease."

"Sympathy for the Devil" rattled the door in its frame. Above was a glowing red light that read ON THE AIR.

I looked at Carol. "It's just wired to the lights in his room, maintenance did it kind of as a joke, but at least you can always tell if he's home or if you need him to answer the door. He's even got a text-to-speech recorder for when he needs to use the phone." She raised a hand and flipped the light on and off.

Nothing happened for a few moments, and then the volume of the music dropped a bit as Carol reflipped the switch. "He's used to us asking him to lower the volume on the music."

She continued flipping the switch, and finally the knob turned and the door opened approximately three inches. There was a lot of hair and one luminescent blue eye, which stared out at us.

"Hi, Mike Bursaw?" Vic ran her tongue over her teeth and smiled a Pepsodent smile, making a quick movement with her hands as he continued to stare at her with the one eye. She signed. "Can we come in?"

His hand, decorated with numerous rings and bracelets, the index and middle finger being taped together like a bird's mouth, came out the door as he signed back.

Vic, undeterred, made the same gesture and a bit more. "No,

really?" She persisted, her hands dancing. "We're from the sheriff's department and have a few questions?" He didn't respond but didn't close the door either.

I spoke as Vic turned to look at me. "You know the Stones didn't play the song for seven years after the stabbing at the Altamont Speedway Concert in '69?"

She translated, and he opened the door a little more.

I began again. "Bobby Kennedy was killed the day Jagger started writing the song, but you probably know that."

She translated, but the door didn't move.

Vic stared at him and then joined in singing and signing the chorus. "Whoo, whoo . . ."

The door swung open a bit, and she leaned forward, peered inside, then pushed it open and disappeared. We followed. I went in after Carol and stood there looking at the floor-to-ceiling racks of old 45s. "Good Lord."

There were thousands of records that took up every inch of available wall space, all carefully arranged in the wire racks with labels noting the artists. Fishing nets and tie-dyed fabric covered the ceiling and incense burned on a sideboard where an elaborate turntable spun the Stones, seven more singles stacked above the needle, ready to drop.

Magic Mike was nowhere to be seen but soon returned through a beaded curtain that covered an opening that looked like it had been sledgehammered through the concrete blocks. He was carrying what I assumed to be a cup of tea and handed it to Vic. Then he glanced at us.

Carol nodded, and he disappeared again.

I gazed around the room, especially at the psychedelic-looking painted floor with sweeping stars and galaxies. "I feel like I just fell into the Velvet Underground."

Carol slipped sideways and looked into the homemade expansion. "We may be the only ones who've been in here since the Nixon administration."

He returned with two more mugs with fluttering tea tags and then gestured toward the four beanbag chairs that slouched on the floor. Doing the best I could to leverage myself down, I joined the others as we sat and got a better look at Magic Mike Bursaw.

He wore a wool watch cap, his hair, a mottled explosion of black with gray streaks blossoming from under the elastic and trailing over his shoulders and down his back, where it joined with a massive beard of the same color that sprouted out from his face and dropped down to an impressive stomach. He was wearing a pair of brown sweatpants and a faded Hawaiian shirt.

Both hands were completely encased in rings and bracelets, and he studied all of us for a moment, but mostly concentrated his attention on Vic.

The record changer finished up with the Rolling Stones and dropped Marianne Faithfull's "Monday, Monday" as we sat there drinking tea. Getting Vic's attention, I promoted the line of questioning I wanted to pursue. "Ask him if he knows Charley Lee Stillwater."

She made a few quick gestures, and I watched as he responded.

Vic said nothing, so I asked. "What'd he say?"

"He wants to know if we like our tea."

"Tell him it's great, but he needs to answer my questions."

She translated, and he responded with a quick gesture as my undersheriff turned to look at me. "He wants to know why?"

"Why, what?"

Carol ventured. "Why answer your questions?"

"No, I suppose why do we want to know if he knew Charley Lee Stillwater."

She made a series of gestures to which he responded, and she made a face. "No, he wants to know why we like the tea; he says he makes it himself from the herb garden in the old chicken shed. He says it's a pu-erh, fermented and oxidized."

Carol nodded toward the back of the building. "The National Register of Historic Places chicken shed."

I nodded. "Tell him it's the greatest tea I've ever had in my life, which is not much of a stretch."

To our surprise, Magic Mike laughed heartily.

Carol nodded. "He reads lips pretty well."

I sighed, shook my head, and turned back to him. "Did you know Charley Lee?"

He nodded.

"Did you know about the painting he had?"

He nodded.

"Did you help him show it to the Wavers?"

He nodded again.

"And then put it back in the cubby behind the closet where Charley kept it hidden?"

Mike nodded once more.

"After he died, it was taken from his room, right?"

He shrugged.

"Do you have any idea who might've taken it?"

He shook his head.

"Did you ever see anybody talking or visiting with Charley Lee who seemed suspicious—people who shouldn't have been around here?"

He smiled, finally gesturing, and Vic translated. "You mean the Russians?"

"Possibly. Which Russians?"

He raised his face, then sipped his tea, and signed as Vic translated. "There was one man who was very heavy set, with another who had a head of wild-looking hair, and a woman."

"Blonde, small, attractive?"

He glanced at Vic and signed. "Not as attractive as me, evidently."

"When did he see them?"

There was a flurry of signing. "Charley Lee would talk to them on the porch of the administration building or out where the benches are near the old missiles park." She paused for a moment. "He showed the woman the National Register of Historic Places chicken shed where he grows the herbs for his tea." He turned back to Vic and gestured some more. "He'd like to know if we'd like to see his chicken coop."

"Maybe some other time." Dropping the hand signs, she smiled. "Apparently, it's pretty unique. He says he captures the rainwater in a cistern and uses that for a gravity-fed irrigation system."

Carol nodded. "It's quite a layout."

"I'm sure it's very interesting."

Vic watched him sign some more. "He says the chicken manure makes for a very rich soil content."

"I'm sure." I put the mug on the floor. "Mike, when were the Russians here last?"

He gestured, and Vic spoke. "The woman and the man with the hair were here about a month ago, and then the fat guy showed up asking some questions about a week ago. He showed him the historic chicken coop."

"The heavyset guy, Serge Boshirov, did he seem nervous or anything?"

He answered in the negative.

"Somebody killed him this morning."

He didn't seem surprised by the news.

"Yep, and it would appear that the guy with the hair, Count von Lehman, is also dead."

He said nothing.

"You don't have anything to say about that?"

Not so surprisingly, he remained silent.

"You seem kind of involved in all this."

He took a moment to respond with his hands as Vic spoke. "Not really, he says he just knew Charley Lee and helped him when he needed it, that's all. Not against the law, is it?"

It was about then that "I Fought the Law and the Law Won" dropped onto the turntable, the 45 catching traction as the needle fell.

"Nope." I studied him, and Vic signed my words. "You're sure the woman was with Serge about a week ago?"

He took his time, his face hidden in all the hair, and then stared at me and slowly nodded.

I stood and looked at the record spinning. "That singer, Bobby Fuller, died in '66 overcome by gasoline fumes from an open gas can in his unlocked car, no keys in the ignition. His body was covered in bruises, and he was soaked in fuel, a number of his fingers broken. The L.A. county coroner ruled his death a suicide, but then three months later they changed the cause of death to accidental asphyxiation." I moved toward the door as the women joined me. "Personally, I think the record label mob connections were responsible, and they were getting ready to torch the car with Fuller in it when they got interrupted."

Bursaw still sat, looking up at me and signing as Vic spoke. "And you're telling me this because?"

The two women joined me at the door as I ushered them out and then turned to look back at Magic Mike. "It's a big, dangerous world out there, and it's important to have friends."

"By the way, I know you're the one who called Bass Townsend and informed him that his grandfather was dead."

I turned the doorknob in my hand and slowly closed the door behind us as the song played on.

14

When we arrived back at the office, Barrett was sitting on my dispatcher's counter. He was reading a copy of *Outdoor Life* with his hiking boots on Ruby's desk.

I stopped at the top of the stairs. "What the hell are you doing here?"

He looked up from his magazine. "It's Friday."

"It is?"

"Yep."

He stared at me as Vic joined us, and I turned to her. "Is it Friday?"

"All day."

"Nobody tells me these things." I turned back to the kid. "One of your jobs is going to be telling me what day it is."

"It's Friday."

"You only have to do it once a day."

"Got it."

"Get your feet off Ruby's desk." Starting toward my office, I muttered. "What time is it?"

"Am I responsible for that too?"

"Sometimes."

"This job is far more wide-ranging than I thought."

I glanced up at Seth Thomas on the wall above the old fireplace and noted it was two minutes before five p.m. "Ruby leave early?"

"Wow, two minutes before the hour is early around this place?"

Vic nodded. "We run a tight ship."

Barrett lowered his feet and stood, then walked around the counter, and I had my first look at him in the uniform of the Absaroka County Sheriff's Department. I had to admit, the kid looked pretty sharp. "You know you don't have to wear that when you're dispatching, right?"

"Yeah." He glanced at himself. "I kind of like it—helps to remind me that the job is real."

I tried to hide the smile as best I could. "The *thrill of the badge* is what we used to call it, but it can get heavy after a while."

"I'm kind of enjoying it." He actually polished his star with a cuff. "Ruby said I was doing so well that she was going home."

"Five minutes early?"

"Yeah, it's not much in the way of confidence, but it's something."

I continued ahead to my office. "I'm sure you'll be fine."

He followed us, making it as far as the doorway, where he hung an arm. Vic occupied the guest chair, and propped her boots on the edge of my desk. He glanced at her. "How come she gets to put her feet up on the desks?"

" 'Cause I do what I want, Meat."

"Meat?"

"As in rookie or new meat."

He folded his arms and leaned on the doorjamb. "When do I stop being meat?"

"When you cease being a liability. Of course, for some guys that can be a fucking career." She glanced up at him. "Now go away—the real cops want to talk."

He sighed and looked at me. "One more thing . . . Um, I was wondering if there was anything else I can do? I mean there are long times when I'm just sitting out here."

"Not like TV, is it?" I studied him with a smile. "'They also serve who only stand and wait.'"

He stared at me.

"John Milton, Sonnet 19."

He continued to stare at me.

"There's a department library out there in the main office. I suggest you continue your reading?"

"Or badge polishing." Vic flipped her fingers at him in dismissal—one in particular.

Shaking his head, he swung away with a smile.

I lowered my voice. "Kind of hard on the kid, weren't you?"

"Not really." She turned to look at me. "So, how did you know it was Mike that called Bass?"

"Bass said the man had a mechanical voice and that he had simply stated that Charley Lee was dead and hung up, something a man who was deaf would do, being incapable of hearing the person on the other end." I raised my face and turned a bit, looking out the window. "I have an undercover operation in mind, but it needs to be done under the cover of darkness, so we have to do something else for a while."

"Like?"

"Well, we could go check on Bass Townsend and Katrina at the Absaroka County Sheriff's Annex over at the Blue Gables Motel."

"Deal."

Suddenly remembering something, I shouted out to the new dispatcher trainee. "Hey Barrett, where's my dog?"

He appeared in the doorway with the dog at his feet. "Is this one of my responsibilities too?"

Bass Townsend and Katrina Dejean were enjoying iced coffees while sitting in the metal lawn chairs at the Blue Gables Inn. I climbed out of the vehicle and headed for the office. Vic called after me. "Where are you going?"

"To get a cup of coffee to wash out my taste buds from that horrible tea."

"Get me a cappuccino. Please? My mouth tastes like ass."

When I got back, Bass was strumming the old resonator guitar in his lap and softly singing an Elmore James tune, "Dust My Broom."

"How do you feel?"

He smiled and looked up at me as I handed Vic her fancy coffee. "Pretty good. I've just been sitting around here entertaining this fine young lady."

I glanced at Katrina before taking off the top of my cup and sipping. "And you?"

Her smile was a little less enthusiastic. "I'm here."

"We need to talk."

"Okay."

"Preferably alone."

She glanced at the others and then back at me. "Yes, sir."

I led the way back to my truck—Vic began talking with Bass as he continued to strum. Flipping the tailgate down on my truck, I gestured for Katrina to sit. "Welcome to my office."

"Nice view." Having a little trouble, she handed me her coffee and sidled up, looking around as I handed it back. "How can I help you?"

I sat next to her. "I've been talking to the boys up at the Soldiers' and Sailors' Home, and there's an individual who claims Serge came by no more than a week ago."

She looked surprised. "Who says that?"

"Never mind for the moment. Do you think it's true?"

She started to speak but then stopped, finally breathing out the word. "Yes." She sipped her coffee. "If something were to happen to Philippe, I can only surmise that Serge was under orders to retrieve the painting, or maybe he was after it for himself."

"Someone broke into Charley Lee's apartment at the Veterans' Home."

She shrugged. "If it was broken into, I can only surmise that Serge did it."

"If he was released from the Sheridan County Jail yesterday and as near as DCI can tell, he was killed only hours later, it would've been kind of difficult for him to get over here and break into Charley Lee's room in that amount of time." I shook my head. "Let's say he did it the night before; what would he have done with it?"

"If he had found the painting, then he would've taken it for himself or someone else."

"Someone like Krovopuskov?"

She looked slightly shaken at the thought. "I hope not."

"Why?"

She put her empty coffee cup on the tailgate. "Well, then it's gone."

"Not necessarily. I spoke with him on the phone an hour

ago, and he's turning his plane around in Helsinki and coming back." I shrugged. "If our runway is long enough."

She looked stunned. "Why would he do that?"

"I was kind of wondering about that myself." I turned to look at her more closely. "Do you suppose he has the painting?"

"It's possible."

"Then why would he come back?"

"Perhaps he left the painting in Helsinki?"

"Nope, I made a call and spoke with the ground security of the private section of the airport and they assured me that nothing came off the plane and the only things that were brought onboard were paperwork, food, and fuel."

"Maybe he thinks he can still get the painting now that Philippe and Serge are dead?"

"Maybe." I waited, but she said nothing. "Which means that whoever has the painting is in danger if Klavdii Krovopuskov is as capable as I'm led to believe." I waited a moment before adding. "You don't get a name like the Bloodletter for nothing."

She turned away, studying the distance. "I don't know where the painting is."

I continued to study her. "Okay, I believe you, but who does?"

Her head dropped. "The only two people I know of who could've had such knowledge are dead."

"And in all honesty, those two unsolved murders are the priority for me." I sipped my now cold coffee. "I think they are connected with the painting, and if I find it, it might give me more to work with as far as finding the murderer."

I put my empty coffee cup down. "Let me pose a hypothetical: if Serge had gotten the painting, where would he have put it?"

"I honestly don't know."

"Where was he living?"

"Mostly at Philippe's."

"In Story?"

"Yes."

"If it's hidden in that place, would you have any idea where it might be?"

"Philippe had a hidden vault in the basement, with a combination lock."

"Do you know the combination?"

"I do."

I glanced up at the road leading north, out of town, toward the tiny hamlet. "So, would you like to take a ride to Story?"

She turned back to meet me, eye to eye. "No."

"I just want to go on record as saying that this is a really fucking bad idea, and when I think something is a really bad fucking idea, it's a *really* fucking bad idea."

I glanced at my undersheriff as we took the Story exit off I-90. "Duly noted."

"A quick reminder, I am the patron saint of really fucking bad ideas."

"Agreed."

"We should tell Sheriff Brandes that we're over here." She shook her head. "You remember him, the guy you said you'd keep in the loop?"

Hitting the straightaway, I resisted the temptation to flip on the emergency lights—after all, we were for all intents and purposes, undercover. "Right."

"But we're not?"

"No."

"Might I ask why?"

"I already did."

"You did what?"

"Called someone." A parked Suburban flashed its lights at us as I pulled in alongside the Sheridan County sheriff's investigator's vehicle. "Howdy."

The silver-haired woman fixed her blues on me. "Don't you howdy me, you outlaw."

"Thanks for doing this, Lori."

She gestured one-handedly with an air of futility. "May end my career."

"We just want to take a look, and I didn't want to trouble your boss."

"Even though my sheriff specifically requested that you trouble him with anything concerning this investigation?"

I made a point of not glancing at Vic. "Something like that."

She pulled out, and we followed, accelerating along the creek as I finally turned to glance at Vic, who sat there smiling to herself. "No comment?"

"Yeah, she's about as batshit crazy as you are, and here we are on our way to the batshit-crazy cave."

Lori turned into the circular drive at the end of the road, and I'm pretty sure we were all surprised to find some lights on in the back part of the house. "That's odd."

Vic sat forward, peering through the windshield. "Sheridan SD could've left the lights on . . ."

"Or DCI."

We both got out with our guns drawn.

Lori joined us at the front of her vehicle, her Colt Python in her hands. "Weird, huh?"

I moved toward the house. "Let's go."

The front entrance was blocked with POLICE LINE tape, which I ducked under before pushing the latch and slowly swinging the unlocked door open. The lights were off in the great hall of the stone building, but in the direction of the kitchen, the light spilled out onto the uneven, flagstone floor.

Stepping forward, I allowed my backup to enter and look around as I held a finger to my lips and continued across the room before running into a heavy lamp that tipped over and crashed to the floor with a tremendous amount of noise.

In the silence that followed, Vic's voice carried through the darkness. "So, do we still have to be quiet?"

Lori snickered, and I continued toward the kitchen door, swung it wide, and looked into the room, lit by a single light that hung over the center island. The DCI tape still cordoned off certain areas, and the room looked exactly as it had when I'd been here last with the exception of the things the investigators must've hauled off for further analysis, not including the half-finished sandwich and glass of milk.

"Maybe they ran when they heard you rearranging the furniture."

I sighed. "You have that piece of paper that shows how to get to the vault?"

"I do, oh great leader." Lori snickered again as Vic, tiptoeing toward the library-conservatory in the back, pulled a piece of paper from her pocket and unfolded it.

Giving one last glance at the crime scene, I had a niggling feeling but, not being able to discern what was causing it, sighed again and followed the two women.

Vic approached one of the bookcases and then consulted the sheet of paper before reaching up and pulling a hidden lever that caused the eight-foot installation to make a noise and bump out about three inches. "Wow, now this is getting to be like a real mystery."

Reaching over, I pulled the side of the case and pivoted it open like a door as fluorescent lights kicked on in a concrete stairwell that led to a metal doorway below.

"All right, who's staying up here?"

Lori shrugged. "I might as well, that way if anybody shows up, I've got an actual reason to be here."

I gestured for Vic to go ahead. "After you, my dear Alphonse."

She smiled and then led with the Midnight Bronze Glock 19 Gen 4.

There was nothing particularly interesting about the steps, walls, or ceiling, but as we got closer to the door, we could see the thing was securely anchored into the walls with a heavy steel facing and an electronic keypad where a knob should've been.

Vic consulted the paper and then tapped in the numbers—the keypad lit up and then beeped at us.

"What does that mean?"

She glanced at me and then pushed the door open, the automatic lights flickering to life inside. "After you, Alphonse."

Stepping around her, I nudged the heavy door back and looked in. The basement vault must've run a quarter the length of the house with shelves of canvases in the awakening lights. "Holy frijoles."

Vic stepped in beside me and held up a hand to feel the air. "I'm guessing temperature and humidity controlled."

We moved a little closer to the stacks, and I could see that none of the paintings were actually finished. "What in the world?"

Turning, I approached an area where there were numerous

easels and painting supplies and you could see more works of unfinished art. "It's a factory."

Vic came over, holstering her sidearm. "Fakes?"

"Yep, and very good ones." I stood. "But who? Serge didn't strike me as the artistic type." Turning, I looked past an examination table not unlike the one at the Bradford Brinton and could see a cot and blankets near the wall along with a bottle of water, a towel, and a half mug of tea. "Somebody's been staying here." Kneeling, I felt the mug. "Cold."

Vic joined me. "Serge?"

"Possibly." Walking back to the door, I got ahold of that niggling thought and called up to the Sheridan County investigator. "Hey Lori?"

Her voice echoed down. "Yeah?"

"Do me a favor and check and see if that sandwich in the kitchen is fresh and if the glass of milk is cold."

"Be right back."

I turned to Vic. "Habeas corpus."

"Count Philippe von Lehman?"

"We never found a body, just blood and prints, and I find it hard to believe that the count would've given Serge the combination to this vault."

She glanced around. "What if Serge killed him?"

"Still no body."

"You really think he killed Serge?"

"I don't know."

She shrugged. "Klavdii Krovopuskov?"

"A lot of those Russian oligarchs are buying up this Soviet-era art and repatriating it, and I'm guessing that the count found a way to sell the fakes back to the Russians." I glanced at the enormous collection.

Lori's voice called from above. "Sandwich is fresh and the milk is cold."

I moved toward the door. "Somebody's here."

"No joke."

She suddenly appeared in the doorway with someone behind her, who nudged her forward into the room with us as he stayed in the doorway. "He got the jump on me."

He aimed the pistols on us. "Sorry about all this, but you haven't left me many choices."

Lori purposefully moved in front of Vic as my undersheriff slipped a hand down by her sidearm; I stepped in the other direction. "Maybe you'd like to tell us what's going on here, Count?"

He looked a little worse for wear and tipped his head, the fluff of hair swaying to the side as he stood there in his bathrobe and slippers. "I know this is where the guilty party usually doles out the details of his dastardly plan, but I'm sorry to disappoint you in that I'm completely innocent."

I stepped forward. "Funny, from here you don't look it."

He shook his head and reached out to close the door. "Look, I'm not going to shoot any of you if I don't have to . . ."

"That's what you call innocent?"

Leaning against the door, he placed more of it between us, only his head, gun hand, and foot showing. "I didn't hurt anybody."

"Then explain to me what's going on—if you're truly innocent then you have nothing to fear from me."

He barked a laugh. "You're not the one I'm worried about, trust me."

"Then who?"

"I'm sorry to cut this short, but I'm afraid I have to go."

"What, you have to get back in your coffin before the sun

comes up?" He and I both turned to see Vic with her arm outstretched, the 9mm leveled at the count's head. "Drop the gun, fucktard."

He paused for an instant. "I can't."

"Then we play catch with lead."

He slammed his shoulder into the door as she fired. The door closed with a thud, all three of us there in an instant trying to pry the thing open. I turned to Vic.

"Quick, the combination."

We could hear screaming and a litany of profanity from the other side. "Fuck, fuck, fuck, fuck, fuck, fuck!"

She pulled the paper from the back of her jeans. "I think I got him."

"Fuck, fuck, fuck, fuck, fuck!"

Lori listened at the door. "Too bad you didn't get him in the mouth."

"Fuck!"

Vic punched the numbers into the keyboard, and we waited, but nothing happened. She consulted the piece of paper again and punched the numbers in once more, but still nothing happened. "He must've jammed it."

I called into the door. "Philippe, can you hear me?"

"Fuck!"

"Look, open the door, and we'll get you some help."

"Fuck!"

"A bullet wound is a very serious injury, and we'll need to get you to a hospital . . . Look, if you're really innocent, we can help you." There was whimpering, but nothing more from the other side. "Philippe?"

"What?"

"Where are you hit?"

"My foot. The bitch shot off my big toe!"

I glanced at her, and she shrugged. "I was trying to keep him alive."

I spoke into the door again. "Is there a lot of blood?"

"My toe is gone, and I'm bleeding to death out here!" There was silence for a moment. "You bitch, why did you shoot me?"

She tapped the barrel on the metal door. "Fuck you, asshole. In about a minute I'm going to start throwing rounds through this door and it ain't going to be your toe this time."

I bit my lip. "Philippe, open the door."

"No."

Lori pulled out her cell phone. "As much as it grieves me, I guess I better call the boss."

I spoke into the door again. "Philippe, we're going to have to call someone."

"There's no service down here . . . Fuck. Really, my toe?!"

Lori glanced up. "He's right, no bars."

"These were brand-new slippers."

"Philippe, just open the door and sit down and we'll do something to stop the bleeding—standing on it is only going to make it worse." There was some indiscernible mumbling. "Philippe?"

Nothing.

Vic reholstered her weapon. "It's a solid door, and I don't think the 9mm would go through."

I looked around. "Well, he can't get far on one foot."

Lori peered up and down the aisles of half-finished artwork. Raising her phone, she started off. "I'll check and see if I can get reception anywhere down here."

I glanced at Vic. "Maybe we can find another door or something."

We started off, each going to the perimeter and walking the

length of the subterranean room. At the far end we met, trading off and switching directions until we headed in opposite paths up the aisles.

The amount of faux art was stunning, the variation in styles and subject matter no less so. Whoever had been manufacturing the stuff had been doing it for some time and had been very thorough in their reproductions.

"Walt?"

I walked quickly down the aisle and peered through an opening where Vic stood. She pointed. "Air vent."

"Big enough to get through?"

"For me."

"What if it's just the heating and cooling?"

She shrugged. "Might still lead out of the basement."

"We need a screwdriver."

"There were tools on that worktable. And a ladder by the wall."

"T-25 Torx."

I handed the bit up to her and watched as she put it in the battery-powered drill. "Who knew you were this handy?"

"Four brothers and a father back in Philadelphia who thought you were slave labor until you escaped."

"How did you escape?"

"Took the Nelson-Denny Reading test for the police department." She unscrewed the last batch and used a chisel that was in her other hand to pry the metal. "Watch your head."

The thing came loose and crashed to the concrete floor between me and Lori. "You're lucky you have a skinny undersheriff."

We watched as she pulled out her Maglite, shimmied her way into the duct, and climbed out of sight. "It's a long run to the end of the room, and then it goes up, I think. I'll know better when I get there." We listened as she thumped along in the duct, following her progress until we got to the wall where the door was, and she paused. "It's a reach, so I'll just have to climb up it to see where it goes next."

Standing there, waiting, we listened to the thumping and banging as she made her way out of our hearing.

Lori folded her arms and leaned against the doorjamb. "So, you think he did it?"

"No, he's a nuisance, but I don't think he's a killer."

"Then who is?"

"Good question. The interesting thing is that he stored up his own blood and faked the murder, so who the heck was he so afraid of?"

"This Klavdii Krovopuskov?"

"Maybe."

She leaned against the wall. "Have you met this guy?"

"Once—over in Cody."

"And?"

"He didn't strike me as a killer, but then I've been wrong before."

She laughed. "When?"

There was a loud noise from upstairs, a noise great enough to carry through the house and down the concrete stairwell to us. "Were those gunshots?"

"Sure sounded like it." We both placed an ear against the door, but there was nothing more. "Okay, if we don't hear anything in the next couple of minutes, as much as I dread the thought, I'm going to have to go up in the ventilator shaft."

Lori shrugged. "I'm smaller than you."

I stepped back, glancing down the corridor just as all the lights in the place went out. "Well, hell."

"It's going to be hard to find that ventilator duct in the dark . . . No, wait . . . There's somebody coming down the stairs."

Placing an ear against the door, I could hear someone's footfalls on the concrete. "Vic?"

The keypad began beeping as someone began punching the numbers and, after a moment, the door bumped open into the side of both our heads as the lights flickered back on.

Vic swung the door the rest of the way and looked at Lori. "I hope that wasn't a brand-new Suburban you were driving."

15

"You're sure there was someone else in the vehicle with him?"

"Positive. Believe me he wasn't driving without that missing toe."

There was blood all over the place, dribbling up the steps and across the den, kitchen, and through the dining area into the main room where he must've stopped to talk quickly with someone. He'd continued through the door onto the front lawn where we now stood, watching the sprinkler system in the side yard making halos in the overhead lights.

"Well, there's no way out of it now." I turned to Lori. "However you want to phrase it, we need an APB on your vehicle."

I watched as she pulled out her phone and dialed 911. "I'll tell 'em I had an inkling and was having dinner over at the Wagon Box with you guys and asked you to back me up—that is if I even tell them you were here at all." She shrugged. "What's the whippersnapper going to do, fire me?" She held the phone to her ear. "I was supposed to retire, and I'm the highest decorated officer on Six-Week-Wonder's staff. Let him try." She spoke into the phone. "Hi Terry, it's Lori, and yes I've got an emergency. Actually, what I've got is an interesting situation involving grand theft auto . . ."

She wandered away as I looked back at Vic. "Any ideas who it was?"

"Hard to tell with those tall headrests, even with the interior lights on."

"Man, woman?"

"Who knows?" She turned and looked down the road, holstered her weapon, and placed hands on hips. "What are they after?"

"The Custer painting."

She continued walking around as if she were looking for something. "You're sure?"

"It's the only thing that makes any sense. The count is sitting on a bunch of fake Russian artwork, and the only potential buyer for something that big is on his way back from Helsinki in his private jet."

She nodded but continued inspecting the lawn. "Somebody really just wants that painting."

Lori reappeared. "My guys are on the way, so you guys better scoot."

"We can't just leave you here."

"Sure you can. Look, this place is going to be crawling with Sheridan SD in a matter of moments; besides, they can give me a ride home." She punched my arm. "Go catch some bad guys."

"Thanks, Lori."

She called after us as I moved toward my truck, Vic still checking the ground. "Make sure they spell my name right in the paper."

I sat in the truck for a moment and thought about what could've driven Philippe von Lehman to fake his own murder. Who could he have been trying to frame?

I buckled up and fired the ten-cylinder of the Bullet to life as Vic climbed in the other side. "Where the hell do you suppose he thinks he's going to go?"

"I have no idea."

"How can he think he's going to get away?"

"Once again, I have no idea."

"On a private jet, say the one that's winging its way here from Helsinki as we speak?"

"Seems possible?"

"So, the airport?"

"No."

"Think he'd be stupid enough to go to a hospital?"

"Not really."

"The Home?"

Slipping the truck into gear, I pulled out of the wooded area and back onto the main road leading south at a brisk pace.

"You know, if we were in my new truck we could go faster."

"Uh huh." I glanced at her. "You mind if I ask what you were looking for in the count's yard?"

She pointed up her index finger like a barrel and blew away the imaginary gun smoke. "The toe, of course—I'm going to need a key chain for my new truck."

It was late as we pulled into town. I took the north exit, drove down the main drag, and glanced toward the Blue Gables, hoping to possibly see a silver Suburban with bullet holes in the back. "So, what kind of damage did you do to the Chevrolet?"

"Not enough to keep it from running, obviously." She shrugged. "Took out the back window and one in the rear door, so I don't think I got either of them, if that's what you're asking?"

"No. I was hoping the vehicle would break down." Slowing, I looked around the parking lot, but the place appeared to be buttoned up and slumbering.

"So, Bass says he's supposed to look in the safe-deposit box first thing on Monday morning."

"Then what?"

"I think he's planning on heading back to Los Angeles."

"With the million bucks?"

"I'd imagine."

"Well, I wish him luck."

"What did Nikita have to say about the painting?"

I glanced at her. "Katrina said that the count had made arrangements with Charley Lee to buy the Custer painting and had even paid him, but then the old guy had died."

"Do you think the count was the one who broke into Charley Lee's room in an attempt to find it?"

"No, I don't think he's up for those kinds of clandestine operations."

"Tonight's adventures notwithstanding?" She chuckled. "Well, if he was, he's not going to be up for them anymore."

"I think we discovered his hiding place, and he was desperate."

"Okay. So, Serge? And if so, then who killed him?"

"Good question."

"And if Serge found the painting where or with whom did it go?"

"Another good question."

"You're thinking the mystery person in the Suburban might be the key to all this?"

I turned the corner at Fort Street as I glanced at our parking spots. "Whose Chevy half-ton is that?"

"I'd imagine it's Barrett Long's."

"I keep forgetting I hired that kid." Reaching down, I pulled the mic and keyed it. "Base, this is unit one."

Static. "Base."

"You're awake."

Static. "I figured that was a part of the job too. By the way, it's Saturday."

"Got it."

Static. "And coming up on two a.m."

"Thank you."

Static. "Something else?"

"Anything coming in on that APB on the Suburban?"

Static. "They pulled one over on I-25, but it didn't have any bullet holes, so they let it go."

"Roger that."

Static. "When do I get to shoot things?"

"If you hear anything on the radio, patch it through to me."

Static. "Roger that."

I hung the mic back up and glanced at Vic. "Where could they have gone?"

"Anywhere. Just because nobody saw them doesn't mean they're not here. What've we got, two highway patrolmen out with another two deputies from Sheridan County and maybe two city cops? Sounds easy to evade to me."

"I guess."

Heading out of town, I looked up at the Bighorn Mountains, where the moon cast a pale light on the high country above the tree line. I thought about the soldiers who had been stationed in this part of the world all those years ago—I imagined they felt as if they'd been deserted.

I reached the turnoff at the Fort and drove down the rolling entryway up to the administration building where no lights shone. After making the next turn, I stopped before heading for the parking lot.

Vic glanced at the side of my face as we sat there. "Something?"

Slipping the truck into reverse, I backed up until we could see around the south wing of the redbrick building and the rear end of a silver Suburban on the next street over.

"Holy shit."

Turning off my lights, we moved slowly in reverse around the administration building and then stopped about forty feet away, studying the shattered back window and the two bullet holes about two inches apart in the sheet metal of the rear door. "Nice grouping."

She drew her sidearm as I shut off my truck. "Thanks."

Directing my spotlight on the vehicle, I flipped the switch and lit it up as we carefully got out, me drawing my weapon and trailing out to the driver's side with the barrel pointed toward the cab. From all appearances, the SUV was empty, but you never knew until you knew.

Keeping a peripheral on the alleyway, I noticed the historic buildings to the left of the main structure, glowing in the pale moonlight.

Vic moved up on the passenger side, her weapon trained on the open window. Stopping at the pillar, she re-aimed and then drew her Maglite from her belt and flipped the thing up, shining the beam into the floorboards on the other side. "Lot of blood. Hell, maybe I did clip something other than his toe." She traced the beam over the seat, but there were no other stains. "Nope, it's all from the toe . . . Jesus, good thing Lori's got those WeatherTech floor mats with the blood wells." She glanced up at me. "He's bound to be passed out around here somewhere."

I reached in, took the keys from the ignition, and stuffed them into my pocket—no sense in letting Lori get her SUV stolen twice.

Vic had slipped the beam to the street and then had carefully started forward. As she studied the ground, I switched back and forth between the buildings, providing cover in case there was something up ahead. "More blood?"

"Yeah, he went this way."

She moved, and I followed, sometimes turning and glancing behind us.

I could see her standing by an open door, which looked like an employee entrance with a ramp, glass booth, lockers, and time clocks. When I got there, I could see the blood marks on the concrete where the count must've slipped and fallen. "How is he still moving?"

Vic shook her head and pushed open the door. "Maybe he's got help."

We crept up the ramp to the glass security booth, which was empty, then pushed open another door and entered the hallway of the silent building. There was no mistaking the direction that he had gone. We followed the trail, took the ramp down to the library where I'd last confronted the rolling Wavers, then went through the event room toward the stairwell where a sound there kept repeating itself.

The blood didn't go up the steps but rather went around into another part of the building with tile floors. The sound was getting louder, and I finally decided that it sounded like an elevator door, opening and closing.

Vic had turned the corner. She stood there for a moment, staring.

"What?"

Leading with the Glock, she moved forward, and I could see Count Philippe von Lehman's leg sticking out of the elevator, the door opening and closing on it.

The toe was pretty well missing, and another pool of blood surrounded his saturated slipper, or what remained of it. "Nobody's stitching that thing back together."

I stepped into the elevator and hit the lock button to stop the doors from operating and then kneeled down, relieved to find the count still breathing.

"He alive?"

"Barely." Pressing a few fingers onto his cold neck, I felt his weakening pulse. "He's in shock, and he's going to need attention, or we'll lose him."

She crouched down beside me. "We need help."

"Yep." I stood and pulled the FIRE EMERGENCY toggle in the elevator—and that's when all hell broke loose.

The elevator alarm was still going off as I continued up the steps to where Magic Mike's impromptu suite of rooms looked out over the parking lot. Vic had begrudgingly stayed to help with the count as Carol Williams arrived with a gurney and two attendants.

Making it to the second floor, I poked my head around the corner and could see that the door to Bursaw's room hung open, along with some of the others, the occupants standing in their doorways looking up and down the hallway trying to figure out what was going on.

Staying against the wall, I shouted to the residents. "Get the heck out of this building!"

The nearest man in pajamas rubbed his eyes and stared at me. "Is there a fire or something?"

"Or something."

"What's the gun for?"

"Shooting things, including you if you don't get a move on." I gestured toward the stairwell. "You guys have a fire drill procedure?"

Smoothing the small amount of hair he had on his head, he nodded. "Yeah. I guess."

"Then follow it and get out of here."

He harrumphed, "This used to be a nice place to live."

I studied all the residents but didn't see Magic Mike in the crowd. Shouting to be heard above the din, I addressed the entire hallway. "We've got an emergency, and the elevator isn't operating, so if you would, please use the stairwell and evacuate the building!"

Moving as fast as they could—which, in actuality, wasn't that fast—they grumbled but followed orders, decades-old military training kicking in. Fortunately, this wing wasn't as crowded as some of the others, and I was just as glad to be in there all but alone.

Bursaw's door still hung open exactly as it had when I'd first seen it, and I moved forward, my weapon leading the way. The door was undamaged, and the safety chain, gently tapping at the wood as I edged the door open, hung from the frame.

The room looked as it had a few days ago, even the turntable continued to spin, skipping on Grace Slick singing the lyric *feed your head* over and over again. The lights had been left on, and a still steaming mug sat on a side table. "Mike?" I immediately felt foolish calling out to a deaf-mute—never mind that even if he could hear anything, he wouldn't have with all the noise from the emergency alarm.

Moving farther in, I could see that the only other part of the room past the hole in the wall was through a beaded curtain where there was a kitchenette in what must've at one time been a walk-in closet. There wasn't anywhere to hide, especially for someone as flamboyant as Magic Mike.

Starting back for the door, I felt a slight breeze and looked over to see that a speaker had fallen out of the decal-covered window and was lying flat-faced on the balcony outside, the sound vibrating against the tarred surface.

I lifted the needle from the Jefferson Airplane's "White Rabbit." "Take a break, Grace."

Carefully easing my head out the window, I looked both ways to make sure the entire balcony was empty, then climbed out and glanced down at the parking area where a crowd was assembling and Vic was escorting the gurney to a waiting ambulance.

I thought about calling down to her, but her hearing me over the Klaxon alarm and all the people was slim. There was a metal ladder attached to the side of the building, so I moved that way, placed a foot on a rung, and hauled myself to the top roof.

The entire surface was pale from some kind of weatherproofing and glowed in the moonlight like a vertical, gold-plated trampoline. I was relieved to see railings at the ends of the overhangs, and that there looked to be a walkway leading to the higher level above the balcony—at least if I fell from there, I'd only land a third of the way to the pavement.

There was a noise to my right, beyond the top of the roof. I carefully climbed up and peeked over but still couldn't see anyone. The roof dropped off on my right and stretched toward the older buildings and an area that used to be the parade ground.

There was the noise again, as if someone were crying out.

Straddling the peak, I crab-walked to the right and was faced with another down slope that went the remainder of the old building before dropping off to a flat roof that ran the expanse of the rest of the structure, including a narrow part that led to another building to the west near what looked like a garage and the historical buildings. I felt like some Bighorn Batman as I stood there listening, but there were no more noises.

Figuring there really wasn't anywhere else to go, I took a step, not one of my best decisions, and watched as my boot slipped out from under me, and I sprawled to the left before toppling over the edge. I slid headfirst on my back, but stretched out my arms and legs in hopes of getting enough traction on the weatherproofing so that I wouldn't slip over the eaves onto the secondary roof below. The ploy worked, but now I was spread-eagled about halfway down the slope, a tenuous thread of friction holding me in place for the moment.

"Well, hell."

I stayed like that, looking at the next drop, before edging down about four inches, this time not coming to a complete stop but instead continuing to slide at about ten inches an hour.

"Damn."

Placing the back of my hand on the surface of the material, I slowed and squelched to a stop.

"Having fun?" With the heightened level of East-Coast sarcasm, I didn't have to look to tell who was addressing me. "This is an interesting perspective."

"Thanks." I raised my head ever so slowly and felt my hat slip off and slide away; I could see Vic standing at the peak of the roof with her Glock hanging at her side as she considered the material that covered the surface and subsequently, my situation. "This shit is slick."

Trying not to move, I called back. "Yep."

She glanced around. "Why the hell would you use this stuff on a roof?"

"Believe it or not, I was just asking myself the same question."

"I saw you climbing the ladder outside the balcony to Magic Mike's room and figured you must be up here somewhere."

"You don't happen to have a rope or tow strap on you, do you?"

"No. Of course, if I had my new truck, I'd have plenty of room . . ."

"Shut up about the new truck, will you?"

"My, aren't we cranky."

I very slowly started to move but felt a tiny squelch and began sliding again. "Any idea how far I'm about to fall?"

"Maybe about twelve feet down to the next level—I'd try and get turned around—backward, headfirst landings don't usually end well."

As I tried to turn, I gained a little speed. "Thanks for the help."

"No problem."

I'd gotten about halfway around when I reached the edge and tumbled off, grabbing at the gutter with one hand. I watched as it jerked itself loose from the eaves, the ten-inch nails pulling from the old wood like stitches being ripped from a hem.

"Well, hell."

Still holding on to the gutter, which in no way was designed to hold my weight, I landed on my feet, sort of. One ankle gave way, and I rolled on it, causing me to fall down a set of three steps that led to a doorway before landing on my back and staring up at the sky and at Vic, who was backlit by the outrageous stars—or maybe those were the ones in my head.

"You all right?"

Taking a moment to catch my breath, I exhaled until I was sure my lungs were going to collapse before breathing in like a bellows and then coughing out the words, "Great, really wonderful, thanks."

"I think I'm going to try another way."

Releasing the gutter and struggling up, I coughed some more. "I can't say that I blame you."

"Did you get a look at whoever we're supposedly chasing?"

Rolling onto my knees, I stood rather slowly, discovering that my right ankle didn't really like me anymore. "No, but I'm pretty sure it's somebody that's got Magic Mike because he knows where the painting is."

"Why would they be on the roof?"

"Because we broke up whatever they were doing, and they crawled out the window to get away."

"So, you don't think the painting is there?"

I picked up my hat and took a step, finding that my ankle, though unhappy with me, would carry some weight. "No."

"I'm headed back down. I'll circle around and meet you at the west end of the building, since if they're up here, that's where they're headed."

"You know, I'm starting to think this manhunt crap is highly overrated." Waving a hand at her in dismissal, I limped forward. "I'll drive them your way."

She disappeared, and I started off toward a structure that housed the elevator, the shaft having a skylight at the top. There was a large cottonwood to my left that blocked off the view of the building in that direction, but I figured I'd be able to see a good deal once I got to it. It took forever to get there on my weak ankle. There were no other lower roofs that I could access, so I supposed I was going to have to look for hatches or stairwells that led down.

There was a door leading into the shaft with the skylight, but it was locked, so unless the assailant had a key, this was a no go.

Glancing around some more, I could see another roof over what must've been an entryway for the building to my left. Limping off in that direction, I could've sworn I heard more noises and picked up the pace as best I could.

By the time I got there, I could definitely hear voices below me. I stepped to the edge and yelled down, figuring my voice would cover ground faster than I could. "Absaroka County Sheriff's Department, halt!"

There were more noises, but they weren't sticking around.

"I said halt!"

Predictably, there was nothing.

Grumbling, I limped over to the edge and looked down at about a six-foot drop to the next roof.

Sighing, I holstered my Colt and sat. Then rolling onto my stomach, I draped my legs over the precipice and edged down. I dropped, trying to keep my weight on my good ankle.

It worked, and I stood there finally looking at the ground,

which I figured was about ten feet down—who the hell was I chasing, the Flying Wallendas?

One of the limbs from the cottonwood stuck out past the corner of the entryway roof, so I limped over there, reached out, and tested the weight. It was sturdy, and if it held me it would be easy enough to climb down on the other limbs and gently lower my damaged ankle to the sidewalk.

Grabbing hold, I swung out and got my boots on the next one down, edging closer to the trunk and then lowering myself to another branch and then another until I was on the lowest one, which was five feet or so above the ground.

Again, I tried to get my weight on my left ankle, but the dirt was uneven, and my right hit first. I crumpled and just lay there trying not to yell.

Finally sitting up, I carefully stood and started limping toward the corner of the building where the noises had last come from and where the sidewalk ended. There was another building and a parking lot across the street, and I was about to turn the corner when somebody came from the other side and I pressed my .45 into his face.

"Jesus!"

Pulling back, I realized it was just one of the watchmen. "What's your name?"

"Gene Weller! It's me, Gene Weller, Sheriff."

Lowering my weapon, I looked past him. "Hi Gene, how are you?"

He sputtered some words out like a teapot about to boil over. "Other than just now I'm doing pretty well—what the hell is going on?"

"I'm after somebody."

"I'd offer to help, but I think I just shit my pants."

Moving past him, I started limping in the direction of the parade ground. "If you see my undersheriff, would you tell her you saw me heading this way?"

"Will do, is there anything else?"

"Tell her I'm in pursuit, and I need all the backup I can get."

He nodded, and I continued off past the line of cars. It was possible that they were thinking of stealing a car, since I'd taken the keys to the one they'd stolen to get here.

Limping across the manicured lawn, I looked to my right and could see what I thought was two individuals darting behind one of the historic buildings. It was one of those out-of-the-corner-of-your-eye things, and I wasn't even sure that I'd seen what I thought I had, but it was something.

Holding the Colt aimed at the stars, I made a solemn promise to not shoot anybody just because I didn't want to chase them anymore—at least for now. I figured the distance to be about fifty yards and just hoped I would make it before my ankle called it quits.

The pavement ended about two buildings before the parade ground to my right, where there was a barn that seemed to have been converted into a garage or workshop. There were old vehicles and large equipment, but the building that interested me was the one to the left.

The chicken coop.

The historic chicken coop.

The only chicken coop on the National Register of Historic Places.

Magic Mike had invited us there, and Carol had pointed it out a couple of times. Hell, it was the most notable location in the entire fort, and it sounded as though somebody was tearing down the place. There was also noise from behind me, and all I could hope was that it was Vic.

There was a crash up ahead, and I lodged myself against the white clapboard building at the corner, where I could see the wire-net door hanging open and movement inside the coop along with hearing more crashing and thumping.

I loped as best I could across the space between the buildings only to trip over the bracing at the bottom of the doorway and crash onto the floor of the coop.

Fortunately, I landed on something. Unfortunately, it was Magic Mike.

Rolling to one side, I swung the .45 up and around the room only to find the rest of the place empty. I could see a massive PVC pipe that half hung from the rafters and recognized it as part of the irrigation system. The plumber's tape that had been used to suspend it had been pulled down, and it looked like the pipe's endcap had been pried off as the thing hung there, still swinging.

Pushing off the ground, I lodged the Colt into my holster and reached down. Pulling Bursaw's hairy head from the mossy, herb-filled ground, I was relieved to see his eyelids flutter and watched as he breathed. Then grabbing the front of my jacket, he attempted to speak. "Mmmmhh . . . Ahmh."

Snatching my Maglite from my belt, I shined the beam on my face so he could see what I was saying. "Are you all right?"

Fuming with frustration, he nodded.

I gestured toward the large plastic tube above us. "It's the painting. They've got the painting, right?"

He nodded again and began to sign. "Mmmmhh . . ."

I shook my head as I pulled him toward the interior wall.

When I propped him up, I could see the blood on the side of his face where he'd obviously been struck. "Hush, and don't worry about it—I'll catch them, trust me."

He nodded and looked up at me very seriously, finally lifting his hand like a child and imitating a pistol.

"Armed?"

He nodded again, finally smiling, blood in his teeth.

Pulling out my .45, I smiled back. "Aren't we all?"

His smile quickly faded as I started to go, and he held out a hand. "Mmmmhh . . ."

Lowering the flashlight, I paused at the door and looked down the slope that led toward the creek-side trail that meandered toward the mountains. "It's okay, I know who it is."

16

It was dark under the canopy of trees that hung over the banks of Clear Creek, and even with the sporadic light cast by the moon, it was like looking through a jigsaw puzzle—albeit, one that could kill you.

My ankle was about to capsize me, and I felt like I was pogo-ing on a raggedly nerved stump. The trail was wide with pea gravel the size of, well, peas and smooth as a parking lot. It helped, but not much as I crunched my way along wondering what anybody thought they could do from here. It was possible that they had an accomplice up ahead, but I doubted it—this whole enterprise stank to the high heaven of desperation.

So, the painting had been hidden in the fake irrigation system of the historic chicken coop after being liberated from Charley Lee's apartment, or maybe even before that. Either way, I was going to have to ask Magic Mike.

There was a bend in the trail, and I couldn't help but stop for a moment to catch my breath even though, for all I knew, my assailant was standing a dozen feet away and aiming at my head. They knew I was coming and could've easily taken me by surprise already, but I had a feeling they were running scared, so I had to kick it into gear and get moving, which I did.

The trail led up the canyon and into the mountains, but

there were a few pull-offs beside the walkway where the gap got narrower and someone could be waiting up there with a vehicle, but then the only other option was back into town. The same was true of the trail and I turned back toward town, wondering if I was headed in the wrong direction.

I stood there for a minute thinking about the odds and what would be the logical choice, but then there was the hunch. I couldn't help but think that if it was who I thought it was that they had headed out of town. With all the ruckus at the Soldiers' and Sailor's Home, I was pretty sure that they had chosen the other direction.

It was a hunch, but I'd followed hunches my whole life, and so far they hadn't done me too much wrong.

I started off.

While walking, the thought occurred to me that the perpetrator might have hidden the painting somewhere out here. I just wasn't sure if anybody would leave twenty-four million dollars under a bush.

I was hobbling around another bend when I could've sworn I heard someone talking up ahead. Stopping at the center of the trail about a hundred feet short of a bridge with a pipe rail fence, I listened. There was definitely someone talking, but with the noise of the stream and the echo from the canyon walls, it was difficult to tell what direction the voice was coming from. I limped forward and was pretty sure it was coming from up ahead, but it was a long straight stretch and I couldn't actually see anyone.

The voice was steady, the tone the kind people used while speaking on a cell phone. I looked around wondering how they had gotten service, and slowed, peering into the darkness of the sheltered path at the bridge buttress.

I fought the urge to call out and identify myself, but even as sure as I was about whom I was chasing, I was still unsure as to how desperate they might be and figured I might be rewarded with a bullet.

The voice stopped, and so did I.

It was possible that they'd heard me crunching along on the gravel, and if they were at the side of the trail near the creek where the shadows were deeper, there was the chance that I'd walk right past them, so I did what all good hunters do—I waited. I waited until I couldn't stand it anymore and then I waited some more until I heard the amplified sound of crickets, much louder than actual, living crickets might make.

"I know you're here."

Nothing.

"I heard your phone."

Nothing.

"There's nowhere to go."

Nothing.

"Trust me, I know this trail like the back of my hand, maybe better."

Nothing.

". . . To be honest, I haven't studied the back of my hand in a while."

"Oh, for God's sake shut up."

I smiled. "Expecting a call?"

"Maybe."

I moved forward, zeroing in on the voice near the bridge. "You're armed?"

"Yes."

"Me too."

There was a pause. "So, how are we going to do this?"

"I don't want to shoot you . . ."

"I don't want to shoot you either."

"You didn't let me finish—I don't, but I will." I let that one sink in.

"I don't think you'll shoot me, even for a twenty-six-million-dollar painting."

"Twenty-four."

"The price is going up."

"Don't count on it—you're a killer, and I'm not likely to forget that." Aiming into a dark copse of conifers by the buttress, I breathed in their scent, along with an expensive cologne. "You killed Charley Lee."

"Did I?"

"I'm assuming by bribing the security guy, Gene Weller, who probably didn't know what you were up to."

"What was I up to?"

"Injecting Charley Lee with suxamethonium chloride."

"Prove it."

"I have. The elements of the drug are only traceable in a urine sample taken from a living subject. Unfortunately for you, Charley Lee used the bathroom but then forgot to flush, instead stacking his books on the seat." I stepped closer. "And when Gene Weller finds out this concerns a murder, he'll flip on you like a Busy Bee pancake." I took another step. "Why kill Serge?"

"He was a pig."

I continued to move forward, even though I was pretty sure he was aiming right at me. "Not a good enough reason."

Silence. "He was making a mess, and it was only a question of time before he began talking."

"Still not good enough."

"The painting was paid for."

"Not by you."

Conrad Westin stepped sideways, an oversize rolled canvas under one arm, and a SIG Sauer P320 9mm pointed at me in his other hand. "Might as well be. How's my partner?"

"Loaded into an ambulance and headed for the hospital."

The young man smirked. "I hope he makes it."

"No hard feelings?"

"He made me what I am."

"A murderer?"

He barked a laugh. "A self-made man."

"You took the artist proof at the Buffalo Bill?"

"I had to. You were getting too close."

I moved forward, hoping to cut him off. "And you started out replicating Russian paintings for von Lehman?"

He nodded, countering my movements, keeping a little ahead of me with the SIG still carefully aimed at my middle. "It was a start, but then I got introduced to a richer clientele."

"Krovopuskov?"

"Among others."

"He's coming back for his painting?"

"Maybe." Conrad shrugged. "The thing is getting heavy."

"I'm afraid I can't allow that."

His phone began chirping again. "By the time you have any say, I'll be in Helsinki, Berlin, Paris, or some other place leading a whole new life."

The phone continued chirping. "You want to answer that?"

"It can wait, I've got time."

I gave a slight gesture with my .45 Colt. "You're forgetting something."

"Not really, but you are." He smiled confidently, too confidently. "That or you never knew."

The first blow was a pretty good one, causing me to stagger forward and almost drop my weapon. The second one from behind forced me to my knees. I tried to clear my head with a shake, but that only made things worse as a vertigo and nausea rose in the back of my throat.

Westin's foot kicked my sidearm from my line of sight as I tried to push myself up, the final blow from behind sinking me flat on my chest as I lay there.

She spoke, breathless from the exertion of clubbing me like a baby seal. "Is he dead?"

"I don't think so. Where the hell have you been?"

I could see her boots as she walked closer to him. "I had to get my car. Where's Philippe?"

"There's been a slight change in plan . . ." He scuffed some gravel toward me. "One of them shot him in the foot."

"Where is he?"

"They got him. Look, it's me and you now."

"Conrad, this is crazy."

"Where's the car?"

"Up ahead, at one of the turnouts."

"Are the keys in it?"

"Yes."

I reached out and firmly grabbed an ankle.

"What the hell?"

Katrina Dejean tried to kick at me, but even as hurt as I was, I held fast, started to stand, and reached up to grab her by the back of her jacket. She swung what looked like a tire iron at me again, but I got my other arm up to block it and crushed her against me, facing him.

I stripped the bar from her hand and flung it at him.

My aim was maybe not the best, but he fell backward into the railing as the metal hit his hand, and he dropped the P320, which fell halfway between us, the bar falling onto his foot. He stood there hopping and thinking about going for the SIG, but I was too close.

He clutched his wrist, and the painting fell.

I tried to focus, but my head was killing me, and I could feel the blood spreading down the side of my face. "Hurts, doesn't it?" He looked at the 9mm again. "Don't. Don't even try."

He stared at me for a moment and then nodded, stooped to pick up the painting instead, and backed away on the concrete surface of the bridge. "Fair enough."

Katrina struggled and then stared at him. "What the hell do you mean, fair enough?"

He shrugged. "Honey, there's nothing I can do."

She struggled some more, stomping on my foot and throwing her head back into my chest, but I held her fast. "You rat-bastard! Help me!"

"Darling, I would, but he's too big, and I can't get to that gun without him getting hold of me." He continued backing away in a limp, cradling the canvas with two hands. "You say the keys are in the car?"

She screamed. "You son of a bitch!"

I shook my head, still trying to clear my vision. "You're not going to make it."

"No joke—I think you broke my wrist, not to mention my foot." He backed away. "Well, I guess I've got to give it a shot, huh?"

I tried moving forward with her, but there was no way I was

going to catch him wounded as I was and burdened with a hostage. "Look, Westin—"

He laughed.

"There's nowhere to go."

"See you around, Sheriff."

She screamed again. "Conrad!"

"Love you, babe." He gestured toward her hand. "You can keep the ring."

"You bastard!"

He turned and limped across the bridge toward the mountains as we stood there, her struggling against my grip as I studied the railing.

Reaching behind me, I pulled my cuffs from my belt and snapped one over her wrist before pushing her toward one of the pipe rails. She struggled some more but sensed there wasn't any way she was going to stop me as I flipped the cuff over the steel railing.

Stepping to the side, I dodged as she kicked at me, still glancing around for my sidearm, but to no avail. "Let me go, you bastard!"

Taking a deep breath, I started off but had to catch myself on the other railing, almost toppling over it and falling into Clear Creek.

"Let me go, and I'll go get him."

Holding on to the railing for support, I walked back and picked up the SIG Sauer he'd abandoned, glanced at her, and then started off at a very uneven pace.

"You'll never catch him, you idiot."

I grimaced back at her. "Well, I guess I've got to give it a shot, huh?"

She screeched some more, but for the life of me I couldn't

really hear her through the ringing in my ears. The tire iron whizzed by me, striking the ground ahead.

I knew I'd forgotten something.

Trudging forward, I picked up the pace, ignoring the pain in my ankle and the increasing one that ran through my head like a camp ax. I mumbled to myself. "I should've shot the little bastard."

I tried to keep my balance, but I was wavering, and I knew it. I went around the next bend into another straightaway, and I could see him up ahead, impaired, but moving a lot better than I was.

I raised the 9mm and held it on him but figured no, not until there weren't any other options. Instead, I fired the semiautomatic into the air in the hopes that someone might hear it and find us. The report bounced off the canyon walls, and I had to admit it would be hard to tell where the shot had originated.

Stuffing the SIG into my jacket pocket, I started off again, but it was harder to get going this time, the heels of my boots digging into the fine gravel. I tried to keep moving, but the sound in my head had become a high-pitched whine. When I shook it, I drifted to the side of the trail and almost fell over.

I took a couple of deep breaths and started off again.

Stretching my jaw, I thought about how many times I'd been hit in the head but took assurance that it was my hardest part—or so everybody told me. Reaching up, I felt above my ear and ascertained that yes, I was bleeding and at a pretty good rate. Nudging my fingers against the flap of skin and hair, I pushed it up and held it as I walked. Usually I occupy myself by trying to estimate how many stitches it was going to take to put Humpty Dumpty back together, and I was thinking about a dozen. Feeling the warmth of the blood trailing down my fingers and into the palm of my hand, I reassessed at maybe eighteen.

Perhaps I'd start wearing a helmet, even at the office—most accidents happening close to home and all. The whining in my ears was getting worse, so bad that I took my hand from my head and held my nose as I blew in an attempt to clear my ears. Big mistake. I almost fell to my knees, my sense of balance completely leaving me.

Maybe twenty.

Just then, I felt something passing on my right, so I reached out, quickly yanking it back, when something moving fast struck it from behind. I felt like I'd been thrown into traffic as I spun around and was smacked by something that made me fall backward. Suddenly, I was seated, skimming along above the gravel at a surprising speed.

It was like a dream, one of those flying dreams, but the ride wasn't smooth, not at all. My head bounced up and down with some kind of vibration, but other than the whirring noise there wasn't any motor sound.

"Hang on, Sheriff!"

I wasn't sure who was talking, but we sped forward. I spread my hands out and gripped anything I could, my fingers wrapping around metal tubing of some sort.

"Is he armed?"

My head jostled and felt like it might disconnect at any moment as I tried to figure out who was talking to me. "What?"

"Is he armed?" I looked back and saw that the driver was my fellow marine, Delmar, doing his best to hold on to me and navigate the trail in his tricked-out electric wheelchair. "Hell, does he have a gun?!"

"No, no he lost it back at the bridge, but I've got it now—at least I think I have it, if I didn't lose it when you ran over me."

The sergeant major laughed and shouted in my ear. "Gave you permission to come aboard, you mean?!"

Coming into a curve, I felt myself sliding to the right, the motorized wheelchair on two wheels.

"I don't think we'll catch him with the two of us on here, but we might. I've been working on this bad boy. Stole a motor out of an old washing machine they were throwing out, so we are good for almost twenty-five miles an hour!"

"God help us."

"What?" We slammed back on four wheels, and I almost slipped off before Delmar could get hold of me and I could get a foot on the platform below. "He looks to be impaired so maybe we've got a chance!"

I could sort of see that we were gaining on the other veterans, and farther up, I could just make out Conrad turning the corner. I felt Delmar put the wheelchair into another gear, and I shook my head at the absurdity of it all as we rapidly gained on the others.

Whizzing along, I glanced up at the crimson and gold of the Corps flying above our heads and couldn't help but feel a momentary surge of pride in the old warriors, who had somehow figured out where I was and had charged in to afford assistance.

We bumped along, and I could see that Kenny, the navy chief petty officer, was wearing his N-1 Deck Jacket for the event and his cap was reversed so as to provide less wind shear. "He's up ahead! When he saw us, he panicked and dropped the painting. He picked it up again, but we're gaining on him!"

Ray, the air force master sergeant, was wearing a blue, one-piece flight suit with a natty white scarf neatly tucked to give the impression of an ascot. "He's making the turn, Delmar! If he's smart enough to take to the woods, we've lost him!"

"Roger that!"

Clifton, army command sergeant major, the only one dressed like a sane person in a weathered Carhartt and his ubiquitous boonie hat, called after us. "Go get him!"

The trail took a rise, and there was another bridge leading north, across the creek, running toward what I recalled to be the location of the first turn-out. If the Wavers didn't get him before then, we stood little chance.

Delmar was now pushing the makeshift chair to its limits, and I was getting worried that we might fly off the trail.

Westin turned to look at us and when he did, he tripped and dropped the canvas again. As luck would have it, the canvas began rolling toward us, but as luck would have it, not far enough; Conrad limped after it, finally scooping it up and glaring back as the super-motorized motorcade advanced.

He had to avoid us, but he had to get to the car parked somewhere up ahead—which meant he had to cross the bridge before he could do anything.

I figured a good hundred yards, and at the rate we were gaining we might just catch him.

It was then that we seemed to slow.

"Damn it to hell!" Delmar fiddled with the speed adjustment, but it appeared to be doing little good. "The washer motor takes a hell of a lot more electricity than the standard motor—should've daisy-chained a few batteries together!"

The speed was tailing off at a steady rate.

My head was starting to clear, and I figured on foot was the only way, so I gestured for the marine sergeant major to let me off. "I'll take it from here!" As the chair ground to a stop, I stepped off the small platform at my feet and stood there for an instant, attempting to get my bearings.

As I waited there wavering, Delmar studied me. "You sure you're going to be okay?"

"Fit as a fiddle." I took a step and lost my balance and promptly fell, face first, onto the gravel.

He gave me a polite moment before asking, "Um, you all right?"

Elbowing up, I pushed off the ground. "I might be a little out of tune."

Kenny, Clifford, and Ray were on us now, the army command sergeant major the first to speak. "What's he doin' down there?"

I stood and realized I wasn't going to make it. I pointed toward the figure in the distance. "Get him."

They lurched forward like a cavalry charge.

It was going to be close.

Stumbling forward, I reached up and straightened my hat in an attempt to keep in as much brain as possible and then turned to glance at Delmar, who sat there in the broken down chair. He saluted. "You'll send somebody to get me, Lieutenant?"

I returned the salute. "We never leave a man behind, Sergeant Major."

Pushing off, I set my boots in a line and started making slow progress.

I was trying to focus on my footing, but there was shouting ahead, and I couldn't help but look up. What I saw choked a laugh in my throat. The three servicemen had circled Conrad, and every time he attempted to get past, they cut him off.

He'd picked up a branch from beside the trail and swung it at the motorized men as they circled like a war party on the concrete surface of the bridge. They would dodge in and then back up when he swung, and I was amazed at how deft they were. After one particular strike, Kenny revved his chair in, running over Conrad's foot and then circling back out of the way.

It must've been the one that had been hit by the tire iron, and I watched as he grabbed at it while attempting to defend himself and keep hold of the painting.

Stumbling forward, I approached and watched as the men grouped into a barricade to keep him from crossing the bridge. Westin had his back to me and limped a few steps my way before turning, looking more than a little surprised.

"Howdy."

He gestured menacingly with the branch that was about the length of a baseball bat. "Stay back."

Reaching into the pocket of my jacket, I pulled out the SIG and palmed it in the moonlight so he would be sure to see it. "It's over, Conrad."

He swung the branch at me and began crying. "I don't think so."

"Then you're a bigger idiot than I thought."

He screamed. "You won't shoot me!"

"Yep, I will. I'll shoot you in the kneecap just because I'm tired of chasing you."

He tried to wipe the tears away with a shirt sleeve and swung back with the branch. The Wavers looked unconcerned. "I'll hit one of them and kill them."

"That's supposed to make me not want to shoot you?" I took a few steps toward him. "It's over. Drop it."

He did as I said, the branch clattering at our feet, but then he moved toward the railing with the oversize canvas—we all listened to the water rushing down from the mountains that stood above, dark and silent. "What if I throw this into the creek?"

I sighed and stepped toward him again. "An iconoclastic and irreplaceable work of art? As an artist, I don't think you're going to do that."

He looked into the water and his lip continued to quiver. "It's not fair."

I reached behind me for my cuffs but then remembered I'd already used them. "Generally, it never is."

He turned to look past the three men in the wheelchairs, who looked a lot less forgiving than I did, his voice like that of a child. "But I almost made it."

I stepped forward and took hold of his wrist with my bloody hand, and he winced. "No, you didn't."

EPILOGUE

We watched the private jet taxi out to the end of the runway and then turn, getting ready for the attempt at takeoff. Readjusting my hand on the hammer of my .45, I fingered the bandage in an attempt to assuage the itching. "Thanks for finding my sidearm."

"All in a day's work." She glanced back at the plane. "Think they'll make it?"

"I don't know. It was kind of touch and go yesterday when they landed in the weeds at the end of the runway."

"Yeah."

Mumbling to myself, I sighed. "Twenty-four."

Reaching down, she ruffled Dog's ears and then stood straight, stretching her back and breathing in the scent of the dry grass at the end of the tarmac. "Twenty-four what?"

"Twenty-four stitches in my head. It was a bet I made with myself, about how many it would take to close. I was betting twenty."

She continued to study the plane. "You do realize that being so conversant with wounds that you can estimate the amount of stitches needed to retain vital organs is not normal, right?"

I laughed. "What's normal in this line of work anyway?"

"Good question."

Walking out to the flight line, I slapped a hand against my thigh to break Dog's concentration as he was paying far too much attention to a western cottontail out there in the grass at the edge of the pavement. He joined us as we watched Klavdii Krovopuskov's jet rev the thrust, unlock its brakes, and shoot down the runway like a house afire, powering into the clear Wyoming sky and banking away from the Bighorns and toward the east. We watched it until it became a speck and then slowly walked back toward our tiny terminal.

She glanced at me. "So, Kiki the Bloodletter had nothing to do with the painting?"

"A passing interest, but when he found out there might be some shenanigans going on, he backed out."

"So, what does the Bloodletter do exactly?"

"Plumbing fixtures."

"You're kidding."

"Nope.

"Well, that would explain why there were no traces of him in the intelligence community." She walked and I limped through the gate of the chain-link fence and turned the corner, making our way toward her vehicle as she continued to study me. "Stop making that face."

"What face?"

"That face you make every time you get in my truck—the one where you look like you're going to die."

"It's an honest response."

She hit the remote and a chirp issued from the Banshee, the name I'd given the blacktop beast.

I stood there looking at it. "Why is it when I really want something the county commissioners always say no, and when I really don't want something they always say yes?"

She placed her hands on her hips and looked at her reflection on the glossy flanks of the speed demon. "I floated the rumor that I was going to go on a ticket-writing spree if they didn't fund it."

"Did it eat up the entire budget for the year, or can we still buy ammunition?"

"Two bullets apiece till January."

She opened the door and started to climb in before calling over the bed. "Stop making that face."

"I can't help it. I'm fine, but Dog is far too young to die."

She climbed in, and so did we after I closed the appropriately named, passenger-side suicide door. "Your dog is getting hair in my new truck."

"I'm afraid you're going to have to get used to it." I moved the cardboard roll to the side, sat, snapped on my seatbelt, and wished for a helmet. "So, Chuck Yeager, do you think we could keep it under the speed of sound?"

She hit the keyless ignition button, and we listened to the throaty bellow as she blipped the throttle. "I honestly think she's as fast as Krovopuskov's jet if you'd just let me cut her loose."

I braced a hand against the dash. "Let's not find out, shall we?" Pulling the thing into gear, she eased out of the spot and wound her way down the hill into French Creek Canyon toward town, the half-ton hugging the curves like a panther. "I don't like these seats."

"What are you talking about? They keep you from sliding all over the place like the ones in that three-quarter ton Conestoga wagon you've got."

"I like my Conestoga wagon."

Static. "Unit one, this is Base."

I glanced around. "What the heck?"

Static. "Walt, are you on your way to the bank?"

Vic shook her head. "On our way, Ruby. Do I need to get there quickly?"

I raised my voice. "Please, don't say yes."

Static. "Roger that. No, but Wes called, and he said that Mr. Townsend was there at the bank and they were waiting."

Vic nodded and spoke to the windshield as near as I could tell. "On our way."

Feeling myself being pushed back into the kidney-hugging seats, I looked around. "Where's the mic? For that matter, where's the radio?"

"Built in. The mic is up here on the sun visor. There's also a computer stand, but I thought that might be too much for you."

I glanced out at the rapidly passing and changing world. "You're right."

I wasn't sure if I'd ever been in the basement of the Bank of Durant, but if I had I'd forgotten it. We were seated at a central table adjacent to the private viewing area with the frosted glass where Bass Townsend-Stillwater had disappeared.

I'd voiced the opinion that considering recent occurrences, it was possible that somebody should be in the room with the man, but Wes had said it was protocol for the recipient of the safe-deposit box to do the initial opening in private.

The result was predictable.

"Are you shitting me?" From behind the door, Bass spoke again. "Are you shitting me?"

I glanced at Wes as he adjusted his glasses and then laced his fingers, placing them on his crossed knee.

The statement floated out from the room again. "You have got to be shitting me."

I glanced at Vic, who covered a smile with her hand. "Now, at this point we should all place bets . . ."

There was some jostling at the door as Bass stuck his head out. "Um, Mr. Haskins, am I allowed to invite all of you in here?"

Wes stood. "Certainly."

"I think there are some things you need to see."

Crowding into the small space with the tiny table and two chairs, I stood against the wall as Vic joined me, and we looked at the assorted items Bass had taken from the metal box, including a rather large stack of bills held together with a rotten rubber band, a medium-size manila envelope, and a small box that had had twine tied around it, which now lay beside the box.

Bass pointed first at the bills. "Is that real money?"

Wes paused for a moment to see if anyone would object and then picked up the stack and examined it. "Looks real to me."

"How much is it?"

"Hundred-dollar bills . . . This is just an estimate without going upstairs and running it through the counter, but I'm guessing close to three hundred thousand dollars." He looked up at Bass, who appeared as though he might have another attack. "Mr. Townsend, how 'bout you take a couple of deep breaths?"

We all remained quiet as the musician did as requested, finally speaking. "I get this money, right?"

"I don't see any reason why not. You'll have to pay taxes on it, but as near as I can tell it's yours free and clear. The million dollars for the painting will be tied up with the fortunes of Count Lehman, and the specifics on that will have to wait until his court dates and subsequent sentencing." He glanced up at me. "There will be a trial?"

"For all three individuals, most assuredly."

Bass folded his hands in his lap. "Who gets the painting, the *Custer's Last Fight*?"

"Well, that'll be tied up in probate for a while, but unless the federal government comes up with some kind of proof of ownership, which I seriously doubt, it will be yours."

"Mine?"

"Yours, exclusively."

He nodded. "What if I wanted to do something with it?"

"After probate it's yours to do with as you wish."

"What if I wanted to donate it to the Soldiers' and Sailors' Home up on the hill?"

We all looked at one another and then back to him. "Mr. Townsend, that's a twenty-four-million-dollar painting you're talking about."

"I know, but it seems to me that everybody that's ever had anything to do with that painting has come by bad luck. I don't think I want to risk it. Besides, without those men in the wheelchairs that came to the rescue, it would've been gone, and I wouldn't have the painting, would I? And if I kept the painting, it's possible that this Count whatever-his-name-is could say the million was mine and the painting was his?"

"I suppose anything's possible."

He tapped the cash. "Sheriff, I haven't ever had this kind of money in my life, and I know if Charley Lee was here, he'd say better a hog on the hoof than a pig in the poke, you know?"

"Yep, but Bass, you could have all of it."

"I know it sounds crazy, but I'm not so sure I want it with all that bad luck." He looked at me. "Hell, you know what I could do with just that three hundred thousand dollars?"

Vic weighed in. "Less than you could do with twenty-four million."

"Yeah, but then I'd have to guard that painting, try and sell it . . . I don't know, but it sounds like a lot of trouble."

Wes cleared his throat. "I'm sure that arrangements could be made."

"I'd rather not, really."

"Mr. Townsend, what if we made provisions for the painting to, say, be on loan from you to Fort McKinney. That way you could retain ownership while the servicemen up at the Home could admire the piece?"

He snapped his fingers and pointed them at me. "Hey, that sounds good."

"I'm not sure how Carol is going to feel about being responsible for the painting, but I'm betting we can get insurance."

He glanced down at the other items on the table. "There's some other stuff."

"Do you want us to see it?"

"Please. Take a look at what's in the envelope. I'm not sure what it means, but it looks old."

Wes reached over and opened the end, carefully sliding a slip of rough paper from the envelope, tattered on the ends and with a portion at the middle missing where it had been folded. Gently, the banker turned the sheet over to reveal writing that had been scribbled in haste.

> *Benteen, where are you?*
> *W. W. Cooke*

We all stood, silent.

Bass leaned in closer to examine the note. "Who is W. W. Cooke?"

"Lieutenant Cooke, Custer's adjutant at the Little Bighorn . . . If this is real, it would be the last known message from Custer before his death, even more recent than the one that hangs in the library at West Point." I stood up straight, leaning my back against the wall. "Giovanni Martini, the bugler for the Seventh carried the first message to Colonel Benteen, but then Sergeant Daniel Kanipe carried another, and then there were rumors of Captain Jack Crawford carrying a final message that may or may not have gotten through." I glanced down at the scrap of paper. "This may be that final message."

"There's more." He cleared his throat. "In the box."

We all looked at the tiny cardboard container.

Bass swallowed and gestured toward it. "Um, you might want to see what's in there next."

Wes leaned over, carefully taking off the lid and staring at the contents and then up at me with an eyebrow cocked. He placed the box back onto the surface of the table and then slid it toward us.

Peering in, I could see, nestled in slightly yellowed cotton, a shriveled portion of human flesh.

Vic looked over my shoulder. "Is that a finger?"

"Yes, I believe it is."

Bass spoke under his breath. "Are you shitting me?"

"I'm no expert, but from the condition, I'd say this is quite old." Picking up the box, I looked closer at the grisly artifact. "A pinky, I believe."

"It's got a ring on it."

I glanced at Bass.

"Be my guest, I'm not touching that thing."

Reaching in with thumb and forefinger, I plucked the digit

from the cotton and held it up to the light, the golden ring falling off onto the table, clattering and chiming as it rolled in an uneven circle, finally falling over and lying still.

There in the minimal light of the safety-deposit examination room, the wider part of the ring winked up at us in tarnished gold, the color not unlike the eyes of my undersheriff.

A signet ring engraved with the spiraling initials GAC.

"I'm just glad it wasn't his penis with an arrow stuck in it."

I tried not to focus on that image as she drove up the hill toward the Soldiers' and Sailors' Home, carefully placing the cardboard tube onto the new dash. "Nice of him to give the artist proof to Henry."

"That's a lot of shit he's giving away." As she drove, she glanced at me. "Is Henry really going to have it framed and hang it in the bathroom at the Red Pony?"

"Probably." I moved the small cooler from the carpeted floor to my lap. "I guess it's real, but who knows? Anyway, the Bear will do what he always does: whatever he wants."

She slowed the missile and put on her blinker to turn left into Fort McKinney where four familiar figures sat waving at traffic and waiting for us. Pulling up in front of them, she put the Banshee in park and stepped out as Dog hopped into the front and I hobbled my way around the elongated hood with the small cooler.

"That is one fine looking truck." My unofficial Uber driver, the sergeant major of the marine corps, ran his eyes over the new unit. "Black, though, hard to keep clean."

"Shut up, Delmar—it's got white doors." The army command

sergeant major, Clifton, smiled at Vic. "Beautiful lady, beautiful truck."

"How fast does it go?" Kenny, the chief petty officer wagged his head in admiration.

Folding her arms, she leaned against one of the white doors with our freshly applied star. "Faster than he'll let me."

"I bet." The air force master sergeant, Ray, glanced at me with a raised eyebrow. "Whaddaya got there, Sheriff?"

I stopped with Vic, the cooler dangling from my hand. "Oh, something I found on the road."

Delmar pivoted his newly restored chair for a better look at me. "Can we have it?"

Kenny nodded. "Salvage laws of the sea, you know."

Ray agreed. "This stretch of road is under our command."

"What kind of medication are you guys on?"

Clifford laughed. "The best the federal government can buy."

"You guys get me in trouble with your CO, and I'll be back but not with gifts." I walked over to set the cooler in Delmar's lap but then paused. "You guys will save one for Magic Mike when he gets out of the medical unit?"

"Yes, sir, Lieutenant."

"All right, then." I put down the cooler. "I just wanted to say thank you for what you did. You could've stayed up here in mothballs, but instead, you put yourselves in considerable peril by assisting me with the apprehension of a dangerous criminal and restored a valuable piece of American history to its proper owners." I stepped back, presented them with my snappiest salute, and ignoring the pain, clicked the heels of my cowboy boots together.

They sat there looking at me, and then one by one they

raised their hands and returned my gesture of respect, honor, and recognition.

"Gentlemen, you are relieved." I dropped the salute, and we watched as the Wavers peeled off, one by one, wheelchairs motoring down the pathway toward the old fort with just a touch, perhaps, more dignity.

Vic strolled up and joined me in watching the military-branch flags bobbing as they rolled along like caissons. "So, what is it, anyway?"

"Excuse me?"

"This crappy painting that people were ready to kill each other for—I mean why not go out and steal a real work of art like the *Mona Lisa*?"

"Well, this one wasn't quite so closely guarded either in the closet or the chicken shed."

"You know what I mean."

"Well, I'd imagine it's the same reason it got painted, toured around the country, and hung on that saloon wall in Saint Louis, and why Augie Busch ran off a million copies of the thing—contact."

"Huh?"

I turned and limped back toward her truck but was struck as I always was by the power and majesty of the mountains that guarded our little town. "Contact with an important part of American history. Pick a side, but it was a turning point for both cultures and popular or not it still resonates into the modern day."

"I think most school kids nowadays don't even know who Custer was."

I turned to look at her. "Sitting Bull."

"Nope."

"Crazy Horse?"

"Nope."

"More's the pity." I stood there at the front of her truck. "Hey, can I borrow your phone?"

She gave me a strange look but then pulled it from her pocket and handed it to me. I dialed, listening to it ring.

Looking north I thought about the obelisk and the scattered stones on that hillside and ruminated on a band of nomadic people who, even though they won the battle, had lost their way of life. Sitting Bull knew, even with all his dreams of falling soldiers with no ears, that the other US military boot would drop, and the gains made in this great battle would only be a footnote.

"Daddy?"

I held the phone a little closer. "Hey Punk, I've got some sad news . . ."

ALSO AVAILABLE

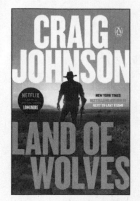
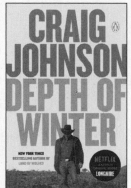
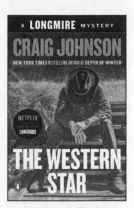

HELL AND BACK

DAUGHTER OF THE MORNING STAR

NEXT TO LAST STAND

LAND OF WOLVES

DEPTH OF WINTER

THE WESTERN STAR

AN OBVIOUS FACT

DRY BONES

ANY OTHER NAME

A SERPENT'S TOOTH

AS THE CROW FLIES

HELL IS EMPTY

JUNKYARD DOGS

THE DARK HORSE

ANOTHER MAN'S MOCCASINS

KINDNESS GOES UNPUNISHED

DEATH WITHOUT COMPANY

THE COLD DISH

SPIRIT OF STEAMBOAT

WAIT FOR SIGNS

THE HIGHWAYMAN

 PENGUIN BOOKS

Ready to find your next great read? Let us help. Visit prh.com/nextread